Full
Faith
& Credit

by James R. Cook

Published by
Blue Book Publications
8009 34th Avenue South
Minneapolis, MN 55425

This novel is a work of fiction. Names, characters, places, and incidents either are the product of the author's imagination or are used fictitiously. Any resemblance to actual persons, living or dead, events, or locales is entirely coincidental.

Library of Congress Cataloging in Publication Data
Cook, James R.
    Full Faith and Credit / James R. Cook
        p. cm.
    ISBN 1-886768-49-8   99-091925

Manufactured in the United States of America
March 2000
10 9 8 7 6 5 4 3 2 1

Cause and effect, means and ends, seed and fruit,
cannot be severed;
for the effect already blooms in the cause,
the end pre-exists in the means,
the fruit in the seed.

Chapter 1

———

It was a tough year for Richie. He was living off capital. An elderly business acquaintance had once warned him "never get into a situation where you're living off capital." In other words, don't spend your savings and, as Richie acknowledged to himself, he was running low. He didn't like the worry or the haunting fingers of anxiety that troubled him in the night. He had expenses.

His new company managed money in commodity trading accounts and was a tough sell. He was pioneering and that's always a grind, he consoled himself. Truth was, Richie wasn't managing much more than the little money he had left and thirty grand from his widowed mother. Well, actually $25,000 after he'd covered a short position in oil that had gone against him.

He steered the Lexus around a gradual curve on the ribbon of concrete that cut through the lush green Minnesota countryside. Home was in a brand-new expanse of urban sprawl tucked deep in the countryside and for ten minutes each way he zipped by rows of corn and soybeans.

At age 43, Richie Stenquist still had the angular good looks and intelligent eyes that had helped him further his career in finance. He kept his blonde hair cropped short and his hairline stayed far forward. Thin, muscular, and one hundred percent Norwegian, he looked like he'd climbed off a Viking raider that very day. It also helped that he was a dapper dresser. Richie hadn't bought a suit off the rack in a decade, opting instead for tailor-mades at $1,500 a throw. He favored yellow power ties that harmonized with his dark suits, and Italian shoes of the softest leather. He looked successful and for a long while he had been.

It wasn't just his smooth Wall Street appearance that moved him into the Minneapolis branch of America's largest brokerage firm. He was clever enough to sail through the training program and passed the Series Seven with a blistering 96. At age 28 he became the number two producer at Merrill's Midwest arm.

After the 1987 crash, his customers slowed their trading to a crawl and he became impatient with the pace of things. Patience was not one of his better qualities. He once remarked, "Impatience has one virtue, it gets things done." And to speed up the pace of his life, he switched to commodity trading. At first he lost money for both himself and his customers. But over time he got the knack of it. He played the grains like a violin in the early nineties and rode the yen up and down in the middle of the decade. He was short copper and wheat when the Asian crisis hit. His customers loved him. Then ever so subtly things changed. He had trouble with the grains in the late nineties, and a big short position in oil at fifteen dollars burned off a slug of customers. Then he hurt himself by prematurely anticipating a recovery in gold. As the century was winding down, his customer base had eroded and so had his bankroll. He still had a small cash position of $ 3/4 million, and two dozen stalwart traders who would listen to him.

That's when he decided to make the biggest move of his life. Others he knew had left the big firms and were making huge amounts of money managing equity portfolios for big investors. His instincts were now finely tuned to commodities trading and he saw a grand opportunity in managing money that was invested in the commodity markets. The big kicker for him was a small piece of any profits he engineered. After a few weeks of pondering, he took the plunge. Within a month he was properly licensed and registered.

Richie didn't count on the rebuff he received from his customers. Most were reluctant to leave the big firm while a handful of others shelled out minimal amounts for him to manage. Then his ability to pick a profitable trend turned sour. He found himself whipsawed by the currency markets, and, when a short on the British pound went wrong, he covered, and bought contracts the other way only to have the pound finally soften against the dollar. It wiped out the funds he'd received from six of his best investors and the heart of his start-up was gone.

Commodity trading is high risk for small players pitted against giant corporate hedgers and professional traders. Ninety percent of commodity speculators lose money. Richie had worked out a highly advanced computerized trading program that had worked quite well at Merrill. But once on his own, it went haywire. At the worst time he made moves that killed him and his customers. After six months nobody was returning his calls.

Richie wheeled up his long driveway onto the concrete apron of his two-story luxury home. He crawled out of the beige Lexus and pushed through the side door into the kitchen. His wife of fourteen years burst into the room with a big smile and planted a wet kiss on his lips. Nancy Stenquist still possessed her girlish figure and the intelligent good looks that had attracted Richie to her. A Danish and German mix, she retired from her job as a surgical nurse after the birth of their first child. Now with two girls twelve and ten, she was a classic soccer mom delivering Chrissy and Kimberly to a plethora of activities.

But Nancy was worried. A curt reminder from the mortgage company and the threat of a cancelled credit card had arrived just that day in the gray metal mailbox at the end of the driveway. The occasional phone call about an overdue bill would send her off in a fit of anxiety. She loved her house and the slight possibility that it would be taken from them aroused her sharpest suffering.

"What happened today, hon?" she queried.

"Not much. Ralston at First Bank called me. No dice with the loan."

"Ouch."

"I know. I'm counting on Fuchs at Bemer," he stated, referring to an old college chum who worked for a local mortgage company.

"How much?"

"I asked for one hundred. You can have five for bills and I can pay the office rent and phone. That leaves ninety thousand for trading."

"How much do you still have?"

"About fourteen. I can't go below ten thousand or they could cancel my trading account. Of course, I still have Mom's."

"What's that down to?"

"Thanks! Twenty-five, I guess."

The conversation trailed off. Soon rattling dishes in the kitchen and TV news echoed through the lower level. Richie greeted his daughters at dinner and heard about the day's exploits of his popular girls. Nancy beamed.

After the girls had left the table they chatted again.

"I've got a hunch I think might work," he began.

"Good."

"The dollar got hit today. GDP was disappointing last quarter and the economy could be slowing a little. The bond market looks a tad illiquid. I'm going to short the dollar against the Euro and yen and hope for a quick drop."

"Sounds good," she reassured. "I know you've been thinking about it."

Nancy was more than a sounding board. Simply by osmosis she knew the ins and outs of commodity market trading and she had acquired a decent knowledge of money and markets. She knew the stock market was at astronomical levels and she'd done just enough reading to understand some of the dangers it held. Her husband had taught her that it takes more and more money and credit to keep a big stock market bubble expanding. Same with bonds. She recognized that the spread between government bonds and lower-grade bonds had widened lately and liquidity problems were emerging. She watched the financial news most mornings and sometimes skimmed the *Wall Street Journal* her husband brought home each day. In every way she was perfect as Richie's counter-part. She gave him good counsel, toned down his sharp edges, and blunted his tendency to act with too much haste.

Richie settled down to study some charts and read one of his economic books. He liked to read and if he was interested in what he read, he remembered it. Richie was also opinionated. He had a strong belief in free markets and read the economists who promot-ed that viewpoint. Over the years he had become suspicious of the great economic expansion that ran through the eighties and nineties. He suspected that stock prices were valued too high and often shook his head at the scale of consumer borrowing and spending that propelled the economy. Years ago he had concluded that a boom driven by easy money and credit sent the wrong sig-nal to business. The Japanese experience proved it. Credit made them overexpand to the point that it created future problems. As credit slowed, as it always did, the economy turned down and a lot of people got hurt. The pain of the bust was always sharper than the pleasures of the boom. Unfortunately, the bust was inevitable.

Now he was at a crossroads. "The acid test of intelligence is whether the things you believe in turn out to be true," Richie told his wife. "There's a big crash coming. I wish I knew when and exactly how it's going to start, but I don't. I'm guessing that sooner or later the dollar's got to take some serious hits. Look at the balance of payments," he continued. "The deficit is over twenty billion dollars a month. Normally that would cause a hell of a crisis. If any other country did it, their money would sink out of sight - I mean worthless. We're lucky! The rest of the world wants our dollars and what a stroke of luck it is for us. We keep printing money and people send it overseas to buy things. Sooner or later there's going to be a dollar glut in the world causing it to get repriced a lot lower. Believe me, when that happens all our markets are going south. That's when we want to be short the whole enchilada." He smiled at her and took an exaggerated breath.

"The kids went to the Dairy Queen with the Andersons," she interrupted. He perked up at the slight huskiness in her voice. Would you like to see my new outfit," she queried. Watching her dress and undress always stirred him and he responded affirmatively with a foolish ear-to-ear grin. In a moment she was back from the closet in a gossamer-thin negligee he'd never seen before. He pulled her down and whispered an outrageous compliment into her ear. She giggled. She's so good at this, he thought as they pressed together.

Chapter 2

———

Richie was up and out the door early. He kissed his wife good-bye almost absent-mindedly, his mind churning with plans for the day. He got on the car phone and caught Freddie Fuchs of Bemer Financial at home, still in bed, sipping coffee and reading the sports.

"Freddie, can you do it?" he asked.

"Yeah, I think so."

"Great! That's great!"

"It's going to be a high rate and we still have to appraise your digs, but I think you got enough equity. I mean just barely, you know."

"OK. Thanks. How long?"

"Come in today, you can have the money at the end of the week. I've got an appraiser going out there tomorrow. OK?"

"Slick. I'll see you before noon today."

"Done."

"Thanks, my friend."

"No big deal."

Richie had rented space in the new Hiawatha Heights Financial

Tower across from the refurbished Foshay Tower in downtown
Minneapolis. As he cruised up 35W the outline of the downtown
skyline poked into view above the trees and sound barriers that lined
the freeway. He was always impressed with the shimmering oblong
scrapers and the big-city sophistication they implied. He loved it
here. Sometimes in the winter he'd complain, but he was accustomed to cold weather and it didn't bother him all that much.
Sometimes in the dead of winter he'd laugh out loud as he thought
of the former Viking coach, Bud Grant, lecturing his football players
on a frozen sideline about how the Inuit in Northwest Territories
could work on a bulldozer in January without hats or gloves. It was
all in your mind, he mused. At least for the first sixty seconds.

He dropped down the concrete chute into the underground
parking and wheeled into his stall. He was four spots from the elevator and quickly crossed into the tiny lobby, pressing the "up"
button. The elevator ding-donged open and he was soon up and
away to the 31st floor. He strode into his small office and greeted
his secretary, Carol Olson, with a quick smile. Slightly graying and
slightly frumpish, Miss Olson had never married and he'd always
wondered why. No matter, she was a skilled secretary and had a
memory that could recall who'd called him in this same week a
year ago. They were friends.

She had made coffee. He poured himself a cup and then sat down
at his huge mahogany desk that was a size too big for his small
office. His view overlooked downtown and the Mississippi River
with its old flour mills and dams. On the opposing shore lay tiny St.
Anthony, a community that was once dominant over Minneapolis.
Beyond that lay St. Paul, and, far away, the St. Paul skyline.

He scoured the financial section of the *Journal* for anything
new. Even the tiniest shred of information could be critical. Most
everything he had digested the previous day on the expensive wire

8

service that came across his computer. He thumbed through a sheaf of faxes, newsletters, financial bulletins, and brokerage firm reports that were germane to his dealings. The dollar had meandered further down against the major currencies. Nothing dramatic yet, but it could be the start of a trend. He was going to make the move and plunger that he was, it would include most of the new loan. If it went against him, he would try to close his position out before he got a margin call. He was usually nimble enough to escape before his losses became colossal. To the untrained observer he was a reckless gambler taking naked positions that could wipe him out. But, he had enormous self-confidence tempered by an awesome grasp of the market and all the facts affecting it, plus a superb intuition that some would come to write off as no more than luck.

Timing would be everything. The dollar had traded in a narrow range for months. The current slump had yet to penetrate the trendline on the downside and thereby signal to the market that a dollar decline had begun. If the dollar stayed flat then the commission and interest charges on the highly leveraged contracts and the borrowed money they included would eat him up along with his monthly operating costs. Richie needed to hit this one on the nose. His clients were gone and he was now no more than a lone wolf trader operating for his own account. Make the wrong moves now and he and his lovely wife would be searching for a small apartment in the city accompanied by two sobbing daughters.

He clicked onto the futures markets and briefly analyzed the screen. Trading in the dollar had just opened and was directionless. He put in a call to Ken Ferguson at First Trading, commodity specialists in Chicago.

"Hi, Kenny."

"Richie, oats are ripe for the picking. Our analyst just concluded that the crop is going to be a bin buster. Our grain traders are freaking. You want to short a few?"

"No, sir."

"Silver looks better here."

"No. No."

"You don't want an idea?"

"Not now."

"What can I do to you. I mean for you?"

"Stop talking."

"Give me an order."

"O.K."

"Really!"

"Yeah. Buy me twelve long October contracts on the yen and twelve on the Euro."

"You only got fourteen grand in your account."

"I'll have another ninety by tomorrow. FedEx."

"O.K. You promise?"

"Absolutely."

"O.K. We buy twelve yen and twelve Euro October longs."

"That'll do it."

"Thanks my friend. Send money and I hope you make out as good as Hillary Clinton."

"I've got a shot."

"I'll call you to confirm. Bye."

Richie pushed back in his chair. He fretted that there could be a glitch with the refinancing. Not likely. In the worst case scenario he could call Mom and borrow part of the money he needed from her commodities account that he managed and was currently idle and he would leave it there until he was virtually certain about a trade. He couldn't lose any more of her money. If he had to borrow it and lost it, then somehow, at some later date, he would square it with her.

Carol Olson called to him through the doorway that he had a call. He picked up. It was Bernie Fogelson, a stockbroker and friend. Bernie was more than a casual acquaintance. Over the years he had become close with Richie and their deep philosophical discussions had influenced to some extent how Richie thought about things. Bernie tended to be a gloom and doomer. He specialized in gold stocks but had failed to make his customers money in them for a full decade. Fortunately, he had taken down some IPO allotments for Internet stocks, had prospered himself and made his customers just enough money so that they would always give him five minutes when he called.

"Where are we eating?" he asked.

"Lee Ann Chins, but not till twelve-thirty. I have to run somewhere."

"O.K., see you then."

Richie made a few more calls looking for information and then made his way to Bemer Financial. It was six blocks and he strolled through the elaborate skyway system that connected the downtown office buildings in Minneapolis. It had started to sprinkle and although the skyway was designed to protect people from winter, it got plenty of use in the summer.

Freddie's secretary had a stack of papers on her desk for Richie to sign. He waved at Freddie, who sat behind a glass wall talking with two men in his office. Within minutes he'd completed the task and had the forms in a manila file to take home for his wife's signature. Normally they both would have had to come in for the closing, but Freddie had waived this requirement.

He made his way back through the skyway to the restaurant located on the first floor of a nearby office tower. It was twenty after twelve and he quickly got a small table that had just been vacated. He ordered an iced tea and waited for his friend.

Although Bernie was a stockbroker, he always went out for lunch at noon. Most brokers didn't leave their desks until the afternoon bell closed trading, but he was not that gung-ho anymore. His grandfather had left him a part interest in a downtown parking lot that supplemented his income.

Bernie's grandparents had left Kiev with six other young Jewish couples prior to the first world war. They settled in New York and, after gaining a measure of comfort in their new country, the couple moved to Minneapolis where they became successful grocery wholesalers. They had one son who was Bernie's father and a daughter. The boy attended the University of Minnesota and, one summer while working at the State Fair, he fell in love with the Minnesota Dairy Princess. She had come from tiny Blue Earth, Minnesota to attend college and become a teacher. Much to his parents' dismay, she was a Swede. They had wanted and expected a Jewish daughter-in-law but, in America, when a blue-eyed Scandinavian beauty captivated a Jewish boy, it wasn't like the old country. Sometimes they married.

When Bernie was seven years old his father died. His dad went to bed one night and never woke up. They said it was an aneurysm in his aorta. It shattered Bernie's grandparents. Three years later his mother remarried and eventually added two half-brothers to Bernie's family. His mother scuttled them all to the Lutheran Church each Sunday, but his grandparents insisted on bringing Bernie to the Temple and celebrating Jewish holidays. From a religious standpoint, he landed somewhere in the middle, but favored services at the Temple.

Bernie's big body framed itself in the doorway of the Chinese restaurant, where he caught Richie's wave. He made his way to the table, plopped down, and huffed out a greeting.

"How's the market?" asked Richie.

"Up about sixty."

"Anything exciting?"

"One of the Fed governors wants to raise rates, but he said the same thing last week and the week before."

"Inflation worries?"

"I suppose, but hell, gold's down, housing starts are off, and the CPI ain't moved in three months. Look at this menu. Lunches are more expensive, but it never shows up in the inflation index."

Richie laughed. He had often thought that prices were rising for everyday goods, but there never was any inflation in the index.

"They're always increasing the money supply. I wonder why the inflation index isn't up," he said, raising his eyes from the menu to meet Bernie's. "It must be productivity gains," he continued, answering his own question.

"I don't think so. That's bogus."

"Look," argued Richie, "Henry Ford made better cars more efficiently all through the nineteen twenties. That's why the prices for cars kept dropping. Productivity gains! That's why there was no inflation back then, even though the money supply was growing. Just like now, only this time we're lowering the price of computers."

Ever the cynic, Bernie rolled his eyes. "As far as I'm concerned, the computer benefits are mostly in. We've had these productivity gains for years. Now we're replacing equipment and adding some damn expensive programming. Let me tell you another thing. Computers make up less than two percent of the goods and services produced in this country. Almost all of our productivity gains come from that measly little slice of GDP. It's a statistical mirage. The way the government measures computer power in the productivity figures is pure unadulterated bullshit! They're winging it." Richie sighed. Bernie cast around the room for their tardy waitress. "Here she comes," he reassured him.

"Gin martini, straight up." It was Bernie's custom to drink one martini every day at lunch with the exception of Fridays when he drank two.

"I'm fine with the tea," said Richie, "but let's order."

After the waitress had gone, Bernie started up again.

"I'll tell you where the inflation is my man. It's in assets. All that money and credit is going into stocks. Why do you think the market's so high? Assets are inflating, right?"

Hell, somebody just paid sixty million for a Cezanne. A realtor I know in Florida just flopped an ordinary beach house in Boca Grande for three-and-a-half million. Give me a break, this is the biggest inflation in history."

A tepid "Yeah," was all that Richie could muster. The conversation meandered until their waitress brought the food. They ate silently amongst the din of conversation from neighboring tables. Bernie ordered a coffee.

"What you doing these days, Richie? You haven't taken a new position in a couple of weeks."

"Yeah, I went long the yen pretty good this morning and the same with the Euro."

"How many contracts?"

"Twenty."

"Hmm. I thought you had the shorts."

Richie began to confess the details of the loan he had taken out to his now-attentive friend who had leaned forward so as not to miss a word.

"So, I'm sending forty grand to Chicago, FedEx. I should have the money deposited by the time the check comes back."

"Interesting!"

"I got no choice."

"Well, that's probably better than Ed Porter's kid."

"What do you mean?"

"You know Ed, the mortgage guy?"

"Sure."

"His daughter and her husband refinanced their house in Blaine. They just owned the place three years and hooked it for all they could get, an extra twelve thousand. What do you think they did with the money?"

"Don't know."

"Bought a Harley, ha ha." Bernie dissolved into laughter. Richie chortled.

"That's the way it's going, pal," said Bernie, suddenly turning serious.

"What do you mean?"

"I mean everybody's doing it. They're refinancing their homes or taking out a second, just like you. Then they either piss the money away or buy stocks and mutual funds." "They get to write off the interest," countered Richie.

"They're loading themselves with debt."

"Well, I'll be paying mine back."

"Sure, that's what everybody plans to do. When a few people lose their jobs during a bad slip in the economy mortgage foreclosures are going to come on like a plague. People don't seem to think they can lose their homes. They can."

"I suppose."

"What happens if home prices take a big drop? They going to stick around or are they going to walk? You going to pay for something that's worth half of what you hooked it for?"

"Probably not."

"Not only that, most of these shmoes got their credit cards maxed out. I mean they got no freeboard. Almost half the people in the country can't even scrape a grand together if they need it.

They don't have it, man."

Richie reached for his credit card and coincidentally wondered how much room he and his wife had left on the card before they reached their limit.

"I know what you mean," he responded.

"I'll tell you another thing. People are spending their savings. I mean, it's like the consumers are out of control. They won't stop buying things. This is the biggest good-times boom ever. It dwarfs anything."

"I know, but people are putting their savings in stocks. That's why the savings figures are negative."

"Then it ain't savings, it's speculation and they can lose it. I mean money in the market isn't like money in the bank."

"You're right."

The waitress returned for his signature with a smile that indicated no problem with the card and inwardly he felt a moment of relief. He took back his card, added a gratuity, and signed the slip.

"You know," Richie continued, "most of that money is in mutual funds. It's pretty safe."

"Less risky is a better way to put it, and it's no way safe as a bank."

Richie muttered an agreement and picked one of the fortune cookies the waitress had left. He broke it open and extracted the strip of white paper inside. "Fear is the root of all evil," he read aloud. Bernie broke open his cookie and extracted the fortune. "It's the same as yours. They didn't shuffle the deck. Anyway, they got it wrong. It should be, 'Evil is the root of all fear.'" Richie rose from the table. Bernie popped up and trundled toward the door behind him.

"Call you tomorrow."

"O.K., Bernie."

"See you, Richie."

One thing about his daily lunches with Bernie, they were never boring, mused Richie. The man had a prodigious grasp of economics and finance. He was a natural-born contrarian and his skepticism of almost everything had stood him in good stead. He'd passed by a lot of bad over-the-counter deals and new offerings that had gone sour.

Some people thought him to be exceptionally shrewd by nature. But it wasn't always that way. He'd worked at a Yellowstone Park concession between his senior year in high school and first year of college. The two owners had convinced him to postpone taking all but one of his paychecks till the end of August when they closed up. On that last day he'd gone to get his paycheck for a summer's work, only to find that his two bosses were gone. There was no paycheck. Out of those bitter tears came a permanent skepticism. He no longer believed anybody.

Within minutes Richie was back at his office checking the markets. The yen had moved up slightly against the dollar while the Euro was unchanged. He was in the money ever so modestly. Carol Olson gave him a stack of phone messages and he worked through them, returning those that were important. He called Nancy and told her he'd be home early. At three o'clock the financial futures were finished trading. He made one final call and headed for the elevator.

"Good-bye, Carol."

"Good night, Richie."

Chapter 3

———

The chairman of the Federal Reserve was tired. He was slumped down on the floral bedroom chair with his feet up on the matching stool. His wife lay in bed propped up by three fluffy pillows, covered by a single sheet and a light summer bedspread. She was reading a fashion magazine. He paid no attention to the low volume of sound or the program running on their TV. Inside he was churning. Today had been his Humphrey-Hawkins testimony and the congressmen had done just what he hoped they wouldn't do. They bombarded him with questions about the booming stock market. He kept backing away from the subject and finally told them he could say no more about the equities market.

The last time he said anything concrete about stocks the market lost fifteen hundred points. Almost immediately they were labeling it as his crash. The media heaped criticism on him, including the talking suits from Wall Street who spoke in unison every morning on CNBC. He hadn't peeped on the subject for almost eighteen months and the market had added on another twenty-five percent.

That was the problem. Three years ago the market had risen into the stratosphere and nothing seemed able to slow it for long. He knew that stocks were terribly overvalued. He also knew that leveraging and margin buying were spurring on the gains. Margin debt was jumping as much in a single month as it used to rise in a year. He worried that a crash would devastate the economy and he knew that the wreckage from the bursting of a financial bubble caused far more economic havoc than an ordinary recession.

Unfortunately, he was in a box. He couldn't talk the market down or issue warnings about the crazy values and wild speculation for fear he'd cause a crash. He was too damn influential. He would get the praise or the blame, and most of all, he didn't want to get blamed for another 1929. Instead he had formulated a policy of constantly warning about inflation and hinting about a pending rise in interest rates. If he could let the air out of the stock balloon gradually, he could keep the record economic expansion rolling along. Hell, everybody knew there was no inflation. Nevertheless, he kept his staff of economists sifting through the financial tea leaves and endorsed any reports that suggested a stirring of inflation. While he had made inflation out to be the ultimate villain, in his heart he didn't worry much about the possibility. So what if there was five percent inflation. The real threat was the crazy market.

"What's the matter, dear?" his wife asked, looking up from her reading and studying his scowl.

"Those Wall Street assholes." he hissed. The chairman knew the value of public circumspection. His speeches were guarded and eloquent. The image of wisdom and control was carefully cultivated. The chairman of the Federal Reserve must be urbane, witty, charming, and a bit enigmatic. At home, however, he was far more earthy, and, when roiled up, cursed profusely. Only his wife knew this and she would never tell.

"I spend all day warning Congress about inflation and a rise in interest rates, and the Dow still goes up one-eighty and the Nasdaq fifty. The brokerage firms have all their analysts telling people not to worry about inflation or a quarter-point rise in rates. They're talking about another twenty-five percent gain this year. They've lost their minds. And that idiot in the White House is telling everybody he's responsible for any prosperity we have. Not only that, most of the Federal Reserve board wants to lower rates. What the hell's the matter with them?" He stopped for breath.

"Don't worry, dear," injected his wife. "You've been doing a wonderful job; just keep it up."

"I may not be able to keep it up. Whenever we stop pumping money out, liquidity starts to dry up. The junior-grade bonds are taking some hits again, spreads are widening on corporates, and all the rest. I can't lower rates or the dollar will fall out of bed. It's a hell of a predicament and nobody seems the least bit worried but me. You know, I'd like to serve one more term."

"You will, dear."

"Then we'll retire."

"Sounds wonderful."

"Then I'm going to write a book."

"Really."

"How I Saved Western Civilization From a Million Bad Economic Ideas." His mood had turned lighthearted. She laughed.

The thing he loved was her great sense of humor. He liked to make her laugh. She still giggled the same way after twelve happy years of marriage. Joan Goldfarb had come a long way from Levittown, Long Island. Some of her co-workers ridiculed her when she was a young girl because of the speed with which she wheeled a rack of women's dresses from one part of the garment district to another. She moved up the ladder almost as fast, and by age forty she was part owner of a couture house that was attracting international attention for their popular dress designs. For a decade she rubbed shoulders with the glitterati until the day in Washington when she was introduced to the chairman. She had known her share of bright guys but he ran much deeper. He talked in depth about things she knew only superficially. One year later they were married and splitting time between her condominium in New York and his apartment in Washington.

She reached for a Kleenex on her bedstand and gently blew her nose. "It's not that bad, is it dear?"

"Probably not."

"You usually don't fret about things."

"No, I don't."

"Well, what is it then?"

"I don't know, it's just an uneasy feeling I have."

"That's foolish."

"I guess so."

"Do you mind if I turn out the light, dear? I'm getting so tired."

"Go ahead, love. I'll just stay here awhile."

She clicked off the TV and then the light. A night-light burned in the bathroom. He could still see dark images in the room. He sat a long while in the semidarkness, deep in thought.

They called him the Wizard in college. He aced his courses and his undergraduate skills were much admired by his professors. He soon had the economics chair at Cornell, the youngest professor to ever become a department head at a major university. To everyone's dismay, he left his post and moved to Manhattan. The plan was to work as a bank economist and at the same time make judicious investments and become rich. He never took the job. Once in Manhattan he looked up Oscar Bloom, an obscure writer and political thinker who later came to be known as the founder of the neo-Libertarian movement. Bloom claimed to have taken the best parts of both political parties and melded them into the wave of the future. It hadn't worked out that way. His conservative belief in limited government and liberal view of social issues never gathered enough adherents to challenge the entrenched political parties. But, at the inception of the movement, the intellectually stimulating environment attracted some good minds. For a few years the chairman had been at the center of it.

Eventually he left New York and shuttled between a think tank in Los Angeles, the Treasury Department in Washington, and Manufacturers Hanover, a major New York bank. With each move he honed his skills as an economist and improved his fortunes. He disconnected from the Libertarians, but still held free market views and considered himself a classical economist in the mold of the Englishman Alfred Marshall, the influential head of the Cambridge Economics Department at the turn of the century. A modern economist embraces at least some of the views of many economic predecessors and the chairman was as familiar with Adam Smith and David Ricardo as with Marx or Malthus.

Prior to his appointment as the Fed chairman he had crossed his personal Rubicon. For many months it was rumored that he would get the job. Yet, he was at odds with the reigning Keynesian dogma that placed the government at the throttles of the economy. He favored a more laissez faire approach and felt certain that even John Maynard Keynes, the British economist who originally formulated a method of government intervention in the economy, would be aghast at the extent the government had now intruded. The Federal Reserve, for example, was supposedly independent of government, but any Fed chairman who strayed too far from the easy money policies promoted by the government would quickly get the boot.

He wasn't even certain there should be a Central Bank. Moreover, he had been a firm believer in gold money and the gold standard, and their absence made inflating the money supply all too easy for the politicians. It was Keynes who won him over. Of course, Keynes had died in 1946, but there was plenty written by him and about him. It wasn't just Keynes' economic theories that influenced him. The man had been breathtakingly brilliant and a wit to boot. He was Samuel Johnson as economist.

Keynes's good friend but philosophical enemy, Freidrich Hayek from the London School of Economics, told a story about how a group of them were sitting for dinner one evening with Hayek, separated by three seats from Keynes. Across from Hayek was seated an astronomer and since Hayek had recently read an article about a lost manuscript of the astronomer, Copernicus, he was able to engage in a lively discussion with the astronomer. As he related an obscure point, Keynes, busily engaged in a discussion down the table but apparently monitoring Hayek's conversation interrupted. "You are wrong, Hayek," he intoned and explained a small correction that Hayek had overlooked. Years later when Hayek won the Nobel Prize, the chairman had remembered the story and laughed.

Keynes had dealt with the Great Depression, an experience few modern economists could relate to. He advocated that the government step in and spend because the public, fearful of the future, was saving too much rather than spending, as they must to keep the economy going. The government would, for a while, take the place of the consumer and the government would do the spending. That's what had happened in the nineteen thirties. Whether it had worked or not was an open question. What had taken place, for sure, was that government had taken a much larger and permanent role in the economy.

The chairman had also been aware of Hayek's views that emanated from a group of economists in Austria. Their business cycle theory pointed to the expansion of money and credit as the reason for booms and busts. When credit expansion was curtailed, a recession or depression developed. This thought had been foremost in the chairman's mind as he considered that the job at the Fed might be leading him into a minefield. Yet, credit expansion and money supply growth had been going on since the end of the second world war and no terribly serious crisis or lasting damage had occurred other than periodic recessions. In fact, things had steadily improved and the economy was booming. Perhaps it would continue this way into the foreseeable future. He took heart at Keynes' response when asked about developing problems for the long term. "In the long run," Keynes had responded, "we are all dead." It became a famous remark in economic circles and when the chairman became certain that the long run still had a great distance to go, he took the job.

Quietly he rose from the chair and moved to the bed.

Chapter 4

———

Taiwan and mainland China exchanged harsh words the day following Richie's currency plunge. It was heated enough to put the U.S. Pacific Fleet on a low-level alert. The dollar, always a haven in an emergency, moved up strongly against the yen and staged a mild rally against the Euro.

Richie was in agony. In only one day he found himself in trouble. As his losses mounted through the day, he wrestled with the idea of closing out his position and cutting his losses. He seldom hung around to take a big shellacking, but in this case he continued to hold through the day. The coming week the August trade figures would be out and he based his dollar short on a healthy suspicion that there would be another record month for the trade deficit. He needed to hang on until then, but if the dollar kept rising he was going to get a margin call. In effect, he had lost almost half his money before he even got it.

The following morning he rose at five, sat down at his computer and checked Globex, the twenty-four hour electronic currency futures trading system. Next he went to the kitchen, put the coffee on, slipped out the back door and ran for thirty-five minutes in predawn darkness. Back in the house he poured himself a coffee, slid into the leather chair in his study and, glistening with sweat, dialed London. The operator at Johnson and Pixley, world-renowned precious metals dealers and currency traders, answered on the second ring. He asked for Mickey Halliday and, in moments, the currency specialist was on the phone.

"Mickey, hi, Richie Stenquist."

"Hello, Richie."

"Listen, I've got a short going on the dollar, I'm long on the yen and the Euro, and it's moving against me a little bit here. Anything you can tell me?"

The two of them had been exchanging information and rumors for the past five years, ever since Richie had called him about an article Mickey had written in the *Commodity Trader.* They knew each other's information to be reliable.

"Sounds like Taiwan backed down a bit overnight, Richie. Actually, the yen's perked up a little here in the last minute or two, must be on the news."

"Good." Richie's spirits soared. Moments before he had checked Globex for early trading news and the yen had been down slightly.

"Any other news?" he continued.

"Yeah, a guy over at Smith, Miller just told me he'd heard a rumor that Cayman Partners was in trouble. They're a medium-sized hedge fund. Offshore, you know. Word is they're mostly short on the Euro, puts, and contracts. If they move to close them out, it may give you a lift."

"Terrific."

"You have anything for me, Richie?"

"Not much. One little thing. The guy I have lunch with every day is tight with an analyst in Toronto. Told him, for sure, the board at Red Lake Properties is going to close their Keno Mine in Nevada. Announcing it tomorrow. Subtract a hundred and fifty thousand ounces of production."

"Thanks, Richie. Probably won't have much effect on the gold price, but it's good to know."

"O.K., Mickey, thanks a lot."

"Stay in touch, Richie."

"Good-bye."

That was the best phone conversation he'd had in awhile, Richie thought to himself. He should be able to hold on until the news release came out next week on the trade deficit. It's hell when you're so thinly capitalized, he mused further. Nevertheless, he had faith in himself and would continue to live and work with the risk until he got rich or went down in flames.

He trotted out to the end of the driveway and brought in the morning paper. The local business scene was upbeat. Everybody was making money and lots of it. The job market was tighter than ever. Yesterday, the governor proposed a plan to lower state taxes. A couple of local software companies announced a merger that had sent both their stocks up twenty percent in a day. Retail sales were rosy. There were two cars in every garage and two chickens in every pot. It was economic nirvana. Still there was noticeable weakness in bonds, and the poor liquidity in lower grade issues had widened spreads to punishing levels for the sellers.

Nancy was up. She asked about his trading positions and brightened on the improved news. Soon she was reciting her plans for the day. As he headed for the shower she settled in the kitchen to make him breakfast. Although he planned to go to the office, he would be going through the motions until he saw the coming news on the trade deficit. It would be a long week.

Four days later, on Monday morning, Richie strode into the office. This was the week the trade data came out and with his futures trades now back to even, he felt optimistic. Carol Olson could sense that he was pumped up in anticipation of a profitable week. Richie dropped into his chair and checked the screen. Both the dollar and the bonds were weaker. A subprime lender in Houston had gone under and the wire service offered that as an explanation for the bond weakness. Trouble persisted through the morning with the bond market pressuring down stocks and the dollar.

After walking across the street for a shoeshine, Richie returned to his computer screen and, with surprise and elation, he watched the bottom fall out. The Dow was down two hundred in lockstep with tumbling bonds and a weak dollar. What was going on, he wondered. Finally, a notice funneled across his screen that the mammoth Argonaut Bond Fund, a specialist in High yields, had announced that highly leveraged positions in their bond portfolio has been responsible for significant losses that threatened the solvency of the fund. Mass resignations had taken place in the management company. With an hour left of trading Richie watched his Big Board give up another hundred points, while bonds declined sharply and the dollar plummeted. "Yahoo," he shouted, startling the preoccupied Miss Olson.

At five minutes after three, Bernie Fogelson called. " Did you see that? Man, the computer stocks got slaughtered today, Richie. We got a guy here that covered a margin call with his life savings. One more down day and he's toast."

"I think we're going to go down again," answered Richie.

"Me, too."

"Everything's so overvalued."

"The tech stocks have been giving up ground all month and they're still goofy."

"The Argonaut deal really spooked the bond market. Rates jumped pretty good. Did you see the dollar drop against the yen?"

"Unbelievable! Hey guy, you're looking good on these dollar contracts."

"Yeah, I've got a double."

"Cool."

"I'll be watching Globex on the computer late tonight and early tomorrow. It'll be interesting."

"This is such a bubble, Richie. It could really get dicey."

"We've been saying that a long time."

"I know, but you can only be right once on the kind of heavy crap we've been talking about."

"You going to make any money on this?"

"Hell, gold stocks were down. All the metals got pounded, so did the grains, even oil."

"What do you think it means?"

"Too early to tell."

"Maybe some kind of deflation."

"Maybe."

"It's a house of cards, Bernie. They better not let it go too far."

"Sometimes, when things get too far out of whack, there's nothing anybody can do. I mean, they don't even understand it."

"A few of them do, Bernie. They know some of the things we know but they're going along with it because they're not sure."

"You never know, in a couple of days this could be just a blip on the screen."

"Maybe. But one more down day and I'm going to start pyramiding."

"You got big balls, Richie."

"I hope I still got them by the end of the week."

"I'm going to short a couple of high techs myself."

"O.K., Papa bear. Good luck."

"Talk to you tomorrow."

Richie stopped at the flower shop in the lobby on his way home. He bought a dozen bright red roses for Nancy. On the drive home he contemplated the day's events. Perhaps his luck had changed. In a sense he was gambling, but speculating was a better term. Speculation was a more intelligent and informed kind of gambling. He was going to push his luck, but despite the high risk involved, he knew that in a fast-moving market he could make moves that were mostly right.

Early the following morning Richie glued himself to Globex and the latest reports on business TV. Dow futures were way down. The dollar, continuing its fall overnight, fell hard against major currencies, dropping while he watched. Yesterday's results would surely continue into this day. He began to formulate a strategy to capitalize on the events he saw unfolding.

He was on the phone to his broker, Ken Ferguson, when the U.S. markets opened and with the profits now existing in his current account he doubled up on his contracts. He knew this pyramiding was dangerous. The additional leverage would work against him the minute the market went opposite to his position. He would multiply his profits if right, but compound his losses if wrong.

The day unfolded with the bear in control and it stayed that way throughout the trading session. A full-blown dollar retreat was underway, while the bond market was in serious decline. Dow stocks were pounded, down two hundred and ten points. The Nasdaq fell eighty-one. It was a huge day for Richie. He needed for it to continue one more session because on the following day the trade report would be out and the dollar should then continue its tumble. Somewhere there would be intervention. The U.S., Japanese, and European governments would try to reverse the dollar decline in short order. He had a sense for when, but it was a timing thing that he would have to negotiate perfectly.

It went down pretty much as he hoped. The next day the slide in the dollar continued, but at a slower pace. On Thursday the government announced that the trade deficit had ballooned to almost thirty billion. Down went the dollar once again, crashing furiously against the rising yen and Euro. His long contracts on the two currencies exploded upward and his profits swelled. When the dollar route seemed unstoppable he called Ken Ferguson and sold out the entire position.

"Hey, man, super trade," said the broker.

"Thanks. I'll call you next week."

No sooner had his order been executed than large purchases of the dollar began to take place, suddenly stemming the currency's decline. The dollar turned in its tracks and began to rise. The intervention Richie had suspected was big and powerful. The governments were at work. The dollar snapped back but within a few days the rebound in the dollar peaked and began to stabilize.

Now Richie stepped in and bought one hundred-fifty contracts, half on the yen and half on the Euro.

"Man, you got ice water in your veins," said Ken Ferguson as he took the order.

"I don't think it's over."

"I hope you're right, for your sake."

The Dow trickled down a hundred points more and ended the week with a loss of six hundred points. The Argonaut bond debacle was old news now. The Feds were looking to indict several of the principals. There was a huge loss, and the investors were not protected by government insurance. The only ramification was the continuing liquidity problems in the bond market and the widening spreads in mortgage-backed securities, corporate bonds, and asset-backed securities. Bond investors were switching to quality, and the low-grade bonds were suffering. As bond prices plunged, their yields rose to enticingly high levels but the market still had a bad case of nerves and buyers were sparse.

The last thing the overly sensitive markets needed was any further bad news or rumors. At that inopportune moment a rumor flashed around that the Sausalito Bond Trust, a medium-sized fund, was postponing redemptions for sixty days. Their customers couldn't get their money out. Confidence evaporated on the news and so did stock prices. Once again bonds dropped, but the effect on the stock market was more severe. The Dow plummeted five hundred and ten points, recovered somewhat in the last half hour to close down four hundred and twenty-five on the day.

The currency markets did not react until the following day when the dollar nose-dived once again. World stock markets were also weak but as they lost ground the dollar stabilized. Then as the major foreign bourses recovered from the initial shock of the New York markets big decline, the dollar fell again. The next day brought more of the same. The Dow plunged another three hundred and forty while the dollar dropped to under one hundred yen.

That night Richie took Nancy out for dinner. Their animated conversation continued late into the evening. This was a day to remember and they celebrated their good fortune.

Chapter 5

———

Victor D. Rappaport exuded an aura of supreme self-confidence. His successful morning TV show was the most watched financial show on any network. It ran each weekday for one hour directly before the stock market opened, starting at eight-thirty eastern time. Not only did he have a huge television audience, he had a large following through his fan club and newsletter, *The Rappaport Report*. The former was ten dollars, but the latter cost one hundred and forty-nine dollars annually. For that amount you could read Victor bragging in print about his infallible skills at stock picking. The newsletter format offered his favorite stock selections. Next he heaped scorn on any member of the unwashed public who might disagree with his views of a perpetual boom. Then he trashed those investments he didn't like, especially foreign bonds, his favorite whipping boy.

The director of his show, who disliked him immensely, would often say that Victor proved, "Your greatest enemy is your own vanity." For Victor was not just egotistical, he had moved beyond that. Years of capital gains and profitable advice had caused him to become grand. Convinced of his own mental superiority and financial genius, he became, in his own mind, the center of the financial universe. Everyone else was in orbit around him. No prince at the court of Louis the Fourteenth had a more arrogant or regal bearing. He was soundly disliked by the employees connected with the production of his program as well as the editorial staff of the newsletter. He treated them all with disdain. Victor was no longer in touch with the feelings and aspirations of other members of the human race.

On the morning following two days of steep market drops that had caused Richie and Nancy to linger over dinner, Victor had invited two high-profile guests onto his program. Melanie Pearson was the best-known financial analyst and money manager in the country. She gained notoriety through fifteen years of prescient market commentary and chalked up two impressive market calls at crucial turning points in the Dow arguing accurately for the resumption of the bull market.

She had come to New York from the Tampa office of Harriman Securities. She was an impressive-looking woman with blonde hair, an attractive face, and ample bosom. She was glib or articulate as the situation required and she wrote powerful market analysis and commentary. On TV she came across like a movie star. In every office that she had worked, the men longed for her or secretly loved her. She had never given any of them a tumble and stayed faithful to her husband, a meek fellow who managed a car rental agency.

She had been trained to be bullish and believed in the primacy of the stock market. She had more or less gone with her firm's recommendations in the early years. Later, she branched out and wrote about technology stocks. Many of her recommendations doubled and redoubled. She had a hot hand and soon became a personality. She was bullish when others grew timid, but unlike those analysts who predicted a permanent bull market, she remembered some lean days for her father who had also been a broker for a New York firm. In nineteen seventy-one her mother had to start working to pay the bills. Her father had been deeply depressed by his meager paychecks. She knew that a change for the worse was possible, but not probable.

The other guest that morning was the ever optimistic Anthony Fairbanks. Author of the famous Wall Street manifesto, "Adam Smith Gets Rich," he was also the manager of a huge portfolio of stocks for wealthy investors, all of whom gave his firm a minimum of $500,000 to get started. He was New York born and bred and had started work at age eighteen as a gofer for a major brokerage firm. Long ago he had left Queens for the Upper East Side and now lived in his expensive condominium overlooking Central Park in the toniest Manhattan neighborhood.

The program opened with the usual lengthy speech by Victor Rappaport that quickly turned into a diatribe against those faint hearts and backsliders who doubted the persistency of the bull market. He was especially incensed by an article in the *Economist* pointing out a growing dent in the value of tech stocks. Now almost breathlessly, he turned to Anthony Fairbanks.

"Anthony, you've been through your share of downturns. Certainly you're not running for cover now, are you?"

"Not at all, Victor. In fact we're looking at this as a buying opportunity."

"We've seen a ten percent decline come on rather suddenly. Does that worry you at all?"

"Not really. I would call it an old-fashioned correction of the type that we have come to expect periodically."

"Are your customers worried at all?"

"Actually, we've seen just the opposite. A number of clients are planning to send us more money."

"What moves do you expect to make at this juncture, Anthony?" purred Victor.

"We think we see some outstanding values here and we plan to become quite aggressive over the near term."

"Apparently you're not concerned that the market could deteriorate further?"

"Not in the least. You always want to take advantage of these dips. In fact, some of our best gains have come when we bought the dips. Heavens, if it goes lower we intend to buy more. Personally, I plan to jump in with both feet. Quite frankly, I don't see that happening. In the last few days stocks have become cheap again. These bargains attract today's more sophisticated investor."

"Yesterday we had a guest that thought thirty to forty times earnings on the S & P stocks might be too rich. What say you?"

"We have no inflation. Technology is driving this market. Productivity is rising. There's plenty of money still uncommitted and everyone in the world wants to invest here. This is a new era, a golden age, if you will. We love equities at these levels and so it seems does everyone else. Heavens, forty times earnings is going to be a bargain in the years ahead. We don't see this thing stopping anytime soon, Victor."

"Thank you, Anthony, for those words of wisdom. Our other guest this morning is that femme fatale of finance, Melanie Pearson. Melanie, you've been a phenomenal forecaster throughout the past decade. What are your thoughts now?"

"We're a bit cautious here, Victor, especially in the technology sector. Overall we expect that we're getting close to the lows for this pullback and once we see a trend reversal we'll be buyers again."

"Sort of an amber light."

"Yes, yes, but one that we expect will be green quite soon."

"Anything in particular you like here?" he asked, his eyes dropping to her bosom as the camera went to her. Lascivious thoughts flashed through his mind. Victor could never break the habit of frequently glancing down at her breasts. Once when she had been a guest, his director had mildly rebuked him for his frequent stares.

"We're very fond of utilities now and since the slight deflation over the last few weeks has lowered the price of oil, we've been buying the airlines again."

"Melanie, you've made some great calls during prior market breaks. You have a reputation as a wise soothsayer. Could you give us your prediction now?"

"I think this current correction, which came as a consequence of bond market difficulties, has probably about run its course. I see this market moving dramatically higher between now and the end of the year. Victor, I fully expect to see new highs on the Dow. We are staying fully invested and we urge everyone else to do the same. These periodic corrections should be looked at as buying opportunities. If you get out of this market now, you'll probably be sorry later."

"Thank you, Melanie, for your thoughtful comments. Let's take a break."

After the commercials the conversation continued. Then came reports from network analysts from around the globe. Victor gave more of his profound thoughts on the market, actually referring to them as profound. A junior broadcaster read the news and a second announcer gave earnings reports, along with merger and takeover news. Finally, Victor and his two guests wound up with a synopsis that essentially repeated their earlier comments.

"Thank you all," said Victor, nodding with a wide smile into the camera, "and happy investing."

"O.K.," nodded the director.

Across the monitor screen the market began to trade.

"There's the opening bell, let's watch awhile," he suggested as both of them continued to sit and trading began. The lighting went off on their set and their sector of the studio went dim.

"Well, we've told the dumb bastards what to do," said Victor. "Let's see if they follow orders."

"It's going to be one hell of a rally," offered Anthony Fairbanks. "I'm standing by my predictions one hundred percent." It was a subtle attempt to ingratiate himself with Victor and edge out Melanie as a market guru. However, it would never work with Victor as a wave of arousal swept over him as he grinned at Melanie. She was oblivious to his passion. She didn't know it, but Victor had head problems. One was too big and one was too small and both kept him from accurate thinking.

It was straight down from the opening bell. Weakness in Europe continued in New York and as the three of them stared at the screen the bottom fell out. Within minutes the Dow was down one hundred and dropping fast. Then it was down two hundred and before an hour had expired, three hundred.

"Shit," uttered Anthony Fairbanks, who had sat transfixed throughout the hour. "I have to get back to the office. We don't need anybody pulling their money out now." He rose abruptly and without a good-bye, disappeared from view.

"I don't like it, Victor," Melanie offered. "This bond market fallout is raising too much hell. My God, the dollar is just sinking out of sight."

"Listen, Melanie. I'm not giving up on the greatest bull market in history. This is just a short-term blip. I'm staying fully invested. I won't sell a share and any money I get will buy more. When I send out my newsletter next week the timing will be perfect. I'm going to turn it around single-handedly. Me, Victor Rappaport. I'll show these sons-of-bitches what clout is. Believe me."

Melanie swallowed. Wow! This guy was a red flag all by himself.

"Victor, I'm going to go. Thanks so much for having me."

"Good-bye, Melanie. I plan to have you on again soon."

His thoughts turned salacious again as he carefully watched her exit. He sat in the half darkness alone, fantasizing and watching the screen. It was getting worse, he noticed as he yawned and stretched. Nothing, however, was going to rattle Victor Rappaport, even the final close down an unbelievable eight hundred and twenty-four points. It was the biggest one-day drop in history, but he stood firm, he wasn't going to let it bother him for a moment. When he gave a buy signal, things would rebound.

Chapter 6

——

The shocking eight hundred and twenty-four point drop in the stock market on that fateful Wednesday left investors reeling. Brokerage firms were overwhelmed attempting to notify customers of margin calls. However, by Thursday morning most margin players knew they had to raise more cash or sell something. Brokers had worked late into the night conveying the bad news.

Mutual fund redemptions were soaring. Clogged phone lines meant that most people couldn't get through to liquidate their funds. Late in the trading day quite a few brokerage firms had closed their switchboards. Trading had become impossible. Sell orders weren't getting executed. Internet trading ground to a halt. Hoards of sellers were shut out of the market. All of this meant a huge wave of sell orders were piled up at the opening bell on Thursday. Exchange officials and floor specialists look toward the start of trading with trepidation. World Stock had crashed through the night. The Nikkei in Tokyo collapsed almost a thousand points. Hong Kong's Hang Seng index and the Straits Times index in Singapore were off between three and five percent. The Paris CAC Forty and the Dax in Germany were down equivalent amounts. The London FT Exchange tumbled precipitously. The Argentine Merval and Brazilian Bovespa simply closed trading for the balance of the week.

Waves of selling at the open took the Dow down six hundred points by midmorning. A press conference at twelve-thirty eastern by the Treasury secretary, the Exchange president and several brokerage firm executives promising absolute liquidity took the steam out of the selling. A rally commenced and the market screamed up three hundred points. Piles of backed-up orders were liquidated into the surging market and volume soared to the highest one-day level in history. It was a high-water mark that would stand for three decades. However, by the closing bell the averages fell once again, ending down four hundred and twenty-six points for the day.

Despite the assurances by officialdom, and the compelling words of brokerage firm spokespersons who were seen on every talk show, newscast, and financial program, it was clear that investor sentiment had changed. Margin players had been wiped out and high-tech investors had seen the values of their stocks evaporate at a greater rate than the big cap stocks. Billions had disappeared. Borrowing to buy securities had backfired like never before and the big players, hedge-funds, brokerage firms, and banks were suffering just like the small guy. Their losses were multiplied by the leverage. Derivative protection for the big players had often broken down as sell orders were held up. Trading restrictions implemented by the exchange shut down index arbitrage trading. Too much money had vanished to prop things up and spark a recovery anytime soon.

Friday's market opened with a wave of selling. It was a day that came to be known in history as "Papa Bear," with the previous day named "Baby Bear," and the Wednesday before called "Mama Bear." The three bears were the triumvirate that broke the back of the bull and ended the greatest stock market boom in history. By two o'clock the Dow had dropped a mind-boggling one thousand and fifty points, triggering a circuit breaker or trading curb that shut down the market for the rest of the day. It was said that by three o'clock the bars in the vicinity of Wall Street were jammed with shell-shocked traders, investors, and brokers who, in drowning their sorrows, set a record for receipts at these lower Manhattan establishments.

In Wichita, Kansas, Mary Clark Whittington called an emergency meeting of the Tanager Investment Club. The club's eleven members had only one year before moved their entire five hundred and forty thousand dollar portfolio, that had taken fifteen years to build, into Internet and technology stocks. As best she could tell, the club now had stocks valued at one hundred and eighty thousand dollars. Since none had been sold, a decision must be made on whether to hold or sell. Any buying was now out of the question.

As Mary Whittington dialed the members, her stomach was turning over with anxiety. Her husband, Dr. Robert Whittington, a successful dental practitioner, had invested heavily into the same kinds of stocks that the investment club owned. Trouble was, he had borrowed against their home and piled the proceeds from the second mortgage on top of the money they had originally moved from their money market accounts into stocks. It was all the money they had. Age fifty-eight was no time to start over again. She kept running the numbers through her mind and unless she was figuring wrong, they were wiped out. The equity left in their stock account was a fraction of what they owed. Not only that, Bob had recently cut his practice to the bone, based on the fat profits he had racked up in the stock market. She didn't know if he could get back into it again, or ever recapture his business and old income level.

Louis Ascot answered the phone on the first ring and listened to Mary Whittington explain the reason for her call. "I'll be there," he responded. He had been sitting with his face in his hands, stomach churning. Louis had retired early from Kansas Power and Light. He took the buyout money and plunked it into mutual funds. He put his self-directed retirement plan into the same funds. Then he put all his savings into mutual funds. He did so well that he wanted more. The only other source of equity was his home. It was paid for. Against the wishes of his wife, he put a mortgage on his house at one hundred percent of the appraised value. He invested the money in mutual funds. The house payments were quite high and since he had no income, he planned to liquidate a small amount of the mutual funds every quarter and make three months worth of house payments.

In the last three days his world had turned upside down. Some of his mutual funds had lost half or more of their asset value. Still he hadn't sold. Despite the relentless sobbing of his wife, he remained intractable. But now he was thinking of unloading everything on Monday. He could apply it to the house mortgage and pay most of it off, but then they would have no money. Nothing! The damnable meager Social Security check would be it. No more winter vacations, no more traveling, no more hunting trips out west with the boys. Maybe it would rebound on Monday. He couldn't take a chance on missing that. What should he do? He looked forward to the emergency investment club meeting that evening. He needed advice and other opinions. In the meantime, he watched the stock market reports on TV, switching the channel away from any commentator who sounded the least bit pessimistic.

Richard Cromwell liked poker and took frequent trips to Las

Vegas. Lately he had missed his usual vacation in Nevada because he was getting his fill of action on the Internet, buying and selling stocks. His mother, Anne, who often bragged that they were direct descendants of the seventeenth century English puritan, Oliver Cromwell, had always funded his speculation and his extravagant lifestyle.

Unfortunately, Richard had taken every cent that he had and sunk it into a new Internet stock offering that his broker assured him was an absolute lock. What Anne Cromwell didn't know was that her son had also sold her portfolio of utility stocks that she had allowed him to manage, and sunk the better part of her fortune into the same IPO. Richard and his mother were now the fourth largest shareholders in the company. The stock opened at eighteen and rose that day to twenty-four, causing Richard and his girlfriend to purchase a two-hundred-dollar bottle of wine at dinner that evening. The following week started out choppy and then ran into Mama Bear on Wednesday. By the time Baby Bear and Papa Bear were through, the stock was 3 1/4. Richard had just finished vomiting when Mary Clark Whittington called.

After completing her call with the morose Cromwell, Mary continued to dial her club members. Five of them could not be reached. After several rings to the home of Joyce Gill, a meek hello greeted her. "What's wrong, Joyce?" she asked. Immediately Joyce Gill began to sob. "Oh, Mary, Harry and I have had everything we own under management, you know, at that Pluto Asset Management in Kansas City." She sobbed again, more poignantly than before. "We were doing so good. They had us in technology. I called them today and they told me we've lost three million dollars. All we've got left there is one million. Good God! Mary, I don't know what to do. We'll have to sell the house in Cabo." With that, Mary began to sob relentlessly and tried tearfully to relate her own tale of woe. After the mutual crying session had run its course, the two of them lapsed into a long silence until Mary brought them back to the purpose of her call.

Nicholas Boosalis did not hear Mary's call. He sat in his chair, dazed and depressed. He could not move. Two years ago Nick, as he was called, had sold his medical diagnostics company to a growth company, Baker Labs. After twenty-eight years of struggle, he had finally got the big payday. Nick took mostly stock rather than cash. He had wanted it that way. Baker Labs was a sure thing. When he needed money, Nick pledged his stock at First Prairie National Bank. As Baker stock went up, Nick borrowed more and more to finance what had become a lavish lifestyle. But on the Wednesday that Mama Bear had savaged the market, Baker Labs had announced a steep decline in earnings. Furthermore, they were predicting a loss in the next quarter. The stock fell off a cliff. Baker Labs was now quite undervalued and Nick Boosalis was bankrupt.

Another member of Mary's investment club, Steve Silvestri, also failed to answer his phone. He had maxed out his half dozen credit cards, and bought stocks with the proceeds. Steve had the lowest net worth of any member of the Tanager Investment Club, but he cultivated an image of affluence. Lately he'd borrowed against his condominium and talked a friend at the bank into a ninety-day loan that was thinly collateralized. He'd plopped the money into the market and had been spending most of his time as an insurance underwriter, watching his stocks on the computer. In fact, the boss had warned him about this habit. Steve had missed work the past two days. Nor had he answered the numerous rings from his stockbroker on Friday, calling to advise him that he had been sold out after failing to make a margin call. Steve would never make a margin call again. That's because Steve was dead. That very afternoon he had put a .357 Magnum into his ear and pulled the trigger.

Chapter 7

———

Rain was coming down hard in Minneapolis. Richie Stenquist's Lexus crawled along the freeway, sandwiched between an endless row of cars and trucks. The windshield wipers flapped out a wicked beat. A big semi slowly rolled along in front of him. He didn't like big trucks. When they were in front of you it was impossible to see. At least he thought, this truck was traveling slowly. Usually the big trucks were clipping along much too fast for crowded city freeways. A lot of people were killed by semis driving too fast, he mused. They should have a special limit for trucks in the city, or at least keep them in the inside lane.

He called Ken Ferguson in Chicago on his car phone but it was too early and he wasn't in. Richie planned to make some moves soon. It was Tuesday morning following the week of the Three Bears and he was slightly unsure of himself. On Monday, a weekend of positive spin by economists, stock analysts, and politicians had sparked a rally at the opening bell. But there was too much damage. A Japanese brokerage firm announced a bankruptcy reorganization and in the U.S. several mutual funds were delaying payments to shareholders. Around midday an announcement came across the wire that CK Management, a small hedge fund, couldn't repay its bank loan which was collateralized by stocks and bonds that were worth far less than the loan. A three hundred point rally on the upside turned into a two hundred and ninety point rout.

To date the bear market had sent the Dow stocks tumbling twenty-five percent. But it wasn't this index alone that had investors aghast. Most of the other stocks had gone in the tank, with many down fifty to ninety percent. The big caps were wounded, but the small and medium caps were near death. Foreign markets had recovered on Monday but still looked weak. The bond market stabilized when rumors of an interest rate cut circulated. That news left the dollar weaker. Then the dollar recovered as foreign buying blunted the drop. These crosscurrents troubled Richie and made him uncertain.

Richie assessed his situation carefully. He had pyramided his first twenty contracts out of profits and added twenty more. Then a few days later he had sold out for a gain of three hundred and eighty thousand dollars. Then he had purchased forty new contracts and pyramided with forty more on the eve of the stock crash, which had also buried the dollar. It was incredibly aggressive but at this moment he was up four million dollars. At breakfast that morning, Nancy had strongly suggested he sell. At first she was stunned by his four-hundred-thousand-dollar gain. But this last transaction had left her pinching herself. Had he miscalculated? She knew he hadn't, but she also knew that he was concerned about a whole different problem than she was. "Let's not lose this," she told him gently. He looked right past her. She wondered if he heard. He was so intense lately.

Richie sat in his office staring at the computer screen. The rain pelted his window and low clouds obliterated the horizon. He was going to sell this morning. He suspected the dollar would weaken further and he'd miss out on some profits, but he planned to take new positions later. He knew his wife and others who had learned of his gargantuan profits were mystified why he hadn't yet sold. He understood their fears, but a few million dollars didn't mean as much to Richie as it did to most people. He thought back years ago to an old trader, Dick Mortenson, who had made a million in silver futures. "Peanuts!" he had exclaimed. Richie chuckled out loud as he thought of him. Who could relate, he thought. Dick Mortenson had never received the ten or twenty million he was shooting for and, so far, Richie hadn't received the hundred million or more he wanted. He would keep trying and in his mind it was an absolute certainty that he would succeed. The money was important. He craved the security and freedom that a fortune would bring. Deep inside him, however, another fire burned. The big money represented validation. He wanted to be the top performer. He wanted the identity, he wanted to be somebody.

Ken Ferguson was having breakfast that morning with four other commodities brokers. They listened attentively as he described his biggest client.

"Listen, the son of a buck has ice water in his veins."

"He's a million ahead and he doubles up. Can you believe it?"

"Now he's four million up in thirty days and he hasn't sold."

"What's he going to do?" asked one of the brokers.

"I don't know, he don't say nothin."

"Man, he hit it just right," intoned another. "How did he know?"

"Pure-assed luck," said another.

"Anybody could have done it," said the fourth. "Just short anything last month and you'd be rich."

"Yeah, Foster, just like you," jibed Ferguson. "Putting everybody you got into index futures the wrong way. What a bath." The group burst into laughter at the expense of the chagrined Foster.

"Screw you," came the lame reply.

"I got to get going," said Ferguson, taking a last swig of his lukewarm coffee. "The main man may be calling. Think of that commission on four mill," he giggled. The others rose in unison, tossing out change for the waitress.

"Man, would I like a customer like that Richie Stenquist," said one broker as he followed the others out. The legend had begun to grow.

After Richie had made his call to Ken Ferguson and Ken had called back to confirm the sale of his contracts, he left the office. He worked his way through the seven blocks of skyway, came out on lower Hennepin Avenue and entered the Minneapolis public library. There he requested a half dozen books pertaining to the crash of 1929, found himself a quiet table and read through the day.

Early the next morning he called Germany for Dr. Klaus Furstenburg, former economist at the Bank of International Settlements. He subscribed to Furstenburg's weekly fax service at a cost of one thousand dollars a year. The doctor provided a classical economic viewpoint and cornucopia of information on currencies, precious metals, and commodities.

"My dear boy," he lectured Richie, "The bubble has burst. It cannot be restored. What is the name of your person that had a great fall?"

"Humpty-Dumpty?"

"Yes, indeed, that is the one."

Richie chuckled.

"What do you see now, sir?"

"More of the same, I think. There will be repercussions for the U.S. economy."

"You certainly predicted what has happened."

"The credit excesses and speculation were absolutely mind-bog-gling. I am dismayed that no one in the U.S. could see it. The state of economic thinking in your country is really quite pathetic."

"What do you think about the dollar?"

"It has been crushed. What is there to think?"

"It looks like we could have a big deflation."

"Absolutely! Deflation, this is the thing to fear. You Americans talk of inflation. It is nonsense!"

The doctor held strong opinions and as he talked he became more emphatic and less patient with Richie's questions, which in the doctor's mind, reflected both a lack of insight and conviction.

"What do you think of gold here?"

"No, no! I would advise to buy German bonds and nothing else."

"I see."

"You Americans, you have been quite clever at manufacturing credit and most efficient in expanding the capital markets. But now I think you will not be doing so good!"

Richie hesitated with his response.

"Good-bye, then."

With that, the doctor simply hung up.

Richie spent the balance of the day on the phone talking with commodity analysts, economists, newsletter editors, and market technicians. He knew a lot of people and was adept at ferreting out information and gathering opinions. It was work he enjoyed.

The stock market staged a brief midweek rally and by Friday erased the losses for the week. But by the end of three weeks the Dow had slipped another thousand points, spreading consternation among those who were counting on a sustained rally. Foreigners deserted the market in earnest, worried about losses both in stock and currency. Mutual fund redemptions were chron-

50

ic as money flowed steadily out, transferring to bank savings and money market funds.

An army of brokerage firm spokesmen plied the networks with assurances that it was a good time to buy.

"Stay in this market, whatever you do," was the oft-repeated advice. Across America shell-shocked investors were busy licking their wounds and frequently sneered at anyone who recommended they buy more stocks.

Richie was watching Victor D. Rappaport on financial TV when he issued his "everyone back in the water" advice. With the strongest possible recommendation on his TV program and in his newsletter he told his audience that his "far-reaching thoughtful advice was the turning point in the market. Expect a sharp rally from this point on, followed by a buying panic," he advised. The market dropped one hundred and thirty-eight points that day.

"Stick a fork in it Richie, it's done," said Bernie Fogelson over lunch a few weeks later. He had busily related story upon story about the battered customers of his firm. That same week had brought announcements of massive layoffs at brokerage firms. A combination of losses and falling volume at some of the major brokerages had eroded the value of their stocks and cast a pall of gloom over the industry.

"We had it too good for too long," offered Bernie.

"Our guys are afraid to call some of their customers. Volume sucks. It's going to be a long winter. If you haven't put anything aside, say good-bye to your lifestyle."

"What happens now?" questioned Richie to no one in particular. "That's what I'd like to know."

"Screw it," said Bernie, "I'm going to Florida for the winter. You should come, too, with what you made."

Richie smiled. He still had work to do.

Chapter 8

———

After several moderate winters an icy blitzkrieg swept across Minnesota. Record cold and deep, drifting snow made life harsh for those who ventured outside. Richie didn't mind the cold. He drove from the warm garage at his home to the warm garage at his office. It was the snow he hated. It made driving hazardous and slowed traffic to a frustrating crawl. It also made it impossible to jog outside and he was forced to do his running inside at the Downtown Athletic Club. After a storm dumped a big snowfall, he had to wait for a private contractor to plow out his driveway. Then a big snow removal truck from the suburb came by to clean off the street. One morning after his driveway had been plowed and he was readying himself to try and make it to work, the city plow came by and threw up a huge ridge of ice and snow at the point his driveway met the street. He made a run at the ridge with his Suburban, planning to break through, but hung the big four-wheel vehicle up on the unyielding snow pile. He stomped back into the house only to be warned by Nancy that the children could

52

overhear his bad language.

A chill had fallen over the U.S. economy as well and each unrelenting month of winter had brought a flock of new statistics and economic indicators, none of them good. The consumers, many who had been feeding their spending off of stock gains, were retreating like Napoleon's army. Consumer confidence fell like the thermometer. Housing starts, which always slowed in winter, had virtually stopped. Layoffs had started in the construction business and at some factories. Unemployment rolls were expanding week to week and automakers were warning of large future cuts if improvement didn't come soon. Worst of all was the high price of foreign goods that cost so much more now because of the fall of the dollar. For that reason, inflation had perked up.

The president had openly badgered the chairman of the Federal Reserve to lower interest rates. He had been joined by labor leaders and special interest groups who publicly criticized the Central Bank. However, the Fed balked, fearing that lower interest would have a negative impact on the dollar and send it lower. So much foreign money was invested in government securities that the Fed chairman could not risk the wholesale exit from U.S. markets that lower interest rates might provoke. In addition, low-grade bonds were still illiquid and continued to pressure up rates. New bond offerings were drying up and a couple of quarter-point drops in interest rates wouldn't cure what ailed that market. Investors insisted on exceeding high returns from anything less than blue-chip debt instruments. In effect, the capital markets were slowly shutting down for American business.

Gloomy profit forecasts punctuated the morning financial news each day. Individual companies announced sobering earnings results and saw their stocks retreat. Then they were hammered once again when analysts downgraded their future earnings.

Billions continued to flow out of stock and bond funds into money markets, banks, and foreign bonds. The major New York banks had seen their economic health deteriorate. Most had taken big losses in their trading departments. These banks had become accustomed to making a large percentage of their profits through their trading activity. Their huge derivative positions had proved incredibly profitable. This nontypical banking activity had started to backfire with mounting losses from leveraged trading positions and financial strains among the counterparties on those derivative contracts that hedged interest rates and currencies. The brokerage firms were in much the same boat with their once lucrative trading departments suddenly the source of mounting losses.

In November, Richie had begun to concern himself with the large tax that was going to come due in April on his four-million-dollar short-term capital gain. He was going to owe almost two million to Uncle Sam and he saw payment of that tax as a serious impediment to his trading plans for the coming year. If he could figure a way to forestall the taxes just one more year, it could prove to be enormously fruitful to him. He needed the money for a while longer because it would buy him a lot of contracts. He racked his brain for a month and finally came up with a plan.

Duke Peterson was an old pal of Richie's from his slow-pitch softball days. When he was single, he and Duke played ball on the same team, drank beer together, and sometimes competed for the same girls. For a while they had shared an apartment. Their softball team was sponsored by the Apple Valley State Bank where Duke was a vice-president. In those days he was already a savvy banker and someday would become president. It also helped that his father owned the bank.

Richie had called him for an appointment and Duke met him in the lobby with a smile. They shook hands. Richie knew that a part of his enthusiastic greeting was accounted for by the two million dollars he had on deposit in Duke's bank. Also, they were still good pals and got together socially once or twice a year for dinner. Their wives had become friends. Duke's father had retired to Florida and turned the bank over to him. The old boy was ninety-one and hadn't seen the north country in a decade. Recently his mind had slipped badly and Duke had hired a full-time nurse for him. Once they were seated in Duke's office, Richie began.

"I need you to do me a favor."

"What kind of favor?" responded Duke with a hint of trepidation.

"I would like you to accept my deposit of coinage, a great deal of coinage."

"What do you mean?"

"I'd like to deposit some bags of coins."

"Why, what's in them?"

"A thousand dollars worth of silver coins."

"O.K. How many?"

"Six hundred."

"Six hundred bags of coins?" Duke's voice reflected amazement.

"Yes, I'll have Brink's deliver them into your vault."

"My God. Then what?"

"You deposit them in my account."

"Why?"

"It will help me a great deal."

"We can't do it, Richie."

"Why not."

"We can't count that many coins. I don't have the staff."

"You don't have to count them."

"We do if we deposit them."

"No, all you have to do is weigh them. If they get fifty-five pounds of weight there's one-thousand dollars there."

"That's a big job."

"I'll pay for it."

"We can't keep them in the vault for you, Richie, and deposit them in your account. It's against banking regulation."

"Federal regulations only," pounced Richie, "a state bank can do it. It's perfectly legal."

"How do you know."

"I checked."

"I'd have to confirm that. But, jeez man, six hundred bags of coins, what a pain in the ass. How long would we have them here?"

"Sixty days."

"That's all? Then what?"

"Brink's picks them up."

"You'll need a fleet of armored cars."

"Brink's uses big eighteen-wheelers on this size load."

"Man, you got all the answers. But, it's going to be embarrassing having this many bags of coins coming in to the bank."

"Why? We'll use the side door. Only a few employees will see it."

"What else?"

"I'll be taking my money out of the bank to do this. But I'll put it back in right after I get rid of the bags."

"Why, what's going on? Why are you doing this?"

"O.K. The bags are silver coins. They once traded on the commodity exchange. You remember the old ninety percent silver coins they used prior to nineteen sixty-five? Like the silver Kennedy halves?

"Sure."

"I've got a big coin dealer in California who owns six hundred bags that he's partially financed at a bank that specializes in financing precious metals. I'm going to buy them, take delivery here, and deposit them with you."

"What am I missing?"

"I got a huge tax liability. I need to postpone it."

"How?"

"The bags are worth sixty-five hundred each, mostly because of their silver value. There is a premium on them over their silver value."

"I don't need to know about that. What are they worth?"

"Let's keep it simple, if you melt them they've got almost sixty-five hundred dollars worth of silver in them."

"And you are going to turn sixty-five hundred times six hundred," Duke quickly punched the numbers into the adding machine on his desk. "You are going to turn three million nine hundred thousand dollars into six hundred thousand once we hand you a deposit slip for the face value of the coins."

"Correct."

"It's illegal!"

"No, it's not. How can it be illegal for your bank, or any bank, to accept a deposit of U.S. coinage?"

"Well, it may not be for us, but for you, my friend, it's tax fraud."

"No way, Duke. Maybe they can claim it's a sham. Hey, they can claim anything, but can they do anything to me for depositing their money in a bank and carrying it on my books at its face value?"

"I don't know."

"They can nail you if there's a specific law prohibiting it. I've done my research and there's no such law. The first time through with something like this they just make you pay the taxes, that's all. And I'm going to pay them eventually, just one year late. All I'm doing is rolling it over into next year."

"I suppose you'd have to get audited for them to find it," volunteered Duke.

"That could happen. I'm racking up some big numbers and that attracts them. But, hell, that big tax return is still two years away if I can do this with you."

"You're a bright lad. I'll check with the bank's attorneys. I'm going to put it to them like this: A big customer of the bank wants to deposit six hundred bags of silver coins each worth six and a half times their face value. We can only credit him with the one thousand dollars face value, of course. We have the vault space, so that's not a problem and we'd like to earn the storage fees. We don't know how long they will be on deposit. We don't know why he's doing it. We don't know what he plans. I'm not mentioning anything about taxes and I will forever deny any knowledge of your tax scheme. If he says O.K., and he'll give me a letter to that effect, I'll do it. The storage fee is three hundred dollars per bag each year, payable on the day we begin to store them. There is no pro rata cancellation of the storage fee."

Richie smiled across the desk at him. "When will you know?"

"Call me in two days. I'll call him right away."

"O.K., and thanks."

With that, Richie sauntered out of the bank. Perhaps it will work he speculated as he crossed the parking lot toward his car. Taxes are a penalty on progress, he rationalized to himself. He needed to keep that money one more year.

Two days later Richie called the bank. "Believe it or not," said Duke, "the lawyer says it's completely legal for us to store the coins and give you a deposit slip at face value. He faxed me a letter to that effect. You can go ahead with it. I'm going to turn this over to Mavis Jandro, she'll be in charge of the project from the bank's standpoint, O.K.?"

"Fine. I'll talk to her now, if I can."

"Hold on, then."

"Thanks a lot, Duke."

Richie bought the silver bags. Brink's trucked them to the Apple Valley State Bank. It took three semiloads and for two days they trundled them through the side door of the bank into the vault. The bank employees passed it off as an eccentric ploy by a friend of the bank. They understood that sometimes you have to bend over for a big depositor. When Richie gave Mavis Jandro a check in the amount of eighteen thousand dollars for storage, it made more sense to everyone.

Richie shorted futures contracts to cover any losses he might suffer if silver went down while he held the bags. At year-end Richie's financial statement showed a $600,000 bank balance at the Apple Valley State Bank. The $3,900,000 had disappeared for sixty days. Then, in early February, he reversed the process and sold the coin bags back to the coin dealer. The bank was emptied of the coin bags and he had his millions back.

"Never again," said Duke in a loud voice for everyone in the bank to hear when he spotted Richie at the teller window. "We thought you were going to store these coins with us for years."

"Don't worry," responded Richie. "I won't do it again."

Chapter 9

———

Once he had his funds back in the bank Richie began to think in earnest about a new money-making strategy. The downturn in the economy had snowballed and first quarter GDP was certain to be negative. He knew this would hurt the dollar but he didn't have enough confidence to reinstate his big short position against the dollar. He'd taken a stab at a few stock index futures with mixed results as the stock market bobbed up and down.

On the home front, Nancy had become thoroughly disgusted with the winter weather. "God, I'd love to be able to sit outside for a while," she moaned to Richie over dinner.

"Maybe we should go to Florida," he said offhandedly, figuring that the girls' school requirement would be a roadblock for such a trip. Nancy had immediately expressed that concern, but talked on about how good the girls were doing in school. "It wouldn't hurt them to miss a few days," he added.

Richie had nothing more to say on the subject, but his one comment about Florida was all that it took to put Nancy into high gear. By the time their next day's dinner rolled around, she was equipped with a load of persuasive facts.

"The second week in March the teachers have a meeting on Monday so there's no school that day. I talked to a few teachers and they could give the girls their assignments for that week in advance. They wouldn't miss much if we're gone.

"I called the Four Seasons in Palm Beach and they have two rooms available side by side. I've got them on hold. Northwest has four seats available to Fort Lauderdale, two in coach, two in First Class on that Saturday. I'm holding them for twenty-four hours. We'd have a wonderful time." Richie laughed. The two girls smiled nervously, glancing between their parents, waiting for a verdict.

"O.K. with me."

A loud cheer reverberated through the house.

Stan Carlson, a neighbor, gave them a ride to the airport. Parking at the airport for a week was expensive, so it was better to catch a ride from an obliging neighbor and take a cab home at the end of the trip. Stan was a money manager for IDP, a huge financial entity with headquarters in Minneapolis. He and Richie had become friends at neighborhood get-togethers, and often they would sidle to the fringe of a backyard barbecue, sip their beer, and talk about markets. Stan was a bright guy and while he admired Richie's independence and knowledge, he considered him to be on the fringe. He'd heard rumors that Richie had made a big score in currency futures, but felt that this was more luck than anything else. Richie just wasn't mainstream enough for it to be anything more than a fluke. He liked the guy but his economics were too far out and he had this weird view that the economy was going into the tank someday.

Events of the past half-year had proven Richie at least partially correct, so Stan Carlson was glad to give the family a ride and get

a chance to talk with Richie. He begrudged the fact that some of
Richie's predictions about the economy were unfolding, but, after
all, it wasn't Richie who was responsible. It was the buttheads in
Washington who were running things.

"I think the worst is behind us," he told Richie as they talked.

"Fund redemptions are slowing a little and all that pension
money keeps pouring in." "That's a hell of a rudder in rough seas."

"Yes, it is," agreed Richie.

"We're buying the cyclicals and the big caps."

"What's the price earnings ratio on the S & P now?" Richie
knew the answer but wanted to ask the question so he could
respond to Stan's answer.

"It was down to nineteen but it's twenty-one now."

"That's still high."

"Twenty times earnings is high? No way. When you figure the
value of future capital in this high technology economy, it could
be cheap, Richie."

"Maybe, maybe not. When I was a kid, ten times earnings was
the benchmark. Under ten you bought, over ten you sold."

"That's way too conservative. Back then they never dreamed of
computerization. Now there are microchips, pcs, the Internet, and
what about medical technology, telecommunications and satellites,
you name it. Everything's bigger and better now."

"Value is still value. I don't know how anything can be worth a
hundred times earnings, even technology."

"Look at the capital markets," continued Stan. "This country
has the most innovative and efficient capital markets in the world.
The corporate bond market is hundreds of times bigger than it was
just a few years ago. I mean, last year close to a trillion dollars of
corporate debt offerings were sold. It's mind boggling," he paused
for effect. "Last year Salesmart sold five billion of its bonds. That's

just one company raising five billion dollars in one pop. I know bond sales are slower now, but they can come back."

"I agree," Richie responded. "It's been impressive. There's been a big change in the way we borrow money. We used to be leery of debt in this country, but not anymore. They used to say you can't borrow your way to prosperity. People quit thinking that way. But I just don't believe people begin to comprehend the enormity of the debt load we're piling on. If things keep slowing down it might turn into a tremendous drag. Debt service could get really unmanageable."

"Say what you want, the capital markets have really boosted the economy."

"For all that capital, it seems like foreigners are making most of the goods we use."

"That's the way it is now. We've got a service economy and high tech. We don't need smokestack industries."

"A country's got to make something, Stan. Our manufacturing is way down."

""They've got low labor costs over there, let them make the stuff."

"It's sending the balance of payments out of control."

"Hey, we're helping them. They love our money. Up to last year the dollar's been as good as gold. No, it's been a lot better than gold."

"The world can only stand so many dollars. Money is like anything else, you get too much of it, it loses value."

The airport popped into sight.

"Where do you think it's going from here, Richie?"

"I don't know, Stan. When I get it all figured out I'll let you know," he laughed. "Right now I can't make up my mind what move to make."

"Me," Stan responded, "I'm buying some call options on the S & P and five or six of my favorite technology stocks. A rally is overdue."

"Buy the dips."

"It's always worked before."

"Who knows, maybe it will again."

The car moved up the ramp to the second level departure gate and the passenger drop-off area. Stan slid the car down to the Northwest end where skycaps were busily checking in luggage.

"This is it, girls. Thanks a lot, Stan."

"Bye Stan, and thanks," echoed the family as they quickly extricated themselves from the sedan and pulled at their luggage.

Richie was apprehensive as they entered the terminal. Past experiences with bad weather that had left him stranded in airports haunted him right before a flight and invariably left his stomach fluttering. The weather was bright and sunny, a perfect day for flying. He felt fine after checking in and walking to the gate. Things went smoothly and soon they had boarded and were underway.

When you get off a plane in Florida from the north, the first thing that hits you is the smell. It's a humid smell of the sea that lingers in your nostrils momentarily and then is gone until the next time you arrive. Richie noticed it as he directed his family toward the baggage claim. He suggested Nancy and the two girls await the luggage while he moved toward the car rental booth. On the way he ducked outside through the snappy electronic doors and walked to the curb. It was 72 degrees and he closed his eyes for a moment and took in the sun. Just to be outdoors, after all those weeks of avoiding the cold, was a thrill. They would enjoy the beach, and the running, walking, and swimming. Some days they would simply bask in the sun and read quietly, swaddled in beach towels. Everything has its price, thought Richie, and to enjoy this weather so much they had paid a price. A local resident could never understand or experience the joy of a sudden metamorphosis into warmer climes. People take what they have for granted.

They motored up to their luxurious seaside hotel and checked in. It was expensive, they both agreed, but the pampering, the extra service, and the lovely facility made it worth the cost. They began to settle in for the week and unpack.

"I'm so glad we're here," whispered Nancy and bent over to kiss him as he lay reading a novel on the bed.

"So am I, love. We'll have a good time."

The girls burst into their room giggling furiously and Richie felt happy for them all.

The days slipped past. By Wednesday Richie experienced the first twinge of restlessness. He wasn't bored in the conventional sense, just slightly jaded from repeating the same routine of exercise, dining, swimming, and reading. He put in a call to Bernie who was in Naples at the condominium that he had inherited from his grandparents. His aunt, who was also entitled to a share of the place when his grandparents passed away had sold him her interest for a song. She didn't need the money. Long ago she had married Irving "the lecher" Lepinski who made a fortune as the Minnesota porno king. Anything seamy that you bought west of Chicago or East of Spokane, Irving was getting the heavy end. His aunt had once told Bernie that Irving didn't even like the stuff. His primary thrill came from nuzzling her breasts, which were more than ample. The cops had tried to get Irving on numerous occasions but when the heat reached its zenith, he deftly sold out. Now they spent their winters at their place on Fisher Island, a heavily gated compound for the wealthy on Miami's Biscayne Bay.

"Yo, Dude," exclaimed Bernie when he heard Richie's voice. "How are you?"

"Soaking up the sun."

"Where are you?"

"Palm Beach."

"You are? Can you get over to Naples?"

"It's hard with the whole family."

"I suppose."

"Great weather you got down here."

"For sure. What a winter up there, huh. Really bad?"

"Yes, indeed. You making any money?"

"Not really. Man, this market sucks."

"Deflation?"

"Looks that way, Richie."

"How bad?"

"Don't know."

"Guy gave me a ride to the airport says the worst is over."

"I don't think so."

"Me, either."

"How long you down for?"

"Sunday."

"Hey, man, maybe I'll catch a hop over on Friday and have lunch with you."

"Love it."

"There's a commuter out of Fort Myers to Lauderdale. Just a little twin, but it doesn't take more than a few minutes."

"Please do it, Bernie."

"Can you pick me up at the Fort Lauderdale airport?"

"Absolutely."

"O.K., I'll call you back with the exact time. I should be there by midmorning Friday."

"Great. We'll have a good visit."

"Talk to you."

"Bye."

On Friday Richie picked his friend up and drove back to the hotel. After lunch, Richie and Bernie adjourned to poolside while Nancy and her two daughters drove to Palm Beach to prowl the glorious couture shops, art galleries, posh jewelry and collectible stores that lined Worth Avenue. Bernie slid under an umbrella to shield himself from the sun as Richie stretched out on the matching recliner beside him.

"What do you hear lately?" asked Richie.

"A lot. I don't know how much of it is true."

"Like what?"

"Well, this guy with a condo right below us, he's from New York, big bond salesman."

"Yeah."

"He told me the big brokerage firms and the banks are in cahoots with the government. They've been buying the Dow stocks right along. Government's financing it."

"How would he know?"

"Says his cousin works at the New York Fed. They're in on it, too."

"I don't believe it," offered Richie.

"I don't know. That guy Heller from the U wanted to do it once when he was with Kennedy."

"They never did it then and I doubt they're doing it now. There would be too big a stink if they did it without letting anybody know."

"You're probably right. I'm just telling you what I heard."

"You got to do better."

"Well, one thing I keep hearing is that one or two New York banks are in trouble. You know a couple of them have balance sheets more like a hedge fund than a bank."

"I've heard that, too, but I also heard some big hedge funds are close to tanking and maybe a big brokerage firm."

"Do you know how many derivatives they're sitting on," quizzed Bernie.

"One hundred trillion, something like that."

"Listen, there's a counterparty to every futures contract or swap. If any one of them are insolvent, hell, you don't even like to think about it."

"It could get ugly. If they take risks, I mean, if they're unhedged or even improperly hedged, it can cause big problems."

"Then an accountant guy I know over there tells me the government's tax receipts for the next few years are going south."

"Because profits are down?" asked Richie.

"This guy works for a big eight firm. They had a meeting. They figure there's going to be tremendous losses. Forget about lower profits, there isn't going to be much of any profits."

"No kidding."

"Then he says these corporations can income average and they're going to be getting money back from the government."

"I think they can elect to go back two years," said Richie. "There's no tax revenue from capital gains anymore and all the fat stock options are worthless. Those were all big revenue producers for the government."

"So, there's going to be one hell of a big federal deficit again," concluded Bernie.

"That means they're going to have to finance a lot more debt this year. They're going to have to borrow again to cover the deficit."

"Plus, they've got to roll over damn near six trillion of national debt, Richie. Now the debt's got a lot shorter fuse, I mean they changed it all to short-term bonds to save interest costs. The thing is," added Bernie, "there's tremendous pressure to lower interest rates."

"They're going to do it, Bernie. They have to. The president's going to talk about it in a message to the nation next Tuesday evening."

"I know, but how are they going to sell all that debt if they lower interest rates?"

"And what about the dollar? If it goes down any more Hyundais will be fifty grand." They both laughed.

"I don't think they'll do it. They don't have the guts, the dollar's in too much trouble already."

"Man, if it goes down any more, foreigners are going to buy up America," worried Richie.

"They're not doing that great, but if they get stronger, look out. Either way, if they start switching out of dollars in earnest, school's out."

They stopped their conversation for a moment to reflect on the dollar dilemma.

"What about the markets, Bernie?"

"You see what I see. The big board is slowly eroding. The small and medium caps are at their lows."

"This bond thing never goes away, either," replied Richie.

"Capital is drying up, you can't sell junk. Those huge corporate bond offerings are over."

"You can see it in the economy, housing starts were down again and the money supply is shrinking."

"It's ugly," sighed Bernie.

"I read a newsletter the other day, a guy says we've been destroying capital, not building it. He says by consuming goods instead of building plants we're just eating the seed corn. We've been spending and consuming, not saving."

"Too tough to measure," replied Bernie. "He's just guessing."

"The commodities are getting pasted, too," said Richie, changing the subject again.

"People must be buying gold, it's up a few bucks."

"Coins, yeah. I know a broker at Investment Rarities out in Bloomington. They're selling a lot of Eagles, Philharmonics,

Krugerrands, things like that."

"I don't know about that stuff, how will it do in a deflation?" asked Bernie.

"I know gold popped in the depression, but I think the government did it."

"Maybe what you should own is the thing that goes down the least," offered Bernie.

"Whatever that is."

"Well, it isn't art and antiques. One of the big auction houses cancelled their spring art auction."

"And how's Florida real estate?" Richie asked.

"I never thought I'd see it, but stuff around Naples is definitely down. Just not much buying and lots of stuff for sale. My neighbor lost a lot of money in the market, he's got his condo up for sale and the realtor's telling him he'll have to drop the price."

The afternoon was wearing down. They went upstairs to Richie's room and checked the market close on TV. Then they waited at the front of the hotel watching the affluent guests come and go. They laughed back and forth, needling each other about past gaffes until exactly 4:00 PM when Nancy and the girls pulled up. They exchanged places with them and drove leisurely out to the freeway and down to Fort Lauderdale.

Chapter 10

———

The country was soon to be in depression, thought Richie as he sat in his office reading the *Journal*. It was April and first quarter GDP figures were out, showing a three percent decline in the economy. Retail sales were still in a steep dive. Car sales and new construction suffered even steeper falls. The morning's newspaper brought news of layoffs, consolidations, and restructuring. A lot of people were losing their jobs and the economy was no longer creating the new jobs to replace them.

An interesting article in *Barron's* detailed how a slumping economy was changing the eating habits of Americans. Fancy restaurants that were crowded to overflowing one year prior were virtually empty. There was never a wait for a table, and they were, according to one senior citizen, "blessedly quiet." "I can hear again," noted another retiree who had returned as a regular to a favored French restaurant. The restaurant chains had also seen revenues drop sharply as people began to eat more meals at home. "We can't stand a ten percent decline in sales volume!" claimed one fast food

CEO. "And now we're coming up on fifteen percent. Some of our stores are going to have to close."

Richie had spent most of the week researching the financial strength of various commodity brokers. After months of delay he had worked out a new strategy and since he would be placing big orders, he didn't want any problems. After a week he selected five firms with whom he felt comfortable doing business.

He had asked Nancy to drive in and have lunch with him that day. She was happy to do so since it meant she could dovetail a nice lunch with a shopping trip to Neiman's and Dayton's department stores. They walked the skyway to Murray's Cafe and the hostess directed them across the luxurious maroon carpet to a rich-looking mahogany table.

"I want to tell you what I'm planning to do," he started.

"O.K.," she replied brightly.

"I've been reading a lot about gold lately. It's very unpopular, especially with the big banks and brokers. Economists think it's useless and most governments are washing their hands of it. But little people around the world buy it and hoard it. In our country a few rich people own it, but by in large it's smaller- to medium-sized investors who buy some of it to hedge."

"What are they hedging against?"

"Economic uncertainty, I guess."

"It hasn't gone up lately has it?"

"No, it hasn't gone up, but it hasn't gone down, either."

"Well, that's quite a trick these days," she offered.

"That's what I like about it. The price is holding up, it's contrary to everything else and I'm a contrarian."

"Didn't they used to buy gold as an inflation hedge?" she queried him.

"Yes, back in the seventies. It hit eight hundred and forty dollars an ounce in 1980."

"Well, there's no inflation now."

"No, but there eventually could be, with the dollar's sinking the way it is."

"I've never heard you say that before."

"What I think is going to happen now is the dead opposite of what's been happening for the past two decades."

"Which is?"

"Instead of a big inflation in assets and low consumer inflation, we're going to have falling prices for assets and high inflation in consumer prices."

"And people are going to turn to gold?"

"Some already are, a few Americans are buying gold again. It's only a fraction of the money that's around, but it could be the start of a trend."

"You could own the stuff a long time before anything happens," Nancy challenged.

"I don't think so. When people get worried, they buy gold. Let's face it, there's a lot of worried people nowadays. They may still be in stocks or have their money in the bank, but they don't have the confidence they had a year ago."

"You think the gold price will move soon?"

"I think it's going to start reacting to bad news; any further fall in the dollar or stocks or bad economic news, anything like that."

"You going to go into this in a big way?" she asked hesitantly.

"You know how I do things."

"Hon, what about the mortgage on the house, you promised you would think about paying it off."

"I know you're concerned, and since I'm planning to take some risks I'll make a deal with you."

"What's that?"

"I'll pay the mortgage off if you'll promise not to complain about me risking the four million on this gold strategy."

"Everything? You're using everything?"

"Just about."

"Richie, I love you and have faith in you, but you scare me sometimes."

"I'm never going to do anything crooked that would get us in trouble."

"I know that!"

"And I'm not going to take losses to the point where we can't pay our bills, believe me. We've been down that road, I'm not going there again."

"Promise?"

"Promise." He leaned over the table and gave her a reassuring kiss.

After lunch he contacted Ken Ferguson and explained that he had ordered his bank to wire seven hundred thousand to Ken's firm. He would call back in the morning with instructions on what to buy. Then he called brokers at four additional firms who he had previously contacted. They had sent him papers to open accounts and he had returned them a few days prior.

"Do you have the paperwork?" he asked each one. When they replied yes, he explained that a wire for seven hundred thousand would be coming the next day. Then he called his bank and gave them the wiring instructions.

The following day he called Ken Ferguson and bought five hundred long contracts on gold at $252 an ounce. "We'll have to report this position to the exchange, of course."

"I know," replied Richie. "That's fine."

He used one of the farthest out months for the delivery date, although he did not plan to ever take delivery. He did plan, however, to roll them over before they expired. The next day he called

two of the other brokers and duplicated the order. The third day
he ordered the balance. When it was done he felt a slight shiver
race through his body.

The commodity trading firms required that he put up a thousand dollars per contract, plus keep some money for margin calls
in his account. Each contract was for one hundred ounces of gold.
Through each firm he controlled fifty thousand ounces of gold, or
a total of two hundred fifty thousand ounces. If gold moved up
one dollar he made a quarter million dollars, but if it moved down
ten dollars, he was out two and a half million. A fifteen-dollar
decline and he was finished. He knew that most commodity
traders and experts would consider his strategy to be pathologically
risky. He was crazy, they would be certain. Yet, he felt that watershed events were unfolding and gold had bumped along the bottom for too long. He knew he was the world's champion plunger,
but felt confident with that knowledge.

For two weeks gold treaded water; up a dollar, down a dollar.
Richie went through his daily routine as restlessly as Grant or Lee
waiting for a campaign to begin. A warm spring had set in, but
Richie was too preoccupied to enjoy it to the fullest. His patience
grew thin and he found himself irritated by things that he normally blew off with equanimity. One morning he snapped at his secretary, Carol Olson, only to find himself apologizing a few minutes
later. In the afternoon he ran out and brought her back a small
vase with three peach-colored roses.

Finally, gold rose two dollars on the news of a big jump in the
bankruptcy rate. Credit card defaults had soared with more people
than ever unable to pay down their credit card debt. Consequently,
personal bankruptcies were going through the roof, with mortgage
foreclosures also rising briskly. A sudden glut of houses for sale had
sent home prices into a downward glide. But it was business bank-

ruptcies that had everyone's attention. The market had grown accustomed to Internet and technology companies that once had red-hot public offerings turning belly up. When the once highly profitable department store chain, Mason and Leach, caved in it sent a shudder through the stock market. The dollar dropped, not only against the yen and the Euro, but against most world currencies, including the Russian ruble.

Richie felt a little better. Gold offtake, the amount investors and industry were purchasing, had risen. Around the world the demand for gold was strong and in the U.S. the demand rose from one month to the next. Richie knew that hedge funds, brokerage firms, and banks had large short positions in gold. They thought it was going down in price. A price rise would make the shorts squeamish. Once they started to cover, a big rally might begin. Then other buyers would come in and push things to the upside. He also knew that the gold mining companies had sold most of their production forward for several years ahead. That put a floor under gold because their new production would have to go to cover the forward sale they'd already made. In other words, future production was already factored into the price.

His only fear- and it was a big one- was the inscrutable actions of the Central Banks. They had once owned a third of the above-ground supply but had been consistent sellers for a decade and now owned twenty percent of the world's gold supply. The dicey economic conditions over the past year would surely make them reluctant to sell and suddenly depress the price. He was banking on it.

Bad economic news kept piling up. Then the Alliance Capital and Mortgage Company bit the dust and gold shot up four and a half dollars. The next day oil prices, as measured in dollars, broke out to the upside and gold followed. At $265 an ounce, short covering began in earnest and like a rubber band stretched to the limit in one direction, it snapped back with a vengeance. At $272 Richie was up five million dollars and on the strength of this equity buildup, he doubled his position to five hundred thousand ounces. Each dollar rise would garner him half a million dollars, but now an eighteen-dollar drop would wipe him out. He was brash beyond measure, but he felt a powerful certainty that he was on target.

A rise in the price of something feeds upon itself. The momentum players, chartists, and trend followers spot a strong price movement in one direction and they come to it like metal cuttings to a magnet. Suddenly, for the first time in years, favorable comments were starting to be heard about gold. The sleepy yellow metal was now in play and heading higher. The shorts were feeling squeezed. It's going to break $300, predicted gold expert Frank Perrazo, otherwise known in the gold market as the "Lonely Bull." "You'll never believe it," he joked on CNBC, "my phone rang today."

"Richie, you're a madman," expressed Bernie to his friend over lunch at Market Barbecue. "I'm totally flabbergasted. Look what you've done. I mean it's pure genius, but here's my advice: get out now. Don't take any more chances."

"I'll think about it."

"Jeez, the risk you took. I'd have wet myself." Gold had risen to $289 and Richie now had a bullion position valued at over seventeen million dollars.

"That's an enormous amount of money, why not take it?" continued Bernie.

"The way things are going," he replied, "gold can go quite a bit higher."

"Listen, the way you're pyramiding would give me a heart attack."

"There's a lot of paper in the world, Bernie, but not much gold.

Do you know that at the peak of the stock market, the market cap of the five top Internet stocks and the five top technology stocks was more than all the gold in the world. I mean the whole above-ground supply."

"No kidding. How come you're just telling me that now?" he joked.

"It's still cheap," replied Richie.

"Oh, sure," said Bernie, rolling his eyes. "I hope you're right."

Two days later gold crossed two hundred ninety-two and Richie increased his position another five hundred contracts at each firm. The price dipped back to $289 and within a few more days moved up to $300, broke through and closed at $301.50. The next morning Richie struck again, adding twenty-five hundred more contracts. He now controlled one million ounces of .999 pure gold and, if it moved up another ten dollars, he would make ten million dollars more. In the annals of modern speculation, no person had ever taken such a huge risk and survived. But as far as Richie was concerned, he had only built the foundation.

"The basement is in," he told Nancy, "now we have to build the house."

"Oh, no," she groaned.

Chapter 11

Michael Donahue punched the button on his intercom and blurted out an order for his secretary to get Jack Heath, the company's corporate counsel, on his line. Michael burned with impatience. Three middle managers of his Stanford, Connecticut-based company had just departed from his office. They claimed to represent several hundred employees and had been appointed by a committee to present their grievances directly to him. They had aggravated him greatly and he needed to get advice on the delicate issues they'd raised surrounding their compensation. As the president and CEO of the Hill Corporation, a diversified industrial company listed on the New York Stock Exchange, he needed to respond through a companywide memorandum to all managers within the next few weeks. This was a serious issue and conceivably a bone of contention that could fester among the managers to the detriment of the company.

Jack Heath, founder and senior partner of Heath, Foreman, Ivy and Steinberg stared out the window of the Manhattan skyscraper that housed his law firm. He gazed down toward the United Nations building and the East River behind it. He was lost in reverie; a huge salmon had just latched on to his streamer fly and ripped yardage from his reel. His guide, a grizzled veteran of the Grand Cascapedia, had just shouted that this was the largest fish of the season, perhaps any season, when the intercom on his desk rudely interrupted his daydream. "Mr. Heath, it's Michael Donahue."

He quickly swung his chair around and raised the phone to his ear. "Hello, Michael, how are you?"

"Not too happy, Jack, we've got problems."

"Tell me."

"I just had three managers in my office bitching about their stock options. The managers got together and appointed the three of them to come see me."

"You mean because the stock price has dropped?"

"Yes, they don't see it going up anytime soon."

"They may be right."

"They say that because the price of our stock has fallen, they'll never be able to exercise any of their options."

"Could be, that's the chance they take."

"But, they say they counted on this as part of their compensation."

"Yes, but it didn't work out. It happens, Mike."

"They don't care, they're telling me they took these options in lieu of salary increases."

"That doesn't change anything."

"They got a lawyer."

"Who?"

"I didn't ask."

"What's he say?"

"They got a heck of a good lawsuit. He told them they're entitled to the salaries they would have had if they didn't get the options."

"That's crazy. Some of these guys will say anything."

"He told them we benefited by giving them options instead of salary."

"How's that?"

"We saved on payroll. Lower overhead meant better earnings."

"I suppose to some extent that's true."

"Not to some extent, to a hell of a large extent."

"Really."

"They were happy when they were cashing in those fat stock options and making big money. Now one lousy year and they sound like a union."

"Hmm."

"The stock was eighty-two. Now it's twenty-one. The exercise price for most of them is eighty or ninety, but there's no chance now."

"Not too likely."

"What should we do?"

"I should probably talk to their lawyer, see where's he's coming from. I can stiff him pretty good, tell him they got no chance."

"Why don't you. I'll get his name and number."

"I don't think we should talk to him until after the board meeting."

"That's two weeks."

"Tell them it will be a few weeks before I call."

"O.K."

"We're going to have to tell the board, Mike."

"Oh, Jack, don't tell me that."

"It's not so bad."

"On top of everything else?"

"You mean the earnings?"

"I mean the losses."

"Ouch, things have gotten worse."

"Yeah."

"Well, you can join the party, everybody's earnings are getting hammered. Lots of other companies are losing money, too."

"They don't care about anybody else."

"How come the loss? I thought you were going to make two cents a share."

"We thought so, too, but we got hit by a ton of returns and the interest on our bonds is eating us up."

"Yes, that's something I wondered about."

"We shouldn't have done those bond offerings, Jack." The lawyer felt slightly uncomfortable. His firm had collected fat fees on the Hill Corporation's registrations necessary to selling their bonds.

"It was great at the time, Mike. Maybe it wasn't the best use of the proceeds, but everyone was doing it. Hindsight is twenty-twenty."

"Well, we've stopped the repurchases." Michael Donahue was referring to his company's program of repurchasing the company's stock. At first they had bought back their stock with profits. Then they had drained their cash reserves to buy back more of their own shares. The stock price soared. The officers and senior managers had granted themselves generous options. When the stock price rose above their option price, they converted and harvested handsome profits. Then the corporation began to borrow money by selling bonds. They used these proceeds to buy more of their corporation's stock back, driving up the price further, exercising another crop of options. They bought back their stock that was free of obligations and replaced it with debt that cost seven percent a year. It was the rage among the big OTC- and exchange-listed companies and they were one of the leaders. Now they were saddled with too much debt that had begun to destroy their profitability.

"Things might turn around, Mike. Listen, I'll call you next week to go over the agenda for the board meeting."

"Thanks, Jack."

Of all the luck, thought Michael Donahue a week later as he sat perched in the executive suite on the top floor of his mirrored headquarters. He was reading the *Wall Street Journal* and, wouldn't you know it, the week before the board meeting a front-page story appears discussing the rash of shareholder lawsuits aimed at the officers and directors of corporations that have seen their stock prices collapse. Insurance companies were not renewing directors' liability policies for anyone who served on the board of a listed company that showed any red ink.

When his board heard about the Hill Corporation's sorry results for the current quarter, they would be incensed. Fortunately, the board had only a few business people, half of them were there as window dressing or to curry favor with unions or legislators. His harshest critic would be Don Spivey, CEO of Treadway Energy, and to a lesser extent, Lenore Quist, director of Nature Unlimited, an environmental group.

The following week he saw immediately that he was right. No sooner had the directors trooped in and he had started the meeting when Spivey asked to skip ahead in the agenda to the financial results. Jack Heath, sitting at his side, had objected and suggested they continue working through the agenda and follow the proper rules for conducting a meeting.

"It won't take fifteen minutes," he assured them.

"Get to the point, man," Spivey had persisted. The grizzled old wildcatter had built a major oil producer from scratch and he didn't mince words. "I had my financial people look at your statement and you've got some problems we need to address."

Michael Donahue shuddered inwardly and continued to follow

83

the agenda that Jack Heath had laid out on paper. Sixteen of them sat around the vast mahogany table in the richly appointed board-room. In addition to the fourteen directors, there was their coun-sel, Jack Heath, a secretary recording in shorthand the flow of the meeting, and, sitting against the wall on a lone chair, an attendant who periodically flitted between the directors fetching them soft drinks or pouring water.

Finally, it was time for the financial report. Michael Donahue, a tiny bead of perspiration glistening on his balding forehead, began the dissertation, one that he had frequently rehearsed in his mind.

"Unfortunately, the earlier projections we sent you in the mail have not proven to be accurate. Rather than earn two cents a share this quarter, we will lose two cents." A flurry of grumbles and gasps emanated from the board.

"That's not the worst of it." He wasn't going to pussyfoot around the bad news. Jack Heath had told him to get it out on the table.

"Next quarter's projections indicate a continuation of the down-ward trend in sales. We just can't believe how orders are drying up. Consequently, we expect to lose forty cents a share in the third quarter."

"That's twenty million dollars," interrupted a flush-faced Don Spivey.

"Correct Don, we know that."

"That's eighty million a year," continued Spivey.

"Well, we plan to take steps to turn that around."

"Hell, man, at that rate you'll be bankrupt in a year."

Jack Heath broke in, "They have acknowledged this problem and plans are being laid out to diminish that size of loss. The company has assets, Don. They're worth a lot. They're not going broke."

"Plant closings. Will there be plant closings?" questioned Lenore Quist, the environmentalist.

"Perhaps. Nothing definite yet, but we're looking at everything," replied the harried executive.

"I hope you don't close the Allegheny plant," broke in Chester Herkenrath, former Postmaster General. "My son-in-law works there."

Don Spivey cast him a withering glance. "Can't you be more specific about your plans, Michael?"

"Suffice to say, we're going to cut costs and restructure."

"That's what you did after that Ohio Gear acquisition," interjected Spivey. "How much downsizing can one company do?"

"Everybody's doing it," commented Marvin Stadler, a retired board chairman and director of three *Fortune 500* companies.

"It's the economy," offered another.

"They were doing it before the downturn," countered Stadler.

"Here's the problem," explained Don Spivey. "When one company restructures it can help them, but when everyone does it, they are reducing the amount of business they do with one another. What starts out helping one company expands to the point where it hurts them all. They reduce each other's revenues and profits."

"That may be," said Michael Donahue, "but we don't have any choice."

"How soon will you have a plan?" asked one of them.

"Thirty days. We'll be sending you an outline of our strategy."

"Can you get your costs down enough to catch up to falling revenues and income?"

"We're going to try."

"You've got one big problem that you can't overcome," advised Don Spivey.

"What's that?"

"The interest on these bonds of yours. Your balance sheet's loaded with debt. The interest on the bonds accounts for half this projected loss."

"We've taken that into account."

"I told all of you three years ago that selling these bonds was going to hamstring this company with too much debt. Every damn dime of it was used to buy back the company's stock and make earnings per share look better. The earnings didn't improve through capital investment and improved productivity. It was a paper caper. You leveraged the hell out of the company so the management could feather their own nests. You did it to make your stock options juicier."

"That's not fair, Don," cut in Donahue.

"It's the truth. What do you think my oil company does if we borrow money or sell bonds? What do you think we do with the money?" his finger stabbed the air. "We drill for oil, Michael. We don't buy our stock back to run the price up. You should have been improving your factories, buying new equipment, increasing your capital investment. Now you've got your tit in a wringer. With this sorry financial statement you can't sell any more bonds or any more stock in this market. You can't raise a penny. All you can do is slash and burn. You're going to ruin a fine company and give a lot of poor souls pink slips."

A stunned silence fell over the board. No one spoke for thirty seconds, digesting Spivey's remarks.

"I hope my son-in-law doesn't get a pink slip."

Someone groaned audibly.

"If this is true," commented Archbishop Andrew Gillicudy, "we directors could have some liability."

"I just read an article in the *Journal* about that," said one.

"Yes, I saw that."

"So did I."

"I'm not worried," said one. "A lot of companies bought back their stock. Hardly anyone's investing in manufacturing. We can't get blamed for that."

Jack Heath cut in. "You don't have anything to worry about. We have insurance and we have resources. The company may have to make some adjustments, but it will certainly survive."
Lenore Quist spoke up. "That is probably the case, Mr. Heath. But the way the economy is deteriorating it's going to be very difficult for the next year or two. Mr. Spivey is right to warn us about the company's debt, without it they would be far better off."

"Things are going to get better," offered one gray haired director.

"I hope you're right," she responded, "but I can tell you that I run a charitable organization and our donations have dried up completely. It's scary. At present I don't know how long we will be able to operate."

Suddenly, everyone was talking, breaking into groups and passing comments between themselves. Michael Donahue let them go on for a while, glad to have a moment to regain his composure after the tongue-lashing Spivey had directed toward him. Within minutes he called the meeting back to order and continued his financial report. The last item on the agenda was the issue of compensation and stock options raised by the employees. He explained the managers' disenchantment now that their stock options were worthless. Thankfully no one on the board aimed criticism at him.

"A lot of people made a lot of money off these short-term financial gimmicks," summarized Spivey. "Now it's over. The employees who missed out took a risk. They were happy when it looked like they might get rich. In my opinion, the company has no liability."

"I certainly agree with that," followed Jack Heath.

"Let's adjourn. Could I please have a motion. Thank you. Who will second? Thank you. Meeting adjourned!"

Chapter 12

It was August and Richie stared out the rear window of his home, his mind skipping from one thought to another. Behind the house a pond shimmered in the early morning sun. A mallard hen rose from the pond while her six young flapped across the water, attempting to emulate her flight. She flew back to the pond, sat and rose again. Suddenly, two of her young were airborne with her, circling around the pond and splashing down again. Finally they were all on the wing circling the pond like pilots on their first solo.

She and her greenheaded mate had come to the pond in April. Her first nest, with eleven beige eggs, was discovered by a skunk who feasted on them. Then she tried again, laying one egg a day until there were eight. On the ninth day she sat. After a week a farm tractor crossed over her patch of grass and as she flushed in fear, a wheel smashed the contents of her nest. She rested a few days and then tried once again until finally, in the middle of July, six downy young hatched and followed her down to the pond. Surprisingly, all had survived and now that they were on the wing, they would soon leave together. If she survived the rigors of the fall migration, she would return to this same pond in the spring to try again.

Richie noticed the ducks and watched their awkward first flight. Then he rose and fetched the morning paper. He wanted to read a story in the business section about financial stress in a large Manhattan bank that he'd heard reported on early morning TV. Although the nation's politicians were jawboning the Federal Reserve to keep interest rates low, the Central Bank only controls short-term rates. Long-term rates were on the upswing. According to the rumor, this trend created mismatched swaps and other hedging problems that had hurt the big banks. Richie knew that derivative problems could be kept quiet for a long time. He wanted to find out more.

He decided to call Jerry Eisenberg, the interest rate derivative trader at Yamaha Securities in New York. Years ago the two of them had trained for a month together in the same class of beginning stockbrokers in Manhattan. They had socialized in off hours, became friends, and stayed in contact. Nancy came into the room as he reached for the phone. "Who you calling?" she quizzed.

"Jerry Eisenberg."

Nancy knew Jerry from trips to New York with her husband when they had dined together with Jerry and his wife.

"Ask about Marnie."

"I will."

Nancy sat down to kibitz on the conversation. Moments later Richie hung up the phone.

"Tied up with a big swap. He wants me to call back in five minutes."

"I don't understand this swap business," she volunteered. "All I know is you hear a lot about them."

"Swaps are derivatives. They're used to hedge the interest rate risk on bonds."

"How's it work, Mr. Know Everything? Tell me in one sentence," teased Nancy.

Richie seized the opportunity.

"Let's say you have a fixed-rate home mortgage and your neighbor has a flexible mortgage. You think rates are going down, but you won't benefit because your mortgage is fixed. Your neighbor thinks rates are going up and his interest costs will rise because he has a flexible mortgage. So you decide to swap mortgages. You each get what you want. That's roughly the way it works in the bond market, but in the millions and billions."

"I see," she said, arching her eyes in a way that showed she was impressed.

He smiled at her, but her face suddenly grew serious.

"I told you Charlie Newcombe lost his job," she said, changing the subject to the plight of their neighbor two doors down.

"Yes."

"Debbie thinks they may lose the house."

"You told me."

"Could we help them?"

"What?"

"Could we make them a small loan until he gets another job?"

"He's been looking for two months."

"Nobody needs engineers."

"A lot of people have been losing their jobs lately, Nancy. We going to help them all?"

"No, of course not. But they're such good friends. Debbie and I go everywhere together with the kids. I'd hate to lose her."

"How bad is it?"

"Five payments."

"Behind?"

"Yes."

"How much?"

"Twelve thousand."

"They got no savings?"

"No."

"Nothing?"

"Richie, they're living off his unemployment check. She's trying to find a job evenings."

"He was making a hundred grand a year."

"I know."

"The guy's got two snowmobiles, a boat, two cars, a motorcycle, and an RV. Maybe he should sell one of his toys."

"They've been trying, but Debbie says nobody will pay anything."

"They go to Vail skiing."

"Yes."

"Two years ago they built a swimming pool."

"Yes."

"Man, what a comedown."

"They're hurting, Richie."

"Where would they go?"

"If they lost the house?"

"Yeah."

"They don't know what they're going to do. They're scared."

"They've spent every dime they ever made."

"Today we're lucky, Richie, but not too long ago I was worried like they are."

"I hope our luck will last."

"We've got the money, let's help them."

"I don't know."

"Richie, we've got the money."

"They'd have to sign a note."

"They will."

"What about interest?"

"Come on, Shylock."

"No interest?"

"No."

"Will you do it?"

"Yes."

"That's great. It makes me so happy. I'm going to run over there right now and tell them. Good-bye," she said, skipping out the door and laughing.

Richie returned to the phone and dialed New York again. In moments Jerry Eisenberg came on the phone. They exchanged warm greetings.

"How's it going, Jerry?"

"It's a lot slower than a year ago, Richie."

"There's a rumor floating around about a big bank."

"I heard."

"Anything to it?"

"Maybe."

"What's the problem?"

"They got a mess. They took some big unhedged positions. You know, they were just playing the market like an ordinary speculator."

"They must have lost big when rates jumped up," said Richie.

"That's it!"

"They've also got a bunch of mismatched swaps. It's costing them. Their hedges are out of sync with the underlying bonds."

"I thought they were smarter than that."

"Some of it couldn't be helped. There was a lot more volatility when this all started."

"What about counterparty problems, any insolvency?" asked Richie, referring to the fact that there were two sides to every futures or swaps contract.

"There's going to be some. If a big bank goes down, look out."

"Indeed."

"It's a different ball game now, Richie, that's the problem."

"What do you mean?"

"No liquidity. You can't do a profitable deal. A lot of these swaps dealers have inventories and big overheads. Their revenues have dried up because it's hard to sell bonds and the swaps transactions went south with the bond market. Some of them aren't going to make it."

"If they're desperate they'll take chances."

"If they lose, one pulls down the other."

"All the brokerage firms must be suffering, too, huh?"

"The low volume is killing them."

What about the hedge funds?"

"They got killed, too, Richie."

"How, naked positions?"

"Yeah, they shouldn't call them hedge funds anymore, they should call them unhedged funds."

"Really."

"Don't tell anybody this, O.K.?"

"Sure."

"The Fed's probably going to have to arrange a bailout of at least one big New York bank, maybe a brokerage firm or two, and I honestly think there's a half dozen hedge funds in serious trouble."

"Wow."

"They're either counterparties on swaps contracts, or they can't make margin calls on futures. If the Fed doesn't move it's dominoes, my friend."

"Man, the Treasury will have to print a lot of money."

"Indeed."

"There goes the dollar again."

"And the stocks, too."

"Do not quote me on any of what I told you," emphasized Jerry.

"A lot of people got to know, don't they, Jerry?"

"Some of this I'm surmising from trading activity and some of it's coming from other traders."

"Should be mostly true, then."

"People know, but they just know a little bit of the big picture."

"The tip of the iceberg."

"Exactly," confirmed Jerry. "Hold on a minute."

"Sure."

Momentarily Jerry came back on. "Did a little cross. Gotta take what you can get."

"Thanks for all the info."

"What are you doing, Richie? You making money for your clients?"

"No clients left."

"What?"

"I'm trading for my own account."

"Really. What are you buying?"

"Gold."

"Oy vey," he sighed.

"It's working out."

"Never knew what people saw in that stuff. What do you do with it? Listen, I got to go."

"Thanks. Let's talk again."

"Adios."

Richie reflected for a while on the disturbing conversation he'd had with Jerry. He didn't want anything disastrous to happen in the financial world, nevertheless something bad was likely to happen. He would take advantage of it. Whatever he did would make no difference in the scheme of things. It was going to happen despite any actions of his.

He heard his wife come into the house. She was bubbling.

"Oh, Richie, they are so thankful," she said, referring to their financially beleaguered neighbors. "Debbie couldn't stop crying. I feel so wonderful about doing this. They asked us to go out to dinner with them tonight."

"I've got one question," he said.

"What?"

"Who's buying?" He laughed loudly at his own joke.

"You stinker," she laughed.

He rose and wrapped his arms around her. Then he started a slow shuffle toward the hallway that led to the bedroom.

"You deserve a reward," she murmured.

Chapter 13

The phone rang incessantly at the Miami office of Seacoast Capital Management. Registered in the Bahamas, the offshore hedge fund kept its operating office in Miami. With over two billion dollars under management, they had enjoyed a fabulous run, with gains of thirty percent a year for five consecutive years. The fund started with twenty-five million a dozen years ago, and, on the strength of astute investment decisions by founder Alex Garcia, they had matured into a big player.

Garcia had come to the U.S. from Cuba when he was eleven years old. His father had loaded his mother, sister, and him into an eighteen-foot rowboat, along with five suitcases containing all their worldly goods. He'd pulled the rope on a dilapidated five-horse Johnson a few minutes after midnight, and, as it coughed to life, they left Cuba, never to return. His father had been a successful importer until Castro had taken over. One day a pair of bearded comrades entered his warehouse and told him to evacuate the premises. One of them was now in charge. Ten days later he and his family hunkered down in their rowboat and headed out to sea.

The family had one big advantage over most other Cubans fleeing their island for a new life. Around his waist the senior Garcia carried a money belt stuffed with U.S. one- hundred-dollar bills. He had hoarded his stash of big bills over the years in case of an emergency. Halfway to Florida the motor conked out. The weather had smiled on them and only a mild easterly breeze rippled the ocean swells. His father had rowed through a day and two nights when the family began to fear they were off course. They stopped and prayed, drank the last of their water, and began to row again, altering their course to the northwest. Within hours they began to see the superstructure of ocean vessels poking up like unfinished construction projects on the ocean horizon. They closed on the shipping lane, crossed it, and saw the faintest mirage-like outline of land. Before long they were passing charter boats full of fishermen who stared at the little family with curiosity. His father rowed them right up to the shore of Islamorada in the Florida Keys, altered course at the last minute, and rowed to the small dock of the Holiday Inn. With amazing chutzpah, he jumped out of the rowboat, strode into the hotel, and registered his family as guests. His English was excellent and no one thought much of it or even noticed them carry in their luggage from the boat tied to the dock. Later that night he walked the boat down the shore a few feet, pulled it up, and left it. The following week they walked into the Immigration and Naturalization office in Miami and registered.

His father had struggled at first, but like so many Cuban entrepreneurs, ultimately forged a successful life. Alex Garcia graduated with a business degree from the University of Miami and then gained an MBA from Wharton. After a stint in New York managing money for Franklin, he had left and started his own hedge fund. His fluent Spanish had helped him attract copious funds from wealthy South Americans. Some of the money he had wondered about, but there was only so much he could do to trace the source. He was a money manager, not a detective. He had registered his hedge fund in Nassau just in case some of the money he might eventually manage had a tainted origin. First, he needed to protect himself against any possible prosecution for money laundering, nor did he want to jeopardize anyone who gave him funds. He certainly wasn't seeking money from questionable sources, but if he got some of it by accident, he needed to avoid any problems it might bring.

The phones continued to ring angrily. Periodically his secretary would poke her head into his office with the name of someone on the line and he would shake his head no. He knew why they were calling, he didn't have to hear them recite the rumors. Seacoast Capital Management had failed to make margin calls at three commodity trading houses on huge leveraged short positions in yen. Unfortunately, the yen was on a tear. To make matters worse, they had heavily borrowed low interest yen to buy U.S. bonds, leveraged at twenty to one. Instead of profiting on the interest rate differential, they had been wiped out when the dollar plunged.

For almost a year they had been liquidating their positions and trying to extricate themselves. Their highly leveraged stock portfolio and a massive gold short aggravated their losses. Once everything had clicked favorably for them. Now everything they did was wrong. A few days prior, rumors had begun to circulate that their losses were massive and somebody, somewhere, was going to be holding the bag on their margin failures and capsizing loans from brokers and banks. Alex Garcia had managed to lose over two billion dollars of his customers' money and four billion more that he couldn't come up with.

He gripped the window ledge on the forty-first floor of his

Miami office tower and stared down at the cruise ships docked in Government Cut along the southern tip of Miami Beach. For a moment he thought of smashing the window with his chair and diving out. Then his fear began to ebb. It wasn't the losses and the shame of bankruptcy that worried him the most. It was the phone call. Earlier his secretary had told him, "Mr. Cortez is calling from Bogota." He took the call. Cortez had funneled one hundred fifty million dollars into his company and had always been pleased with the results. Now he was furious.

"My people are not happy," he had hissed in Spanish. "Do you know who my people are?"

"No," came Garcia's meek reply.

"You dumb bastard, do I have to paint you a picture? I am a dead man because of you."

Suddenly he understood. The hair on his neck began to rise and a cold stab of terror churned through his stomach.

"I'm sorry," was all he could muster.

"I hope they kill you slowly," screamed Cortez.

"This was a business strategy that failed. We took risks, every-one knows that."

"Oh, you stupid man, how could I be so naive as to trust your judgment."

"Do you think we're the only hedge fund in trouble? They will see others are in trouble."

"It will not matter," he moaned.

"I'm trying to salvage something. There's a chance we're too big to fail."

"What do you mean?"

"We owe so much that others might go bankrupt because of us."

"So what if they do."

"The government's worried. This whole financial mess may get straightened out in Washington."

"They will give you money?"

"It depends on how big the problem is, how many others are in trouble."

"Señor Garcia, for your sake and mine, I pray you find a solution. I will convey your plan to my people. They are awaiting my call. Perhaps I can cool their wrath for a while. It is hard to know what they will do. They may do nothing, even if you are unsuccessful in reviving your business. On the other hand, they can be quite volatile. They will know that this was an accident rather than a swindle. That will be important. I will do my best to soothe them."

"Good, and I will do my best to keep things going."

"Good-bye, Señor."

Now Alex Garcia waited for his call to be returned from another hedge fund operator in New York, Randolph Schuyler. He frequently conversed with Schuyler, whose fund had grown into the largest domestic hedge fund. Only two offshore funds were larger. He knew Schuyler's Skylark fund had problems but he didn't know how severe they were.

He turned his attention to the market news on his TV monitor. Apparently a flurry of rumors that included his failure were starting to get around. The stock market was falling, with the big caps taking their lumps. Volume ran higher than at any time in the past six months. Pervasive weakness in the dollar and bonds continued. He would get no help from the markets.

Finally, Schuyler's call came through.

"Is it true, Alex?" Schuyler questioned.

"Yes, Randolph, it's true."

"I'm sorry. Have you heard anything about Skylark?"

"Rumors."

"It's worse than what you hear," confided Schuyler.

"It is? How bad?"

"We can't make our margin calls and the banks have called our notes."

"We're both in the same boat. What can we do?"

"For a while I was terrified, Alex, but then the president of our lead bank called. We're not the only ones that can't pay. He told me they're stuck with trading losses in currencies and losses on derivatives into the billions. It's eaten up most of their capital. If they fail, they're taking a lot of others down with them. It gets worse. He told me a couple of major brokerage firms they deal with are in the same boat."

"No!"

"Yes!"

"Here's the kicker. My banker's been talking to the New York Fed. They're trying to arrange a bailout. At first they were talking about just the banks, now they're talking about everybody."

"Yahoo."

"I'm going to Washington in a half hour. My jet's waiting now. There's a big meeting at the Treasury. It's super hush-hush. The chairman of the Fed's going to be there and the Treasury secretary. They're having it in an obscure Treasury building and everybody's coming into an underground garage, and then going up to the meeting room."

"Wow."

"My banker thinks the president might even be there. But nobody can know, you understand? You can't breathe a word."

"Of course, don't worry about me."

"As far as I know, my banker will be there, along with other bankers, some brokerage firm execs, and a couple of senators. They are absolutely paranoid about anybody finding out. They're afraid it will spook the market. Things are apparently much worse than anybody's letting on."

"I understand."

"Listen, I'll call you at home late tonight."

"Thanks, Randolph."

Almost as if the stockholders and fund managers of the nation were tuned into the conversation of the two hedge fund managers, they began to sell stocks. The volume on the exchange climbed as share prices plummeted. Once again trading curbs were invoked, shutting down the exchange and leaving everyone with an uncomfortable sense of illiquidity.

Randolph Schuyler walked into the meeting room at the Treasury Department. He had been subjected to a thorough computerized background check that same day and his person was inspected closely. After walking through a metal detector two times, he was x-rayed and searched. Once in the room he noticed his banker and several others seated at one side of an extraordinarily long table. Sprinkled around the vast wooden surface were high government officers, along with two senators and a congressman that he recognized. Someone in a suit directed him to a seat and whispered, "You sit here." He quickly obliged. No one was talking and he sat silently, staring at the notepad on the table in front of him.

He swiveled his head toward a commotion at the door and watched the chairman of the Federal Reserve stride in. He and two aides seated themselves at the opposite end of the table. The chairman exchanged greetings with some of those seated around him and nodded at others. Within minutes the secretary of the Treasury entered, with an aide following. He greeted the Fed chairman and sat down across from him. Schuyler could now see that the highest ranking officials were all down at the end of the table opposite him. At the head of the table were several unoccupied chairs.

Whispered conversations had started around the table. He

assumed they were still waiting for something. It was now after 4:00 PM and he was sure that if this wasn't such an unusual emergency, the meeting would never take place this late in the day. He could only guess why they didn't begin. Finally, he was startled by a loud voice which announced, "the President of the United States." He looked directly into the face of the chief executive as he walked by him. The president did not acknowledge anyone and moved quickly to his seat. Schuyler suddenly felt inadequate.

"Let's get started. Mr. Chairman, why don't you begin."

The chairman of the Federal Reserve swept the table with his eyes and began to talk to no one in particular. "We have a growing problem in the banking system. A number of failures in the financial area including hedge funds, large speculators, brokerage firms, futures dealers, and swaps dealers can't pay back their indebtedness. Consequently, that has put pressure on certain banks. Superimposed on top of this problem is the fact that some of the large New York banks have taken major losses in their own trading departments. Taken together, it's a looming financial crisis. This, of course, says nothing about consumer debt problems among the public, or mortgage foreclosures which are rising along with both personal and corporate bankruptcies."

"I've said all along," interjected the president in a voice noticeably louder than the chairman, "we should have lowered interest rates more than we have."

"Damn right," piped in Senator Mulroney, the senior senator from Delaware, "we've hurt a lot of people by sitting on our hands. The Fed has to take the blame for this."

"I don't think so, Senator," responded the chairman testily. "Whenever we lower rates we shake up the currency markets. We can't have foreign countries dumping any more dollars."

"Our people are more important than someone overseas worrying about too many dollars."

"Senator, do you understand the full ramifications of a falling dollar?"

"Of course I do. Let their cars get more expensive, we'll sell more of ours."

"It's already gone way beyond the rising cost of imports. We're worried about them dumping our bonds."

"Why would they do that?"

"Because they're afraid the dollar is going to keep sinking and they will be stuck with even worse losses than they already have."

"I don't believe that's anything to worry about. This country is still the greatest nation in the world. That is, if you guys at the Federal Reserve don't screw it up."

One of the aides to the chairman flinched noticeably.

"Senator, with your superficial knowledge of how our economy works, I wouldn't pass judgment," lashed out the chairman.

"What you need is less economics and more horse sense," blustered the red-faced senator.

"Gentlemen," interrupted the president, "stop arguing. From my perspective I'm not sure the senator isn't making some good points here, Mr. Chairman. But, let's get back to the problem."

"Yes, sir," nodded the chairman.

"What's the bottom line?"

"You mean, what are the costs involved in effecting a financial rescue of the endangered entities?"

"Yes, a bailout. What's it going to take?"

"Well, we have several representatives from the banking, brokerage, and hedge fund communities here. They can give us the liabilities for each of their individual operations, and my assistant, Mr. Graves, one of our economists can estimate additional liabilities." He turned to the banker and nodded.

Schuyler's banker stammered, "We have experienced a period of extraordinary economic events that has placed the bank in a precarious situation. Our hedging operation in foreign currency has found that certain transactions were mismatched and...."

"Cut to the chase," interrupted the president.

"Sir?"

"How much?"

"How much?" echoed the banker.

"Yes, tell us the amount." The president rolled his eyes. "How much do you need?"

"Eight billion."

"Eight billion! Are you serious?"

"Yes, sir."

"Are you telling me it will take eight billion dollars to bail out one miserable New York bank?

"Yes, sir."

"What have you been doing up there, rolling dice in the lavatory?"

"No, sir."

"Who else is here?" He looked down at his agenda and then stared at the next banker.

"I'm sorry, sir. We have the same sort of problems."

"How much?"

"Around five billion."

"Good grief."

"What about you?" he stared at a brokerage head.

"It's in the billions."

"You don't know?"

"It could be as much as ten."

"Ten billion?"

"Yes, sir."

"What the hell has been going on? And you," he cast a glance at the next brokerage firm executive.

The shaken executive licked his lips, cleared his throat, and replied, "Not as bad, sir. Four to five billion."

"Not bad, you say. What the hell is bad to you?"

An aide whispered in the chief executive's ear and nodded towards Randolph Schuyler.

"You operate a hedge fund?" he stared at Randolph.

"Yes, I do."

"How big?"

"Four billion."

"You lost it all?"

"I'm sorry, Mr. President, but it's a bit worse than that. We used considerable leverage."

"How big is your problem?"

"We'd like to help our customers, too."

"Let me tell you this. I don't give a shit about your clients who are wiped out. It's the poor bastards holding onto the other end of the bag. I mean, these gentlemen here at the banks and brokerages that were stupid enough to finance you. How much did you bury them for?"

"I believe we've got six billion dollars that we will be defaulting on soon."

"What have you assholes been doing up there in New York? This is the worst circle jerk in history," fumed the president. When he was mad he turned the air blue, and now he was livid.

The chairman interrupted. "Mr. Schuyler also has knowledge of several other struggling hedge funds with similar problems."

"What do you guys do, Schuyler, sleep in the same bed? One of you makes a move and the rest follow. Damned bunch of lemmings."

"Yes, sir. As it stands now, I have two hedge fund operators that stay in close touch with me. One in Miami is out two billion, but

106

owes four billion. The other in Boston has a little more than that. Around five billion they told me."

"A billion here, a billion there, pretty soon you're talking about real money."

"Yes, sir."

"Mr. Graves can summarize the total we think we might be looking at, Mr. President," said the chairman.

"Go ahead," sighed the chief executive.

"Right here in this room we know of thirty to forty billion. From what we can see around the country, it's going to take a total of one hundred and fifty billion to fix the problem in the financial markets."

"One hundred and fifty billion?" gasped the president.

"Yes, sir. That will fix Wall Street.

"Let me also say," intoned the chairman, "that if matters deteriorate further, then this amount will be inadequate to do the job. We must keep the markets at this level."

"It won't be easy after today," remarked the secretary of the Treasury who had remained silent until now.

"The market came down a full ten percent again and trading curbs were invoked."

"We have to announce this plan soon," said the president.

"I'm not sure it won't spook the markets, sir," said the secretary.

"How's that?"

"It's the size of it."

"Hell, it scares me. How are you going to do it?"

"For now we can write checks. Then we have to sell that many bonds to cover it. When the news of this offering hits the bond market, it might scare them. It's so big they may think it will push rates up. They're probably right. We're going to need a higher rate to sell them to any overseas buyers."

"Just get the money dispensed fast."

"I'll need a list."

"We've got one started," said the Fed chairman. "Graves will have it to you by the end of the week."

"Could I say one thing?" requested one of the brokerage heads.

"Why doesn't the government go in and buy call options on the Dow stocks and the S & P index and hold up the market. It would be a lot cheaper than this bailout."

One of the senators who had been silent jumped in, "That's not the province of the Federal government. What would the voters say if they knew their taxes were being spent in the stock market?"

"Today they'd probably be glad," responded the senator from Delaware.

"We couldn't hide what we're doing," said the Treasury secretary.

"It could be done through the banks and brokerage firms," argued the secretary's aide.

"The Fed thinks it's a bad idea," said an aide to the chairman. "We can't support every market the way we support the dollar."

"Everybody think about it," said the president, now pushing to end the meeting.

"Could I ask a question of the chairman?" said a presidential aide. "When should we announce the bailout?"

"Tomorrow. We should have the details worked out by midday. We'll only have a ballpark figure on the amount, but I do think we need to announce it tomorrow. Rumors of these problems are leaking out, and I think they're responsible for what happened today in the market."

"I'm hungry," said the president. Everyone laughed, including Randolph Schuyler, who also breathed a deep sigh of relief. His fat was out of the fire. He had been saved. Later that night he would call Alex Garcia in Miami and explain to him that he had the president's ear and he was able to get Seacoast Capital included in the bailout.

Chapter 14

———

Rumors swirled across the nation about pending failures among financial firms. After rising early, Danny Costello rushed to the midtown Manhattan office of Harriman Securities. As he walked through the glass doors he noticed the lobby was filled with people. "Who?" he furtively asked the receptionist, nodding toward the crowd. "Customers," she replied, "Didn't you hear?"

"No."

"It was on the news this morning. There was a big meeting in Washington about some banks and brokerage firms failing."

"Really. I was in a hurry. I didn't turn on the TV."

"It was secret, but reporters found out. These people know about it already. They're here to sell at the opening bell. They're giving their orders to the brokers personally. They don't trust the phones anymore."

"Wow."

Danny passed through the outer office into the broker area, found his desk and sat down. He checked the foreign market on his computer and whistled softly.

"Look at the futures, Danny, limit down, they can't drop any-more."

He turned to his fellow broker, Paul Aaron, "I was worried after yesterday, but this is insane."

"I know, that story about the banks and hedge funds ain't going to help a bit."

"Is it true?"

"Who knows. Some of it must be," answered Paul.

Phones were starting to ring a full forty minutes before the opening bell and most of the surrounding brokers who had come in early were busily talking to worried clients. Danny's phone rang.

"Hello."

"Danny, this is Myron Fritz."

"How you doing?"

"Lousy. Everything I own is down. You know that."

"Yes."

"I want you to sell everything this morning."

"Everything, Myron?"

"Yes, all of it. I've held it too long. I'm right back to where I was in 1982. I can't lose any more."

"O.K., Myron, I'll put the orders in." He had pulled up Myron's portfolio on his screen. "You want to sell at the market, right?"

"Yes."

"Myron, you bought a big load of Newcastle, Lord Mutual Funds."

"Yeah, that's gone way down, too. I called them yesterday, couldn't get through."

"You going to leave it alone?"

"Do me a favor. Call them and sell it for me."

"O.K., Myron, I'll do it. They're in New Rochelle. I'll call them as soon as we hang up."

"Good-bye, Danny."

"Commissions are going to be big today, Dan the Man," called Paul Aaron. "Enjoy it while it lasts."

Danny's phone rang again. It was Dr. Jennifer Keyes calling from Paramus, New Jersey.

"This market has me nervous, Danny. I'd like to sell all the stock out of my retirement plan. It's down to one hundred and fifty thousand. I've lost half of what I had a year ago."

"Yes, I know," he commiserated.

"What do you think I should do?"

"Maybe you're right, maybe switch into T-bills."

"That's what I want to do."

"O.K., let me write up these tickets. I'm going to sell you out at the market."

"Yes, do. Thanks a lot, Danny."

"O.K., Doc. Good-bye."

"What are you telling these people, Paul?"

"George and Sandy are talking them into holding, Louis got a big order already, he thinks it's a buying opportunity. Me, I'm going with the flow. If they want to sell, why fight it?"

"That's the way I feel, too. I'm taking sell orders."

Paul's phone rang again and he quickly left to answer it.

Danny dialed the toll-free number of Newcastle, Lord Management to liquidate Myron's fund. The line was busy. Once again his phone rang.

"Hello."

"Danny, this is Tammy Wasserman. What do you think's going to happen?"

"I'm clueless, Tammy."

"You're supposed to know these things."

"I know we're getting a lot of sell orders. I've got people in the lobby waiting for the bell. They don't want to take a chance on not getting their order in."

"Heavens."

"You a seller or a buyer, Tammy?" She was his biggest client. She traded a lot and the numbers were big. Her family imported wines from France and Italy and vodka from Russia.

"I'm thinking of pulling the pin. I didn't know how bad it was for some of these hedge funds. I put money in one of them and I can't get it out till the end of the year."

"Ouch."

"I'll call you back later and tell you if I want to sell."

"That's good."

The receptionist had walked back to his desk. "Guy here to see you."

"I'll come out." He followed her back toward her desk.

"Hi, Danny." It was Chuck Capelleti, one of his big clients.

"What you doing here, Chuck?"

"I got a margin call, Danny. I tried to sell out yesterday. The line was busy whenever I called and then when I got through they had trading curbs on. I can't take no chances today. I got to sell or I'm going to owe you money."

"O.K. You selling everything?" asked Danny.

"Yes. The whole bundle."

"I'll take care of it. Listen, I'd have coffee with you, but I got to get this done. O.K., Chuck?"

"Sure, Danny. I understand."

The opening bell was moving closer. He punched his sell orders into the computer.

Once again he dialed Newcastle, Lord. The line was still busy. His phone rang again. More customers with more orders. I hope this isn't happening everywhere, he thought. We'll know soon. The market is about to open.

"Look out below," hollered Paul Aaron. The market opened and dropped like a rock. Within twenty-eight minutes it had lost ten percent and trading curbs shut down any further transactions. Danny's phone was ringing off the hook. His computer indicated there were no confirmations on any of the sell orders he had placed.

"What's going on with these orders? Paul, did you get any fills?"

"One. Only one lousy order. What the hell is going on? I'm going back to operations and see what they say."

"I'm calling our Wall Street headquarters. Maybe I can get someone to explain."

Before he could pick up the phone, it was ringing again. Dr. Jennifer Keyes came on. "Danny, did you sell?"

"No, Doc, they didn't execute my order. I had it in there."

"Oh, no. What's happening? Why didn't my order get taken care of?"

"I don't know for sure, but I think there were too many orders. Then the trading curbs came on."

"You have to get it sold. Keep trying for me, Danny, get me in there somehow, call your downtown office. Please, Danny,' she pleaded.

"I'm trying, Doc. We're only down for an hour. We'll get it done."

"The longer you wait, the more I lose," she said icily.

"Doc, you did good for a long time. We'll get you out."

"You'd better, or you're going to lose a good customer."

"I've thought of that. I'm doing my best."

"O.K., sell me out."

"I will."

"I'll call you at noon."

The next caller was Myron Fritz. "Danny, I couldn't get through till now. Did you sell?"

"No."

"Why not?"

"I didn't get a single trade executed and then the curbs came in."

"What the hell, Danny, I'm losing my ass."

"I know, Myron."

"It isn't your fault, I know that. Be a good guy and get me in first, Dan."

"You went in first."

"Keep me there, then."

"Sure, I will."

"I'm counting on you."

"O.K., Myron."

"I'll call you again here in an hour or two."

"Danny," the secretary was leaning over his shoulder. "It's that same guy again. He wants to see you."

"Tell him I'll be out in a minute."

"O.K."

He dialed the Wall Street office; the line was busy. Then he called Newcastle, Lord. Their line was busy, too.

"Big logjam, Danny." It was Paul Aaron. "Operations tells me the exchange is swamped with sell orders and there's no buy orders to speak of."

"I wonder how long that will last?"

"Sooner or later it's going to get cheap enough."

"These people are getting hurt big time, Paul. I don't know how soon some of them will be back."

Danny got up and worked his way through the office toward the reception area.

"Can you friggin' believe this, Danny?" called one of the brokers. Danny shook his head. Chuck Capelleti was waiting by the receptionist.

"Danny, did you get me out?"

"Not yet."

"Shit, Danny. I got a margin call."

"I know. If we don't get you out soon, you're going to be in the red."

"I'll owe you."

"Yes."

"Lots of luck. I'm tapped."

"We need to sell you out."

"You'd think the brokerage firms would be putting the people with margin calls ahead of everyone else."

"I never thought of that, Chuck. Maybe they are."

"Otherwise they're going to get left holding the bag."

"These trading curbs may not be the best idea," said Danny. "Maybe they should just let the whole thing go. You know, get to the bottom. When people can't sell, they get damn nervous."

"Tell me about it. I don't want no brokerage firm hounding me for money 'cause they couldn't sell my stocks."

"I don't blame you."

"What a mess."

"I'll go back and try again, Chuck. She's going to open again soon. It's only a one hour moratorium."

"Thanks, Danny."

Back at his desk he took more phone calls. The market started trading again. "Pray for a rally boys and girls," shouted Paul Aaron.

The unrelenting decline continued. Within an hour and a half the market had declined a full twenty percent, once again invoking the trading curbs. Every broker was glued to the phone. Several had broken down and were sobbing.

"The Dow is now down over fifty percent from its high," Paul

Aaron advised. "The S & P almost two-thirds. Can you believe it?"

"We trade again in two hours."

At the sound of hollering they both turned toward the lobby.

"There's some pissed-off people," said Paul.

"At least I got some executions this time."

"Me, too."

"They sold out one of my guys on margin. He's going to owe us some money. He got lousy prices."

"That's the only kind of prices there are, Danny."

The phone was ringing again. He worked through the trading moratorium, consoling his customers and promising that he would soon get them out. Some were angry, others just numb.

Paul yelled at him. "My customer just told me that Bloomberg and CNBC are calling it a panic. People are going nuts trying to sell. It's a panic, Danny, a panic!"

"Yeah, I heard you. I can hear them out in the lobby, too. That one son of a bitch sounds like a wounded water buffalo."

Sheila Dorsey, one of the new brokers, came over to them. She had been crying. "You know, the only customers I've got so far are my relatives and friends. My mom and dad are out most of the money in their retirement plan. I can't get my brother sold out and he used money he borrowed from my folks. My cousin won't even speak to me. This is a nightmare."

"Sheila, it's not your fault," said Danny.

"My girlfriend from college called me just now. She says, 'with friends like you, who needs enemies.'"

"I been getting some nasty ones, too," advised Paul.

"People got to be able to sell. That's the problem. There's no liquidity."

"How can there be no liquidity," she asked.

"No buyers," said Dave. "If there ain't any buyers, you can't sell."

"I always thought there'd be buyers."

"There are some," corrected Danny, "just not enough of them."

"Danny," it was the receptionist. "Now there's three people to see you."

"I'm coming."

He saw Chuck Capelleti first. "You're out. We sold everything."

"Thank God."

"Everything was ten, fifteen percent lower than yesterday."

"I figured that. What are the damages?"

"You owe us fourteen grand."

"No!"

"Yes, sorry."

"I don't have it anymore, Danny."

"I'm not going to hassle you; the back room and the lawyers will do that."

"They can't get blood out of a turnip."

"I'm sorry, Chuck."

"O.K., Danny, I got to go."

"See you." I'm losing customers fast today, thought Danny.

Two young guys had been standing behind Chuck waiting to see Danny.

"Danny, you remember me?"

He stared at him for a moment, vaguely recollecting the face but nothing else.

"I'm Lucille's younger brother, Ricky Gromak."

"Sure. How are you?" Danny had dated Lucille for a few months three years prior.

"This is my friend, Dick Cohen."

"Hi."

"What can I do for you?"

"Listen, we both been doing a lot of trading on the computer.

You know, a hundred shares of this, a hundred shares of that. We got all our money into it. Dick here is a programmer. I work three to eleven at Sloan Kettering. We got plenty of time to do it. We were getting pretty good, making some money. Then last year we took some hits. But we hung in there, made most of our losses back. Now we got blindsided. We're losing big time, the worst part is, we can't get our sell orders executed. We'd like to start shorting some things, but we can't get sold out."

Dick Cohen cut in, "Some guys I know said the computers are backed up three or four hours. You can't get no answer. Nothing happens."

"So, here's the thing, Richie. We figured you could take our orders and get us out. Can you do that for us?"

"I can try, but we got the same problems. I got six executions so far today for one guy only. It sucks."

"No kidding."

"I still think you can do better for us."

"O.K., I'll try."

"That's cool."

"You need to fill out some things, you know, address, Social Security number."

"Sure."

"I'll get the forms. You can sit over here. Make me a list of what you want to sell and how many shares."

"O.K."

"Leave it with the receptionist. I'll be on the phone, but I'll pick it up before trading starts again. Call me later to see what happens."

"Thanks."

"Thank you."

The crowd in the lobby had gotten bigger. Other brokers were talking with some of their clients, trying to explain. Most of the disgruntled crowd were standing, while some sat in chairs provided for those customers who still came every day to watch the tape and trade. A woman was arguing with her broker. As Danny walked back to his desk, he could hear her loud voice over everything else. The woman sounded hysterical.

"Danny," called David Aaron as he got back to his desk. "They're making a big announcement." He quickly turned to his screen and watched the news.

"The Federal Reserve announced today at 1:00 PM that the New York Federal Reserve branch and the Treasury Department had developed a plan to assist eighteen banks, brokerage firms, and hedge funds who have recently encountered financial difficulties. The Federal Reserve will be making substantial loans direct to three large banks in order to stabilize them. In the case of the brokerage firms and hedge funds, a capital infusion rather than a loan will enable them to become solvent again. They will be required to use these funds to pay off margin loans and other contracts on which they are counterparties. No money will be advanced to benefit the customers of these firms who may have lost money in dealing with them. The amount of this financial rescue plan as ordered by the president will be approximately one hundred and fifty billion dollars."

A loud combination of gasps and cheers rose throughout the firm.

"Let's start buying," shouted one voice.

"Like I'm going to go out in the lobby and get a flock of buy orders," said David Aaron to Danny.

Danny's phone rang. It was Dr. Jennifer Keyes.

"Danny, did you sell me out?"

"Not yet. Maybe you want to change your mind. They just announced a hundred and fifty billion dollar bailout."

"For who?"

"The banks and brokerage houses."

"I didn't even know they were in trouble."

"Yes, a lot of rumors floating around!"

"I don't care what they do. I just want out. Can you get me out now?"

"I believe so. There should be some buyers."

"You need buyers?"

"Of course."

"Oh, I guess I never thought that much about it."

"That's the problem, not enough buyers."

"Oh, well, listen Danny. Find a buyer for me, O.K.?"

"I will do my best."

"I'll call you again at four."

"Bye."

The market reopened and despite the hopes of brokers and investors, continued its rapid deterioration. It was 2:30 PM. There was an hour and a half to go. "No more curbs today," said David Aaron. "It would have to go down another thirty percent." Within thirty minutes it had collapsed ten percent. The crowd in the lobby had elevated their conversation to a dull roar.

"They're stopping it again," someone yelled.

Danny's eyes swiveled to the screen. "It's stopped," he said to a phone customer. "Let me see if we got you out and I'll call you back."

"Why did they stop it?" he called to Dave. "The next trading curb was another thirty percent down. It was never going to go down that far."

"Here comes an announcement," said someone.

"It's the exchange, they closed it because of a computer problem." Everyone groaned. "Bullshit," said someone.

"They closed it because it's sinking out of sight," said Dave

Aaron.

"Listen to those phones ringing," said Danny. "At least I got a few orders off."

"Me, too."

Suddenly yelling and a high-pitched scream emanated from the lobby. Danny, David, and a few others ran out to see what was causing the ruckus. The receptionist was waving her arms and announced to them breathlessly there had been a fight. "Joey Abramowicz was running out for a sub, he got waylaid by some big lout, told him to stay put and sell his blankedy-blank stock for him. You should have heard his language. Then he conks Joey one right in the face. Joey pushes him away, the guy falls down and Joey ducks out the door. That big guy there. Here he comes."

"What are you assholes gawking at," shouted a large red-faced man. "You crooked bunch of pricks. You got all my money and I want it. Right now! Do you hear me? Now!" The guy's face turned purple with rage. "Yeah, you bastards, I want my money, too," screamed an elderly woman into their faces. The crowd began to push forward toward the alarmed brokers. Danny and Dave quickly looked at one another, devising a strategic withdrawal.

"Call building security," Danny called to the wide-eyed receptionist.

"You son of a bitch," screamed a woman and lunged at Danny, her fingernails clawing at his face. "Give me my money," she bellowed.

Danny twisted her around and pushed her back into the crowd. His cheek carried two small scratches that were starting to bleed. Someone pushed over a desk with a loud bang. "Call the cops," instructed Danny. Another broker was wrestling with a middle-aged man. Now the crowd was chanting wildly, "We want our money, we want our money."

Three building security guards burst into the office lobby and

started giving orders to the people in the rear to vacate the premises. Someone threw a hardcover book that banged into the wall
behind Danny. Two people picked up chairs and waved them
menacingly at the line of brokers. A disgruntled person slammed a
chair against the wall. Suddenly, four of New York's finest burst
into the brokerage lobby and began to shout orders. The big purple-faced guy started screaming curses at them until a shot of
Mace in his mug dropped him like a felled tree. The crowd pan-
icked for the door, sweeping around the police and out into the
hallway. One woman turned to the gaping brokers before making
her dash and flashed her middle finger. A cop hurried toward her,
but she scooted past him and was out the door. The cops were
cuffing the purple-faced guy, who was sobbing outlandishly, when
the brokers began to filter back to their desks.

"That's it for me," Sheila Dorsey called to them. "I'm quitting
right now. I can't believe what I just saw. Who needs it? Say good-
bye to me, boys."

"Me, too," said one of the old-timers, "Screw this. One of you
can have my customer book and listen to these people piss and
moan. I'm too old for this anymore." He stuck out his hand and
shook theirs.

"Amazing," said Dave after the two brokers were gone.

"What a day, and it isn't over yet. I got a lot of people to call."

Danny worked for another two hours and finally was finished
holding the hands of his clients. He made one final attempt to
Newcastle, Lord and much to his amazement, on the third ring
someone answered.

"Hello, Newcastle, Lord. Can I help you?"

"My name is Danny Costello, I'm a broker at Harriman
Securities. One of my clients has requested that I liquidate his
mutual fund."

"We're not taking any more redemption orders this week."

"Why not?"

"Why do you think? Aren't you a stockbroker?"

"Yes, I understand."

"I'm sorry."

"What are your customers saying? They can't be too happy."

"Huh. You should have been here today."

"Why?" asked Danny.

"There was a bunch of customers here this morning looking for their checks. We didn't have them. They got rowdy. After the market closed they just went nuts. Turned into a mob. Somebody tipped over a couple of file cabinets, scattered our files all over. Then someone lit the papers on fire. All retirees, Gray Panthers, you'd never believe it. The New Rochelle fire department had to come. Smoke all over. Nobody got hurt, but it's a mess."

"We had a riot here, too."

"You got to be kidding."

"No, the cops came, arrested a guy."

"Wow. Interesting times, huh?"

"Too interesting."

"Listen, I'll take your number and call you when we can take care of this redemption for you."

"Hey, thanks." Danny gave him his number and hung up the phone. He pushed back in his chair and for a moment closed his eyes. He was bushed.

Chapter 15

———

If last year's crash had rattled world markets, this one was shaking them to their foundation. A panic had set in on Wall Street and from what Richie could tell, it wasn't over yet. Too many people were still clamoring to get out. Mutual funds were forced to slow down their rate of redemptions and checks were now delayed up to a month. The backup in computer trades was totally unmanageable and any stock sale was proving to be difficult. The morning paper was full of stories about the government's one-hundred- fifty-billion-dollar bailout and expert analysis on why it hadn't helped the market recover. The requirement to expend such a huge amount seemed to make people more worried than ever. Stories about several disturbances at brokerage firms and the severe beating of a Miami hedge fund operator were also on the front page.

The president had given a reassuring speech the evening before and the chairman of the Federal Reserve would be giving special testimony to Congress early the next week. The big Asian trading partners were reassuring their people that keeping money in U.S.

markets would prove to be astute. Nevertheless, the dollar had taken a pounding even though interest rates had shot up again. The economic news continued to be grim and a deflationary economic slowdown gripped the land.

Richie had been busy. When the stock market locked up, gold took off. It rose dramatically to $340 an ounce. Within days Richie opened accounts with five additional commodities brokers who were members of the exchange. Then he sold some of his contracts and with the proceeds began to buy at the new firms until he had doubled up on his gold contracts. His profits were already huge, amounting to over sixty million dollars. A one-day rise from $320 to $340 had been worth twenty million alone on his million- ounce position. Now he had two million ounces of gold and the world looked like it was going to crash and burn. He felt no anxiety, nor much elation. He made a conscious effort to control any self-congratulatory sentiments. His wife had concluded that he was one of those exceedingly rare birds that carried a natural inborn humility. Infrequently, she thought, you see such a person in professional sports. Despite the fact that they are making millions, they still manage to keep things in perspective and appear humble. They still stop for autographs and make jokes about their own errors. Most people who make a lot of money tend to become arrogant, she was sure. The best clue to the state of a person's ego was the way they treated others. Richie never failed to be friendly to the little people. "Success carries the seeds of its own undoing," he told Nancy one night. "We need to watch our egos." Nancy had been bragging on the phone to a friend about how much money they had made and was suddenly embarrassed. "The trouble is," Richie told her, "you can't discern your own arrogance in the present, only in the past. It's only after you have some humbling experience that you begin to see that your vanity caused you to do dumb things." How could this man have such wisdom, she wondered.

Richie wasn't perfect. He could be irritable at times and was absentminded to the point of distraction. Sometimes he held grudges and was moody. He'd spend money on his own wardrobe, but after that he could be tight. But these were trifling sins. As her mother once told her, "He doesn't smoke, drink, or chase women. That's ninety percent of the battle, dear." For the most part, her life with Richie had been happier than she had any right to expect. Some of her friends from high school and college had met up with losers and were divorced after months or years of strife and turmoil.

She didn't need all the money Richie had managed to pile up. All she really needed was the security of a house without a mortgage and enough money to pay the monthly bills and take a vacation every year. She understood he needed some kind of validation that was unlike any of her needs. Sure, when the girls grew up she might think about starting her own business, but for now, raising her kids was all the gratification and challenge she needed. She had a great capacity for giving, both to her children and her husband, and although they would sometimes take advantage of her unselfish goodness, they cherished her for it.

That very morning she had run to the Road-Mart while Richie was showering, and filled the car with gas so Richie wouldn't have to stop. It was one of those thoughtful little things she would spring on him that made him happy. He hated stopping for gas and filling his own tank. At times he could be a klutz and on several occasions had spilled a drop of gas or two on himself. He hated the smell and claimed it lasted all day, no matter what you did to get rid of it.

Richie hung around the house long enough to check the 8:30 AM opening of the stock market. She watched with him, fascinated by the dark and gloomy news that permeated the airwaves and satellite transmissions. "It's down again," he told her. "What a horror story." Then he moved to his computer and checked Access, the computerized quote system for international metals trading. "Gold still rising in London and New York," he told her. She knew the dimensions of his trading scheme, but the thought that he could make five or ten million dollars in a day was totally foreign to her. She understood how the futures market worked, and complex financial transactions, but she couldn't comprehend having vast amounts of money in her possession. She'd been raised in a small town in Iowa where a lot of money was a thousand dollars. She had no qualms, however, about being rich. She would enjoy it.

When he got to the office Richie immediately checked his computer screen and was stunned. Trading curbs were in once again. The great selling wave was still rolling in. He picked up the phone and dialed Bernie's direct number. He had been so intent on his trading he hadn't talked to his friend in three days. Bernie had left several messages for him which he had intended to return but never got around to, focusing instead on the nuances of the gold market.

"Where you been?" queried Bernie.

"I was making some moves. I forgot about everything."

"Nice, I hope your moves are working out."

"So far."

"Good God, can you believe this market?"

"Unbelievable!"

"The bear's got us by the balls."

"King Grizzly."

"That's a fact."

"This sucker is one of those kind on Kodiak Island," related Richie. "I was up there fishing once. I'm not much of a fisherman, but somebody talked me into it. I was standing on the edge of a lake casting where a stream came in when this bear comes out next to me as big as a locomotive. The guy I was with jumped in the float plane and wouldn't come back out."

"This one looks bigger than that."

"Maybe. At least mine went away."

"Lot of horror stories, eh?"

"Yeah, I'm glad I'm not a broker anymore. How you doing?"

"To be honest, I'm doing pretty good. I've put most of my people into gold stocks, at least everyone who would listen. Gold was going up when I did it and now it's really jumped. All of a sudden I'm a hero."

"Good for you," said Richie. "I knew you did that in the past, but I didn't know if you were still in it. You like to move around."

"Not anymore. I like being a hero."

"It could go up awhile yet."

"For sure, with this mess."

"They've got trading curbs on again."

"People are pissed," said Bernie. "We got some of them here, coming into our office. They've had trouble liquidating. Some of them are just getting killed. I feel sorry for them. One old guy was just crying his eyes out yesterday."

"That's a shame."

"It isn't going to help the brokerage business, Richie. I can tell you that."

"For sure."

"People got wiped out. Some of them lost their life savings. People are deserting the stock funds like mad. They want out!" exclaimed Bernie.

"You couldn't say anything bad about a mutual fund a couple of years ago."

"Things change. When I started thirty years ago you couldn't say anything good about them. That's the way it will be again. They got burned in stock back then, too. But not this bad."

"What happened that eventually made them so popular?" asked Richie.

"Here's the way it went. The bonds were having problems; overseas loans, bad debts, things like that. So the Fed lowered interest rates. The banks could borrow from the Fed at a low rate and make loans at a higher rate. It increased their profits. In fact, it saved a lot of banks."

"Yes."

"But, the banks couldn't pay any kind of interest on savings accounts. So a few outfits started money market mutual funds that paid more interest than the banks. Up to then you kept your money in the bank. So now people started switching into money markets in a big way."

"Interesting."

"The next thing you knew everybody was starting bond funds. Everybody wanted as much interest as they could get. You could get higher interest in a bond fund, so everybody switched into bond funds."

"Then what?"

"Now people believed in mutual funds again. All of a sudden stocks got hot. Since 1982 the gains in stocks have usually been greater than the yields from the bond funds. So people started switching out of the bond funds into the stock funds. They got lulled to sleep. Some of them didn't believe there was anymore risk in a stock fund than in the other funds."

"Amazing."

"Somewhere along the way all the big brokerage firms introduced their own money market funds and their own stock and bond funds. Then they got their brokers selling them. With those big sales forces people just sent their money to them. Now when somebody gets a chunk of cash they don't go to the bank, they call their broker."

"I know."

"Believe me, they're not going to be so popular after this stock debacle. If they manage to lose a lot of the wealth of Americans because they got overexuberant about stocks, it will hurt them big time."

"I won't argue."

"Now, tell me what you're doing. I mean, is it any different than a few days ago?"

"Not really."

"You still holding all those contracts?"

"Yes."

"You're making a lot of money, I mean millions."

"Don't tell anyone this. I don't want anyone other than you to know."

"O.K., what?"

"I doubled up."

"What?"

"I'm up sixty million so I doubled up."

"What?"

"You deaf?"

"No, I'm in shock. Richie, don't do it. Take it and run."

"Can't."

"Why not?"

"It isn't in me to stop now. I think I'd be leaving too much on the table."

"Jeez, how much do you want?"

"Don't know, Bernie, a lot."

"Listen, take some out and buy some of these gold stocks.

They're the only thing that's hot right now."

"Mmm, I don't know."

"Listen, the big ones are starting to make money."

"I don't think so, I'm better off where I am."

"Well, let's talk about it."

"O.K., hey, I got to jump. Somebody's holding for me."

"Good-bye, Richie."

His secretary, Carol Olson, always took messages unless it was someone important on the phone, then she'd poke her head in and tell him who it was.

"A reporter from the newspaper," she said arching her eyebrows.

"Name?"

"Sarah Gordon. Business section."

"Thanks."

"Hello."

"Yes, Mr. Stenquist?"

"Yes."

"I wondered if you had a few minutes?"

"I do."

"To tell you the honest truth, we're doing a story about commodity speculators, and your name came up."

"Really."

"Apparently you've had considerable success."

"Well, I wonder where you heard that?"

"Some of it's just rumors, but I did get verification from some people in Chicago."

"Like who?"

"I can't say."

"I'm really not too interested in a story."

"There's going to be a story one way or the other. That's already been decided. It's more a question of whether you will help us with the article I'm writing."

"I don't want to be rude, but I like to keep my affairs pretty quiet."

"Listen, I'll be sure and put a positive slant on it if you'll just answer three quick questions for me."

"What could you say negative?"

"You know, the greed factor."

"Sounds like I'm getting blackmailed."

"Not really."

"I don't want my family and neighbors to read that I'm a villain."

"Just three little questions and I promise you'll be the guy in the white hat."

"O.K., shoot."

"Is it gold?"

"Yes."

"Is it a million ounces?"

"Ohh," he groaned.

"Tell me."

"Suffice to say it's a lot."

"I'm going to take that to be a million. That's what we'd heard and I've already got it in the article as a rumor. So what's the difference?"

"I don't like this."

"You're a big boy."

"What's the last question?"

"How much have you made so far and how much do you want to make?"

"That's two questions."

"O.K., how much have you made?"

"What's the rumor say?"

"Fifty million."

"I'm not going to confirm that one way or another. Leave it as a rumor. It won't matter."

"You're fudging."

"That's it, Sarah."

"O.K., if you insist."

"I don't like this story. Everybody's going to know my business."

"It can't be helped. That's what a paper does. How do you think the rich get famous?"

"I don't want to be famous."

"You don't want to be infamous, either."

"What's that supposed to mean?"

"It means that in this article you'll probably look pretty good."

"I'd rather not look any way."

"Well, if you want to stay anonymous, then lose all the money you made. My editor won't care about you then."

"Gee, thanks."

"Anything else you can tell me?"

"No, I don't think so."

"Alright. Thanks for the interview."

"Good-bye."

"Oh, one last thing. Could I send a photographer over to get your picture?"

"I'm sorry. I'd prefer not to have my picture in the paper."

"No problem. 'Bye."

What a pest, he thought. Damn, of all the luck.

Chapter 16

———

Gradually, the selling wave that had overcome the stock market began to recede. After four straight days in which market curbs were put in place, everyone who wanted to liquidate had finally sold. In many cases, the prices were now so low that beleaguered investors decided there was no point in selling. The Dow had dropped to forty percent of its previous high. Now, the volume began to dry up and a terrible apathy swept across the once enthusiastic investment community. People had lost so much that they were short of funds to invest. In many cases the little they had left was now in the bank and couldn't be budged, no matter what blandishments they heard from their broker.

Richie Stenquist was certain there would be further economic repercussions from the crash. He had concluded years ago that the great boom in consumer buying had been fed by the dynamic stock market. Now that people's profit expectations had disappeared and the wealth effect had vanished, a new realization dawned on the public. They were now in danger of an economic

134

crisis and their personal situation was precarious. The specter of poverty had raised its head and they were uniformly worried.

Richie could sense the grave concern in some of his neighbors and friends. They knew the cork had popped and the champagne was gone. He tried to offer solace to a few of them, but found it hard to relate to their plight. He was a nimble trader who could survive virtually any setback and in the most difficult times he could thrive.

The article in the newspaper about Richie had come out on a Sunday. Somehow they had gotten his picture, perhaps taken with a telephoto lens. It wasn't unflattering and Nancy had cooed about how handsome he looked. The story related his recent successes and the rumors that swirled around him. It was neither favorable or unfavorable, but related the facts surrounding his success. Most of the article was background material that explained how such sizable profits were possible. Richie had been embarrassed by the contents, but Nancy had told him not to be silly. There was nothing in the article that could hurt them.

Almost immediately Richie began to get calls at his office, asking for donations, favors, or capital for new ventures. After listening to several harebrained schemes that ate up his time, he began to tell the callers that he did not invest in new deals. This shortened the calls. For a few days it seemed like everybody who called him wanted something. If they weren't driving him to distraction telling about their pet schemes, they were trying to get him to be a guest or speaker somewhere. They all wanted time or money, he told Nancy. She noticed the same phenomenon at home. Several strangers had rung their doorbell, introduced themselves, and began to spin a lengthy explanation of why they were there, which always wound up as a long-winded request for money for an investment or business start-up. She had also noticed that the neighbors seemed a mite warmer to her.

On the weekend following the article about Richie, they attended a barbecue outing at their friends, Charlie and Debbie Newcombe's house. Most of the neighborhood was there and Richie was the star attraction. Everyone nodded, waved greetings, or shook his hand. Richie nursed a beer while his neighbors gathered around him.

"Nice article, Richie," prompted one.

"I didn't ask for it," he told them. "They did it in spite of my request."

"Doesn't hurt anything," said one.

"You don't like publicity?" questioned another.

"I can live without it," he responded.

"Is it true, Richie?" one of them asked. "I mean fifty million bucks. Can it be true?"

"They're guessing a little bit on that. Put it this way, it's a lot for a small-town kid from Minnesota." They laughed, hanging on his every word and basking in the aura of his celebrity. They conversed for a while about generalities and the group split apart for more beer and to converse with other friends. Richie slid into a lawn chair in a shady spot at the side of the yard out of traffic. For a minute he watched the kids at play. The little ones ran recklessly, under the eye of their watchful mothers, and the older ones bunched together on the farthest reaches of the Newcombes' lawn. One of the men was soon kneeling at his side, a slight worried look on his face.

"Richie, you made all that money because the market got clobbered. Now it looks like the economy could go in the tank. Things were going so good, how'd you know this was going to happen?"

"Lucky guess, Eddie."

"It's more than that."

"I've thought for a long time that a big credit expansion can come apart at the seams."

"You mean people borrowing too much?"

"Businesses, too."

"Yeah, it seems pretty obvious now."

"Not to some people. They're blaming it on the wrong things, interest rates and such."

"Man, we are really cutting back at work," said Eddie. "I been there a long time and I thought I was going in this last cut."

"Really."

"Yeah, and I been looking. There's nothing."

"Sorry to hear that, Eddie."

"What's going to happen, Richie?"

"I'm not sure."

"Guess. What do you think?"

"Could be a depression."

"That's just what's messing up my mind. I could be collecting unemployment."

"Not good."

"You got that right."

"You got your house paid for. I heard that," said Richie.

"Not anymore."

"No."

"We refinanced."

"You did?"

"Put it all into my brother-in-law's business. He was doing great, building cabinets, had eleven employees. He needed money to expand. He was going to pay us back in two years. We got twenty-five percent of his company. He had back orders up the gazoo. Now he's closing up. Construction just died. All those home builders are on the ropes. It happened so fast, Richie. I can't believe it."

"He didn't pay you back anything?"

"Nothing, my wife is sick about it. It's ruined the relationship with her family. How the hell you going to sue your brother-in-law?"

"I'm sorry to hear that, Eddie."

"We'll make it, but it's a lot harder now."

"Yes."

"You think it's going to get worse?"

"Maybe."

"I hope you're wrong. Listen, Richie, I'm glad you did so good. Keep it up. I'll talk to you later."

As Eddie sidled away another neighbor, Junior Branson, came over to Richie with a second person in tow.

"Richie, this is my friend, Bobby Nash." Bobby stuck out his hand. "I read about you in the paper last Sunday." Richie shifted uncomfortably.

"Oh, yeah."

"Bobby's a real estate broker. We got to know each other because I'm in the mortgage business."

"Sure."

"You need a new house, Richie? I got a listing on a beauty."

"No," Richie laughed.

"This guy builds a multimillion-dollar house, a regional manager for a mutual fund. Two months after he moved in they fired him. Then all his investments went in the tank. If he doesn't sell it, he's going to lose it. They really cut the price."

"I'm pretty happy where I am."

"I understand. That's the way it is, though, nobody's buying anything."

"That's a fact," interjected Junior, the mortgage broker. "We're dead in the water."

"Nothing cooking, Junior?" Richie asked.

"Tell him, Bobby."

"It's bad, Richie. There's plenty of listings but no buyers."

"Prices aren't holding up, either," said Junior. "The only deals we're doing are under the market."

"Everything's down," continued Bobby. "House prices are off maybe twenty-five percent. Can you believe that?"

"Some people were financing one hundred percent to value weren't they?" asked Richie.

"Yes, some were," said Junior. "We sold a lot of mortgages that I think are underwater now. They better hope these people keep paying."

"What about these one hundred twenty-five percent deals?" Bobby chipped in. "They gave people more than their houses were worth. You think they're worried now? Listen, we got a lot of listings where people can't make their payments. They're behind and they're trying to bail themselves out. If they can't sell, they get foreclosed on. You get very much of that and it drives the prices down."

"If prices get low enough people will start buying," offered Richie.

"I'll tell you what we're seeing, Richie," replied Junior. "Most of these people don't have a pot to pee in. They lost a lot in the stock market or they spent their savings on goodies. I mean the financial statements we're seeing are horrible."

"And bad credit, too," added Bobby. "We get somebody wants to buy a house and once the mortgage company takes a look, they're in hock up to their eyeballs and their credit rating stinks. Then the mortgage company wants a third down. There's no way."

"Home builders are dying like flies," continued Junior. "I've never seen it any worse."

"Tell you a story," said Bobby. "We got this secretary, married to a guy who works at the canning plant. They got a big house, big boat, everything, you know. He gets laid off. They're way behind on the mortgage. What'd they do? They walked. Packed everything up and moved in with her sister, the whole family. Worked out good, she says. The sister and her husband were struggling, too, thought they might lose their house, so the ones who moved in pay them some rent and now they can meet their payment."

"Man, I wouldn't want my wife's sister to move in with me," joked Junior.

Richie decided he'd better mingle a bit and excused himself, moving across the lawn. Two tables filled with food and a barrel of beer resting in ice were the focal point of the get-together. Charlie Newcombe fried hamburgers on a gas grill next to the tables. Nancy was busy talking with two neighborhood ladies. The first northern air of the season had cooled the August heat into a marvelous day in the midseventies. Everyone was laughing, talking, and having a good time.

He decided to eat and pushed his paper plate toward Charlie who promptly placed a burger on his plate next to the potato salad he had piled on.

"You're the man," said Charlie. "You're the man."

Richie retreated to a chair and his wife came over to join him.

"Such a beautiful day, Richie."

"I'm having a good time." He smiled at her.

Later as the sun lowered, the families began to disburse. Nancy and Richie thanked their hosts and said good-bye.

"Don't thank us," said Charlie, "after what you did for our family you deserve all the thanks! We wouldn't be having this party if it weren't for you."

The next day Richie was wounded by a letter to the editor in the Sunday morning paper. It referred to him as a greedy speculator and complained about the fact that he had become rich while others were losing their money. He brooded about the letter throughout the morning, but after talking about it with Nancy, who vehemently disparaged the letter writer, he let it go and forgot it. It popped into his mind again the next day and the same feeling of dismay returned when he read a letter sent to his office that chided him for his greed. That damned newspaper article, he thought. Too bad he couldn't have remained anonymous.

Chapter 17

———

James Cosgrove loved to drive a mile or two under the speed limit in the outside lane of the freeway. The more cars that piled up behind him, the more he liked it. Without him they would be breaking the law and someone had to rein them in. When they passed him on the inside and cast a dirty look his way, he refused to notice. Whenever he drove on the freeway, he routinely went to the passing lane and stayed there. When the speed limit first became fifty-five he'd had several incidents where drivers swerved at him or pulled ahead of him and slammed on their brakes. Finally the incensed drivers made him afraid and he stayed in the middle lane. Now, with the speed limit back up, he had once again taken up his job of policing the fast lane.

Cosgrove worked in the massive gray marble Federal building in downtown Chicago. He was an enforcement agent for the FCTC, the Federal Commodities Trading Commission. His usual fare was nailing brokers who promised extravagant gains, exaggerated their track record, and lied to clients about their accounts. He had been responsible for indictments against numerous bad actors who had practiced fraud. He enjoyed ferreting out wrongdoers and once he got the scent of a crime, he pursued it relentlessly. James Cosgrove was diligent and hard-nosed. He didn't have much flexibility or empathy for miscreants.

His supervisor, Maggie Walcott, approved of his strict application of the law. That's what they were there to do. Cosgrove's character had always been beyond reproach and she trusted him. As Federal agencies go, the FCTC didn't have that much teeth. They were constantly plying Washington for more muscle. Derivatives had exploded and the futures end of it was her responsibility. Her staff was small and she suspected that much chicanery took place that was never apprehended. It never occurred to her that for the massive size of the futures markets, it was remarkably free from sins. Now she had a report on her desk about a character in Minneapolis who had traded himself into a two- million-ounce position in gold or twenty thousand contracts. It wasn't cause for great alarm, nor was it an illegally large position, but it needed to be watched.

Earlier that day Maggie had been included in a conference call with the surveillance head of the commodity exchange clearing house, an FCTC lawyer, and two clearing firm members on the board of the exchange. They discussed the status of Richie Stenquist and his twenty thousand contracts. "He's complied with all our position accountability and information requirements," said one. "We know as much about him as anybody."

"He's in compliance with the Comex rules," said one of the board members. "It's all his own money so there's no possibility of fraud."

"I think we can let him continue. Some of the big gold mining companies have similar large positions."

"It appears he's got enough capital for now."

"Let's send somebody out to talk with him," suggested the lawyer.

"Yes," agreed Maggie Walcott. "That will put him on notice that we're watching him closely."

Her sources told her that what he had done was impossible. Nobody had ever taken such huge positions on such a thin capital base and had it work out so perfectly. It was just too smooth, she thought. How had he done it? Where was the worm in the apple? There was nobody in the Minneapolis office who could handle this. They were totally involved in grains. She would send her best bird dog, Cosgrove, to sniff out this curiosity, and if they found any violations, they would end his run of luck.

James Cosgrove was packing light. He would stay in Minneapolis for only one night. If he found anything he didn't like, he would obtain the records of Richie Stenquist's transactions and go from there. Cosgrove hoped he would find Stenquist compliant and willing to cooperate. With any luck the man would answer his questions and show him his records. He called a cab and soon was on his way to O'Hare. He had an 8:00 AM flight so he should be in downtown Minneapolis by no later than 10:00 AM he calculated.

He walked down the ramp into the waiting 757 and passed through the first-class section. It always offended him to see this separation among the passengers. He would abolish first class if he were running things. Why should these rich dickheads have it any better than the rest of us, he thought. He hated the rich with a passion. His mother once told him, "It's all right to hate, but never do anything hateful." So he disliked successful business people with a passion and while he wouldn't harm them physically in any way he dreamed of uncovering their crooked tricks and sending them to jail. His idol in history was V. I. Lenin, who had dismissed the success of entrepreneurs as no more than luck.

What he really loved about Vladimir Ilich was the way he handled anyone who thwarted his revolutionary movement. "Shoot them," was his frequent instruction. Cosgrove would swoon at the thought of issuing such an order. He imagined himself walking on to the plane with his followers in tow. "Take them outside and shoot them," he would bark as he nodded toward the rich promoters sitting in first class. Here he was, stuck making forty-eight thousand dollars a year and these blackguards were swindling the masses to the tune of billions. Everyone knew most of them were crooked. Lenin did the right thing when he shot them all. Now they were coming back in Russia, but just as crooked as ever. His sister-in-law had once told him they were crooks because ordinary business had been against the law over there, so only the crooks participated. It's not that way here, she had argued. He never liked her after that. He would have had her shot, too. He imagined his brother on his knees pawing at his sleeve, begging for mercy for his wife. The firing squad raised their rifles, his blindfolded sister-in-law screamed in terror, kaboom, her body jerked and slumped forward. "Phut!" He heard a noise and came fully alert. I swear, he thought, the chunky woman next to him had farted. If he smelled anything, he would have her shot, too. He laughed out loud.

"There's someone here to see you." Carol Olson had walked to his door and was looking in at him.

"Who is it?" he queried.

"A Mr. Cosgrove from the Federal Commodities Trading Commission." She was reading off his card.

Richie's stomach knotted up ever so slightly. Why? he asked himself.

"Send him in."

"Good morning, Mr. Stenquist," offered Cosgrove.

"Hello. What can I do for you?" said Richie, rising from his chair.

"I'd like to ask you a few questions if I might."

"Questions?"

Cosgrove reached across the desk and handed his card to Richie who took the card and squinted at it, pretending to read.

"I believe my FCTC registration is up-to-date," said Richie.

"I'm not here to talk about your registration."

"You're not?"

"No, I'm here to talk about your trading activities. May I sit down?"

"Of course," said Richie. They both settled into their respective chairs.

"Mr. Stenquist, it appears that you have had what appears to be unprecedented trading success."

"Perhaps."

"I'm curious, are you using your client's money for this adventure?"

"No, my own."

"Your own? Solely your own?"

"Yes."

"Might I ask the source of this capital?"

"Not really."

"And why not?" said Cosgrove, his raised eyebrows feigning surprise.

"No reason. Actually, the money I started with was mine."

"You mean savings?"

"Yes."

"Well, you certainly must have had a hefty savings account because your large trader reporting form shows position levels at ten separate firms totaling twenty thousand contracts. That's two million ounces of gold."

"Is there something wrong with that?" inquired Richie, a sudden dislike for the man welling up inside him.

"It depends what you have in mind. I'm sure you're aware of the position accountability rules of the exchange? They can order a position reduction if they become uncomfortable."

"I'm aware of that."

"I see you're expanding the number of clearing members of the exchange who you're using from five to ten." Cosgrove used the alternate terminology for commodities brokerage firms.

"What is the purpose of that?"

"To spread the risk."

"What risk? The firms you deal with can't assume any risk?"

"No, I mean the risk to me if one of them fails. I don't want my eggs all in one basket."

Cosgrove's eyes widened as he stared at Richie. Careful bastard, he thought.

"What possessed you to move so heavily in gold? It's been dead for years. Were you privy to any information that others might not have had?"

Richie laughed, "No, I don't think there is any such information."

"It seems like you've met all the requirements for margin and maintenance that these firms require."

"Yes."

"Are you doing anything offshore?"

"No."

"I know you're familiar with the Hunt brothers and their attempt to corner the silver market?"

"Yes."

"You don't have any crazy scheme like that up your sleeve?"

"Corner the gold market?" Richie laughed.

"The way you're pyramiding, it makes us wonder, although you only have three percent of the open interest."

"Not to change the subject, but I never could figure out what the Hunts did that caused them so much trouble."

"You worry me, Mr. Stenquist, asking that question."

"Sorry."

"They had several wealthy associates with whom they conspired to corner the silver market. It was a consortium. They took delivery on an extraordinary amount of silver in order to manipulate the price."

"So you stopped them."

"Yes, of course. Let's get back to the subject. Are you hedging with your gold contracts?"

"No."

"What about arbitrage in offshore markets, writing options, anything like that?"

"No."

"Are you working for any large mining entities, hedge funds, or others who need delivery of gold to cover a short position?"

"No."

"I see you've been rolling your contracts over before the spot month."

"Yes."

"To avoid reducing your position?"

"Yes, I can only hold three thousand contracts in the spot month."

"Not planning to take delivery?"

"No."

"Will you ever?"

"Never."

"It would seem you have quite a large profit. What are your plans now?" Cosgrove knew he was overstepping his bounds.

"I don't know."

"What did you do prior to your commodities career, Mr. Stenquist?"

Richie quickly filled him in on his brokerage background.

"Might I look at the confirmations of your transactions?"

Richie thought for a second and then replied, "I don't see why not. Excuse me."

He walked out to Carol Olson. "Bring me the confirmations for this year," he said, his voice barely audible. "Just the gold contracts for this year."

In moments he had them in his hands. He gave the file to Cosgrove who quickly laid them out on his side of the desk.

"I'm amazed at how well this pyramiding has worked for you. Quite risky but perfectly legal, at least to a point," he said, looking up at Richie.

Richie returned his gaze.

"You're quite a plunger, Mr. Stenquist. Let me give you some advice. If and when this explodes in your face, don't plan to extricate yourself with some unethical scheme and don't get the idea that you're the second coming of the Hunt brothers. If in some way you break a law, I will see to it that you're penalized."

You horse's ass, Richie thought. He fought to control himself.

"I'm not going to break any laws and, frankly, I resent the suggestion that I might."

Their eyes locked, an unspoken antagonism flowing between them. "My work here is done, Mr. Stenquist. I'll be going back to Chicago. Good luck with your speculating."

"Good-bye," said Richie as Cosgrove exited.

Richie sat at his desk, replaying the interview in his mind.

"What was that all about?" interjected Carol Olson.

"Beats me."

"Such nosy questions. I overheard some of them."

"They haven't seen anybody do what I'm doing, I guess."

"It's O.K., isn't it?"

"Sure, but they're suspicious of everyone. The way I figure it, as soon as a person gets successful, it attracts the attention of the government."

Chapter 18

———

The repercussions of the equities decline were rapidly being felt in the economy. A great deflationary slowdown began to unfold. Retail sales that once had been the driving force in the economy shriveled like grapes in the sun. Consumers went on a buying strike. Most of them had been terrified by news of the stock market panic. They changed their buying habits overnight, now trying to save as much money as they could rather than spend it. The malls and shops became silent tombs, where forlorn clerks sat in brooding silence. Among the owners of business establishments there rose a wailing and gnashing of teeth.

In Detroit, Shirley Abernathy watched the line of applicants forming in the unemployment office. Each day there seemed to be more than the day before. A stack of applications for government unemployment insurance rested on her desk waiting for processing. Normally, applying for unemployment was something that could be done over the phone. But the demand had exploded at precisely the time they had switched over to their new computer system. It didn't work. They had been down a week when they were told to have applicants come into the office until the computer was fixed. She now spent most of every day interviewing the burgeoning number of out-of-work applicants. Any hopes of placing the most of them in another job were dashed by the unrelenting shrinkage in the economy and the attendant corporate downsizing.

Shirley was a supervisor and normally would not be in the trenches handling applications. However, the case overload and the computer crash had pressed her into low-level service. Her first interview for the day was with William Stout, an autoworker.

"I don't think we're going back to work any time soon," he told her.

She explained that he would get unemployment benefits for the next six months. For him they amounted to $386 each week.

"That's not much," he groused. "We've been used to living on a lot more."

"I hear that a lot. I'm sorry."

"What happens after six months when they run out?" he asked her.

"I don't know, but if I had to guess, they're going to extend them another three months. The president said something about it just yesterday."

"I didn't figure we'd ever get laid off," he confided. "The Japanese cars cost a fortune now. Ours are cheaper, but people are sticking with the cars they've got."

"Yes, I read that in the paper."

"Thank God we have our house paid for."

"Yes, that will definitely help. Sign here would you, William?"

"Sure."

"Thank you. You'll be getting your first check in three weeks."

"O.K. Thanks. Man, this place is getting crowded."

"Yes," she said, rising to interview another applicant.

Richard Hall, a carpenter, was recently cut loose by a construction company.

"We used to get a lot of overtime," he told her. "I was making good money. Now all they have is a skeleton crew."

"I hear a lot of that," she responded.

"My wife is still working at Donovans, you know, the department store. They've been cutting back there, too."

Soon he was processed and another took his place.

Louis Robinson was a bear of a man who growled at her about the unfairness of the situation. He had lost his job as a restaurant cook.

"They made a mess of this economy, missy," he told her.

"Maybe it will get better," she told him.

"I was out at the shopping center on the weekend. Hardly anybody there. My wife says the prices on everything are high. We didn't spend any money, except for one place had a going-out-of-business sale. There's a lot of empty stores at that mall, I want to tell you."

"I've noticed that," she said, pushing a form toward him for a signature.

Her next interview was a baby boomer wearing a suit and tie.

"When did you lose your job?" she asked.

"This morning."

"You're not looking anywhere else? This application says you're in management."

"I already know there are no jobs for me. The company I worked for made auto parts. They already laid off half the managers. None of them are working. They can't find anything. Why kid myself. I can use a rest anyway."

Next came a fast food worker.

"They told us they're losing money. You wouldn't think people would stop eating fried chicken, would you?"

"I read where people are eating home more," she told him.

Her last interview before lunch was with a well-dressed young woman.

"Goodness, you're a lawyer?" she asked in surprise.

"Yes."

"How did this happen?"

"There's no work for me at the firm. In fact there's not much work for anybody there. They laid off the last six lawyers they hired."

"I've had a number of accountants applying, but you're the first lawyer."

"No doctors yet?" she joked.

"No, they're probably pretty busy these days curing depression," replied Shirley.

"Writing prescriptions for Prozac," laughed the lawyer.

Within minutes she had finished with the young lady and rose from her desk to go to lunch. The evening before she had made plans to meet her brother over the noon hour. He was an economist in the state commerce department. George Robinson had graduated from the University of Michigan with a degree in economics. His first job was in the state government and eventually he landed at the commerce department.

George and his sister Shirley were two of seven children of a Baptist minister and his wife who had flourished in Detroit in the sixties. They had built a large parish of worshippers and raised a successful family. Their youngest son, Kevin Robinson, played for the Los Angeles Dodgers and was a source of great pride to the family. Their oldest son, James, was a Justice on the Michigan Supreme Court and another source of family pride.

Shirley Abernathy had graduated from the University of Michigan with a degree in social work. After two years she found it not to her liking and transferred to the state unemployment department. She rose quickly through the ranks and became a supervisor in her early thirties. She married in her midtwenties to a football hero at Michigan who failed to make it as a pro and gradually turned to alcohol to soothe his feelings of inadequacy. After five years the marriage failed and Shirley was raising a daughter by herself. The Robinsons were a close family and enjoyed frequent get-togethers. George and Shirley were born a year apart and met at least once a month to keep posted on one another's life, family gossip, and current events.

Once they were seated in the sparsely populated restaurant she unleashed a diatribe about how much work she was doing and the unfair rule that reduced supervisors to no more than entry-level clerks.

"You mean you're that overloaded?" he asked her.

"I've never seen anything like it. Every day they just keep coming."

"Well, I know the unemployment rate has gone up over ten percent. It must still be rising," he said.

"It must be rising a lot faster than anybody thinks because we're processing more applications now than ever before. Nobody can remember anything close to this level of applicants."

"Some people are saying it could go to twelve percent," he advised.

"What a time for our new software and computer not to work."

"So, they have you in the trenches?"

"Yes, I'm working like a dog. I go home at night exhausted. Sometimes I'll even stay an hour late just to help some people out. I'm the only employee left in the place."

"That's why you got to be a supervisor."

"I suppose."

"What do these people say?"

"You wouldn't believe it, they're all upset. They're mad at the company that laid them off or they're mad at the government."

"Mostly blue-collar jobs?"

"No, not at all. A lot of white-collar jobs. Heavens, I just processed a lawyer."

"You're kidding?"

"Right before her I got a guy who owned a printing company that went broke."

"That doesn't surprise me. Bankruptcies are going through the roof."

"We have a lot of people who worked for companies that went broke. I hope it quits soon."

"I don't know. There's a lot of bigger companies in trouble now. They employ a lot of people."

"I hope none of them are in Detroit. I'm busy enough."

"Say, did you see Kevin was three for five last night?" asked George.

"I saw."

Their conversation drifted to stories about their family and before long lunch was over. They sat for a few minutes sipping iced tea.

"You remember how crowded this place used to be?" asked George.

"Yes, it's actually quiet in here. What a change."

"I've noticed fewer people everywhere I go."

"I'll tell you one thing I've noticed," she responded. "The freeways aren't nearly as crowded."

"That's right."

"The only place that's crowded is the unemployment office."

"You see the attendance for the Tigers game last night? Under 7,000."

"That's really low."

"Dad was telling me that Kevin said they're worried about it out there. The Dodgers attendance is way down, too. Even the best teams like the Yankees and Cleveland aren't drawing."

"I know that attendance at the Lions preseason game was way down," she said.

"Yes, wait till basketball starts with those high ticket prices. I wonder what they're going to do?" he questioned.

"Speaking of attendance, I heard on TV that the Florida theme parks were nervous. Nobody's traveling as much as they used to. They said hotels, air travel, cruises, everything was way down. Las Vegas is really hurting, too."

"Seems like everything that was overheated cooled off the most," he told her.

"Listen, I better run. The line won't be any shorter when I get back."

"O.K., Shirley. We'll see you again, soon."

George watched his sister disappear through the door. He sat for a while, deep in thought. The unemployment problem gave every indication of getting worse. Where's it going to end, he wondered.

Chapter 19

———

"First it's the damn stock market, then it's a damn depression, now it's a dollar collapse," shouted Calvin Stroud to no one in particular. Calvin, the head government bond trader at the Wall Street giant, Harriman Securities, stared intently at the flashing news and bond quotes. "There's another down tick. Somebody's selling governments in a big way," he announced. "Remember Pearl Harbor," said Earl Lewis, one of Calvin's assistants. A couple of traders seated nearby laughed. "They're really bombing us today, huh, Calvin?" said one of the arbitrage traders.

"Governments are trading off in a big way. I've never seen anything like it," he responded. "They're afraid to keep holding the dollar."

"You're right. The dollar's taking it in the shorts, too," replied Earl, staring at his computer screen.

"Yields are soaring up ten basis points," called another bond trader over the din of ringing phones and chatter from fifteen bond traders crammed together in a corner of the trading floor.

"This is another frigging crisis," responded Calvin.

Large blocks of Treasury Bonds were being offered on the screen. Most sell orders seemed to originate from Asian sellers who had picked up the pace of selling U.S. government securities to the point that it was dramatically forcing down bond prices and driving up yields. It was also driving down the dollar. By itself, a rise in interest rates would have strengthened the dollar except that, across the world, dollar holders were switching into other currencies and foreign bonds.

"Look at the bid drop. This has got to be another load of Asian selling. Look out below," hollered Calvin. "Everybody's dumping."

"What a way to start the New Year," said a trader, referring to the fact that it was the second week in January.

"I can't believe what I'm seeing," stammered Andrew Petrocelli, a new trader. "The world's dumping dollars."

"It can't be," exclaimed Earl Lewis. "It's just a temporary blip."

"I hope it's an aberration," replied Calvin, "but I don't think so. This selling looks overwhelming."

"Aye-yi-yi," whooped a trader down the row. "Look at the dollar."

"It's falling like a rock. This is the biggest one-day decline in history," said someone.

"Fifty yen—fifty yen, it's crossing fifty yen," marveled another.

"It's a stupid panic," cried Calvin.

"A panic out of the dollar?" question Earl Lewis incredulously.

"You got it," Calvin shot back.

"Who'd a thunk it?" jibed another trader.

Calvin took a phone call and punched a sell order from a customer into the computer.

"Rates are rising again on governments, can you believe it?" he called out.

The phone rang again and he took another much larger order,

this time from Archie Fanning on the trading desk at the Federal Reserve. Archie quickly gave him instructions and hung up.

"Here comes the government again." He clicked the huge buy order into his computer. "We'll suck some of it up," he announced.

"Where's the Fed getting billions of dollars to buy up these bonds today?" asked Andrew Petrocelli. "They've been doing it all week."

"Get with it, Andy," needled Calvin. "They're making it as they go."

"What?"

"It's new money. They're being forced to monetize. They create the money to buy the bonds back."

"Yeah, but they're flooding the world with dollars when they do it," interjected a bond trader. "At the worst possible time."

"It's killing the dollar," said Earl.

"The dollar couldn't look any weaker," offered another trader.

"The world's giving up on the dollar, men," said Calvin.

"No way," argued Earl. "It will rebound."

"Too much damage. If you held stocks, you lost half. If you held dollars, you lost half of what you had left. Now you're down seventy-five percent. How long you going to keep holding?"

"They're not stupid over there," said someone agreeing with Calvin.

"They're stupid to have held as long as they did," offered another.

"They don't want to hurt their trade with us," said Earl Lewis.

""Too late now," replied Calvin. "The price of everything they export to us is going to double."

"Man, look at these foreign currencies rise," called a trader.

A currency trader walked into their area to see Calvin.

"You know Izzy Kagin, over in derivatives, Calvin?"

"Yes, what about him?"

"He talked to his brother in Moscow this morning."

"No kidding."

"You're not going to believe this."

"What?"

"They're exchanging their hundred-dollar bills for other currencies."

"No."

"Even rubles."

"Get a life, you putz."

"I'm telling you what he said."

"They actually want rubles?"

"It's not their first choice. They want other currencies more, but they'll take rubles. The dollar has dropped so much, they've been burned."

"A lot of people have been burned," said Calvin. "To a crisp."

Although they continued to banter, they knew in their hearts that the escalating decline of the dollar was a watershed event. It represented a loss of confidence in the U.S. and, like a Pandora's box, unleashed a host of unpleasant economic circumstances that would plague the nation for years to come. Each ugly event seemed to reinforce another. The soaring interest rates drove the cost of borrowing to unmanageable levels. Corporations were seeing their interest charges go through the roof, which depressed their profits. Capital was so expensive that business activity slumped further. Mortgage rates were impossibly high.

"Here's what happened," Calvin explained to Andrew Petrocelli. "The Federal Reserve flooded the world with so many newly created dollars in order to support the dollar that they actually depressed it. It's a vicious circle."

Calvin dialed up the Office of Market Finance at the Treasury to talk with Ken Chang, an economist. He worked with him whenever the Treasury had one of their frequent bond auctions. Harriman Securities was one of thirty primary dealers who could bid on U.S. bonds direct from the Treasury.

"You know what we're in for now, don't you?" the treasury employee lectured.

"I don't think I want to know," said Calvin.

"An inflationary depression."

"Sounds ugly."

"It's the worst of all worlds. All this stuff we import from overseas will cost a fortune, and nobody's got the money to buy it, anyway."

"Maybe the Fed should buy more bonds, prop up the bond market."

"It's a catch-22," said the Treasury man.

"Yes, I know," said Calvin.

"We're flooding the world with dollars at the same time people want to get out of them."

"You can't blame the Asians. Japan and China were clobbered when the stock market and the dollar went south." responded Calvin.

"Now they're losing their market here. We're really whipsawing them."

"What are they saying over there at your place?" asked Calvin.

"Meetings, meetings, meetings. We got more undersecretaries scrambling around than Carter's got pills. Can I tell you something off the record?"

"Absolutely."

"I heard the secretary and the chairman of the Fed had a screaming match this morning."

"No."

"And the president is pissed off at both of them. He's really taking a lot of heat now. Even his own party is blaming him. But the other party, now they are going nuts. There was speech after speech today in Congress. They were condemning him."

"I'm glad I'm not in his shoes," said Calvin.

The trading phones were ringing and Calvin said good-bye. He answered the phone.

"Calvin, this is Manny Weiss." Manny was the head of commodity futures trading at Harriman Securities.

"Hi, Manny. What's up?"

"This dollar thing is nuts, Calvin. Now the Americans are dumping dollars."

"What?"

"We got a huge amount of short contracts coming in on the dollar. Looks like U.S. corporations, hedge funds, the public. Man, it's getting ugly."

"They must be hedging. I thought all that increased activity was hedging."

"It's more than that. They're getting out. I mean Americans are dumping dollars, too."

"You sure?"

"I got a call from the exchange, Calvin. The big position reports are mostly Americans and they're all shorting."

"Join the party, huh."

"It's a dark day for the U.S."

"You got that right, Manny."

"O.K., Calvin, gotta jump. Thought you might want to hear that."

"Thanks, keep me posted."

The hum of activity on the trading floor seemed to grow louder as traders and sales people busied themselves executing customer orders.

Calvin dialed another huge Wall Street firm located in the World Trade Center and connected with the bond trading department. In

December they had won the bid on two billion of a twelve-billion-dollar Treasury offering of ten-year government bonds.

"Hello, Calvin." It was Murray Kempf, the head bond trader.

"Hi, Murray. How you doing? You move all the ten-year bonds?"

"We're stuck with some of them in our inventory," responded Murray.

"You are?"

"We don't have any place to go with it right now. You want some?"

"No."

"See."

"No buyers for reoffers today, Murray."

"You're right, there's no buyers."

"Things will settle down. You got it hedged so wait it out."

"O.K., call me if you can help out."

"I will."

Calvin picked up the phone again. It was the president of the Harriman firm. "Calvin."

"Yes, sir."

"How you doing down there?"

"We got no long position in anything."

"Good boy."

"We're flat and we're staying flat."

"Good."

"How's the company doing, sir.?"

"We got some hedging problems with interest rates, but nothing too serious."

"You never thought you'd see anything like this?"

"Who could have guessed it, Calvin."

"Anything I should know?"

"I wouldn't take on any new customers right now. Lots of rumors flying around again."

"I heard about another hedge fund."

"There's a couple of big insurance companies with problems, Calvin."

"Really."

"They can't unwind enough positions to make debt payments and redemptions. Apparently somebody pulled a lot of capital out of one of them."

"What are the government bond funds doing?"

"Trying to talk everyone into holding on. It should be easy. The yields are so high, but they're getting flooded with redemptions."

"It's the dollar. They're scared to death of it," replied Calvin.

"Some of our big pension customers have called me."

"Me, too, sir. They are angry as hell."

"There's nothing we can do about it. It's the government's problem. They created it, they need to solve it."

"They don't know how, sir."

"That's the hell of it."

"The Fed is buying every coupon pass. It's in the billions, maybe hundreds of billions."

"Monetizing the debt," replied the executive.

"This is more than debt monetization, it's the debasement of the currency. They're pumping billions of new money out to shore up the bonds."

"I know how it works, Calvin."

"Yes, sir."

"Listen, we're going to have a strategy session up here after the market closes. I'd like you to be here."

"Fine. I'll see you then. Did you say your office?"

"Yes."

"O.K."

Calvin popped open a carton of yogurt and tried to collect his thoughts. There would never be a day like this again in financial history, he concluded. But he'd come to that conclusion on several other days in the recent past. Maybe there would be a worse day ahead, but he didn't see how.

Chapter 20

———

Richie had let his gold contracts ride through the fall and early winter. He rolled them over thirty to forty days prior to expiration and kept his twenty thousand contracts intact. He knew that foreigners were on-balance sellers of U.S. government securities throughout the fall. If this selling accelerated, he felt the price of gold would rise and increase the profits on his contracts. He was sitting on a sixty-million-dollar profit. Occasionally one of his brokers would call him with an urgent reason why he should sell. They might have been looking out for his interests or they might have been thinking about a fat commission, but whatever their reason, they failed to sway Richie. Even Nancy had given up and no longer raised the subject.

All through December gold rose. There was weakness in the dollar; nothing dramatic, just a slow erosion. More people were buying gold because of the sorry economic news and this helped push the yellow metal gradually higher. Day after day gold was up a dollar or two and, before the end of December, crossed $400 an ounce. He now had an eye-popping profit of one hundred eighty million dollars. Richie began to pyramid again, adding thousands of contracts at or around $400 an ounce. In a week he doubled his position to forty thousand contracts, or four million ounces. He tried to keep his trading moves a secret, but now all the brokers were talking about him and his phenomenal run of luck. When he bought contracts, the news passed rapidly through the commodity brokerage firms and around the floor of the exchange.

Then came the second week of January, when the dollar crisis and massive selling of U.S. Treasury Bonds burst on the scene. Gold began to climb in earnest, rising in great daily leaps of twenty to thirty dollars an ounce. On the fateful day when the record drop in the dollar led to panic selling of government bonds, gold futures shot up forty-five dollars. Within a few days gold reached $450 and Richie was up four hundred and twenty million. Then he began to buy again. He was able to get another ten thousand contracts by the time it hit $470. Then he stopped and watched gold sail to $530 an ounce. His profits on his five-million-ounce position now amounted to a mind-boggling seven hundred and fifty million dollars. Nobody had ever done anything like this since the Hunt brothers traded silver. The last sixty-dollar rise from $470 to $530 had made him three hundred million dollars alone, and that in only three days.

Despite a series of government announcements and feverish attempts to prop up the currency, the run on the dollar continued throughout January. The daily drops in the value of the greenback were no longer as sharp or dramatic as those manic days earlier in the month, but the bloodied and battered currency was on its knees, slipping a little each day. Gold, on the other hand, which had risen in tandem with the big dollar drops, now continued its spectacular rise as hoards of investors who were attracted to the one thing that seemed to be going up other than foreign currencies, piled into the lustrous metal. Gold which had offset the decline in the dollar in a mirror-like reflection in the opposite direction, now took off on its own. Each ten-dollar rise netted Richie another fifty million dollars.

By now the commodity reporters and business writers were filling the business section with reports on Richie's investment prowess. Much to his chagrin, the extent of his holdings were widely known. As addendums to news articles on the commodity markets, writers would now tack on the fact that speculator Richie Stenquist had enjoyed a profit of ten million dollars that day in the gold market. Much of this was then reported in the general news section of newspapers across the land. When gold hit $580 an ounce Richie had made a billion dollars. It made headlines in the business section of every newspaper in America. Articles in the major financial publications chronicled his success. Richie tried to avoid talking to most of the reporters who called. He instructed Carol Olson to tell them he wasn't in. He did, however, give a brief telephone interview with reporters from the *Wall Street Journal* and *Barron's*. Their articles turned out to be quite flattering. However, his home-town newspaper ripped him in an editorial that blamed the market system for allowing such fantastic profits when so many others were enduring financial difficulty.

Richie changed his office phone number and ordered an unlisted number for his home. He granted one interview with a local TV station. The reporter asked him a series of investment questions. It was the most widely watched TV news broadcast in the history of the Twin Cities. After that he tried to dodge all reporters. He did not want to become a widely recognized media personality. He was being pestered to death by people requesting money or favors and he wanted that to end. He even began to worry about the safety of his family because potential criminals might think he kept gold in his home. Some of them weren't too bright, he concluded, and would not understand how the gold futures market worked. As it was, far too many strangers were knocking on his door and asking for him. One intrusive group had inquired whether they could have a tour of his home and another quizzical visitor had asked him if he kept any gold around. Plus, he was getting occasional nasty letters at his office that accused him of being a greedy speculator.

His success had sparked numerous copycat speculators who were attempting to duplicate some of his gains. This, on top of the appreciating gold market, continued the dramatic rise in the metal to $650 an ounce. Everyone was certain that it would quickly top $700. The economy was in a shambles and gold was now as popular as it once had been unpopular. All of the furor surrounding his success was beginning to bother Richie and even Nancy was restless with the constant publicity and the wearing effect it had on her husband. Richie anticipated further economic problems ahead and he fully expected much higher gold prices. Although his profit was astronomical, he wasn't the least bit embarrassed by his desire to milk his strategy to the fullest. He continuously monitored the financial news and watched economic statistics like a hawk. He read voraciously the opinions of economists, politicians, financial analysts, and newsletter writers on all germane subjects. He did not rest on his laurels but constantly sniffed the wind.

When the government announced in March that there would be a three-day meeting of government officials to organize a plan to alleviate the crisis, his antennas were stretched to the limit. He was perched in his office contemplating the news of this important meeting. Gold was off three dollars on the meeting announcement, but that didn't worry him. Something else was gnawing at him but he couldn't pin it down. Carol Olson, who spent most of her days taking phone messages, called through his door that Bernie Fogelson was on the phone from Florida.

"Hello, my friend."

"Hi, Richie. How are you?"

"I'm O.K."

""Listen Richie, did you know I was famous?" Bernie laughed. "Yes, I'm very famous now. Why do you think?" He hesitated for a moment. "Because I know you."

"Please," said Richie, his voice edged in sarcasm.

"No, that's right. I'm famous because you're my friend. I had a reporter call. Wanted to know about you. Everybody down here keeps asking me about you. I'm famous!"

Richie laughed. "It's not all that it's cracked up to be."

"I'll take it if I can have a billion bucks, too."

"Seems crazy doesn't it," said Richie, "all that money. You really can't get a handle on it. I'm still living in the same house, driving the same car."

"Sell out and build a mansion. Get a chauffeur and a limo."

"One of these days," he laughingly replied.

"I'm serious, Richie. Take some off the table. You're nuts not to."

"Probably, but I'm still going to have plenty, no matter what happens."

"What do you mean?"

"So, I lose a hundred million, how much money do you need?"

"Richie, that's exactly my point."

"O.K., so it must not be the money."

"What the hell is it then?"

"I just like being right, having it all figured out."

"Well, you sure did that."

"I thought it would be great to have everyone know I was super successful, that I was on top in a big way."

"Isn't it? Identity is a big drive."

"In a way, but now I'd like to be anonymous again."

"Sorry."

"I know but I'm wistful."

"You don't sound like a guy who made over a billion dollars. You sound like a mushhead."

"Thanks."

Bernie changed the subject. "Can you believe what's going on?"

"It blows my mind."

"What are they going to do, Richie?"

"I don't know. They're having a big meeting."

"I heard, but I don't think they can fix it."

"They'll probably do something stupid," Richie replied. Bernie kept talking, but for a moment Richie didn't hear him. He replayed in his mind what he had just said. Then, like a lightbulb going on, he knew the one stupid thing they would do. He continued his conversation absentmindedly and Bernie, sensing a change in his attentiveness, soon said good-bye to his friend.

"I'm going for a nice long walk on the beach now, Richie. So say good-bye to me."

"Bye," Richie laughed.

The markets were already closed for the day when Bernie rang off. Richie checked Access, the 24-hour metal futures trading system, for the gold price. The metal had recovered the three dollars it lost earlier and closed unchanged for the day. Richie was deep in thought when Carol Olson interrupted.

"Mr. Stenquist, someone's here to see you."

"Who?" Richie inquired.

"A reporter."

"Oh no, not now, Carol. They'll have to come back."

172

"She knows you."

"Knows me?"

"Yes, she did an article on you previously."

"What article? Tell her I don't want another one."

A pretty face framed itself in the doorway and smiled at him. He noticed her perfect teeth.

"Hi, I'm Sarah Gordon. I did the first ever-article on you. You remember. You wouldn't tell me much on the phone."

"Oh, yes," he sighed. "You're here, so you might as well come in."

Sarah Gordon came into his office.

"Sit down."

She lowered herself into her seat and looked across the desk at him. Their eyes met and appraised one another.

"How are you today?" she inquired, her eyes unabashedly taking in his.

"Fine."

"Up for answering a few questions?"

"Maybe a few," he smiled back.

She was a beautiful woman, blonde, young, and sensual. Richie was a high-testosterone guy. He'd been faithful, but occasionally he would come in contact with other women who stirred the banked fires within him. Sarah Gordon was one. Women could never understand the primal drive that a lovely woman could unleash in a man. It was always there, lurking, waiting, and at times highly disturbing to the soul of men like Richie who practiced monogamy. They made small talk for a while and when they stopped, their eyes lingered too long to go unnoticed and a flash of mutual attraction passed between them.

He felt desire for her building in him and, as she talked, a momentary fantasy ran through his mind. He put his mental brakes on and felt the frustration and mild suffering that these encounters

173

brought on. He sensed that he could have her. It would take some time, but it could be done. He answered her questions, but even as he talked his mind focused on her sexuality. The key now was to take action, ask her to have dinner or a drink. He'd been with numerous women in his life and he knew the game backward and forward. But it was this crucial step he refused to take. It bothered him not to. As the interview wore down, he looked into her eyes a final time with an intensity she noticed and then he lusted for her. He knew this was an infatuation he would not act on and he let it run wild because now he knew it was under control.

When the interview was finally over he withdrew from her eyes and became occupied with other things. She had thanked him, smiled with a slight curiosity and left, tossing a final glance toward him as she passed through the doorway. Once she had gone, he rose from his chair, filled his briefcase with papers and left the office. He wanted to be with his wife.

Chapter 21

———

The meeting took place at the White House. Live television picked up the attendees as they climbed out of their limousines. The chairman of the Federal Reserve, the Treasury secretary, and several senators were the headliners at the meeting over which the president would preside. A smattering of economists from academia, Wall Street and Washington attended, along with relevant cabinet members and assorted high-ranking bureaucrats. The meeting was billed as the administration's response to the economic crisis gripping the country. As a result of the media buildup, hope had returned to the land and the stock market had staged a mild rally.

The president opened the meeting. "Gentlemen, let's begin. We've come here today to fashion a rescue plan for our economy. We must take measures that alter the course of future events. Let us be bold in our planning and fastidious in our execution. The people are relying on us to put an end to the dreadful events that have plagued us for the past eighteen months. In the course of our

175

affairs, let us remember that history may well judge us on what happens here in the next seventy-two hours."

What a politician, thought the chairman. He knew he would be called on next and his report would be the one that everyone wanted most to hear. Unfortunately, they were between a rock and a hard place and only a few of them in attendance had it figured out. The president certainly did not have a clue nor did the senators. He would not tell them. He would skirt around the issue. After all, how could the chairman of the Federal Reserve explain that the country had shot itself in the foot.

"Thank you, Mr. President," he began. "We find ourselves today in a curious predicament. Our market interventions have not worked. In fact, they have backfired. In attempting to provide stability to the markets for our debt securities, we have destabilized them. In attempting to establish a solid underpinning for our bond issues, we have weakened this market and further eroded our currency. We made the attempts as a response to the deteriorating conditions in virtually every market. Clearly they have not worked. Now we must assess the damage and hopefully structure a plan that will alleviate the ongoing pressures on these markets. Let us, in all truthfulness, examine where we are today.

"The stock market now hovers around 4,000. Long-term interest rates are twenty-four percent while short-term rates are eighteen percent. The Federal Reserve has lost control of its ability to control short-term rates. A savage sell-off in government bonds of all maturities has removed this option. We could establish a Federal funds rate at lower-than- market levels, but the banks are not borrowers now and, thus, this exercise is moot. Loan demand has dried up. Open market activity is strictly limited to purchases of government bonds. We cannot sell them nor do we want to sell currently because the interest rates we would be forced to pay are, as I've mentioned, impossibly high. Interest rates on corporate bonds are even higher, and, of course, the price of bonds has collapsed.

"In the broader economy, GDP continues to shrink. We are projecting a double-digit reduction for the current quarter. Construction has virtually ceased to exist, owing to the improbably high mortgage rates. Retail sales are down a third or more. Energy costs have trebled and, as a consequence, travel of any sort has been dramatically curtailed. Layoffs in autos, construction, and manufacturing continue unabated and the unemployment rate is now at twelve percent. Job creation has essentially stopped.

"Corporate bond defaults continue to climb and have become an ongoing problem. Business bankruptcies are at epidemic proportions and personal bankruptcies have now reached seven percent. Mortgage defaults and foreclosures are soaring. Real estate values have plummeted. Ladies and gentlemen, we are in the midst of a depression and this crisis, by any measure, exceeds that of the nineteen thirties." He paused for a moment, looked around the somber room, and took a sip from his waterglass.

"Now for the good news," he continued, "not that there is much. Our balance of payment deficit has ceased to be a problem. We have gone into surplus. Exports are one of the few bright spots in our economy and, quite frankly, they are holding what's left of our economy together. Imports have become prohibitively expensive and exports terribly cheap. Other bright spots in the economy are agriculture, mining, and natural resources. Foreigners are buying our commodities. They would be buying more had they not seen their own economies crippled by the fallout from our economic decline. Naturally, foreign corporations, like our domestic companies, have seen capital vanish because of the nefarious treatment of our dollar in world currency markets. That summarizes our present situation. I have not encompassed all the details of our

predicament, but I have touched on a number of the most important issues. We can discuss these points later."

"Thank you," intoned the President. "I think I'd like to hear
from the Treasury now, Mr. Secretary."

"Thank you, Mr. President. I wish I could give you good news
and introduce a more relaxed atmosphere, but I'm afraid I cannot.
Ladies and gentlemen, I am worried. The balance sheet of this great
nation has deteriorated measurably. You will recall only two years
ago we were contemplating a large surplus into the indefinite
future. That surplus no longer exists and in its place we have a
deficit. Tax receipts have fallen precipitously. In some cases we are
returning proceeds to corporate taxpayers who currently have losses
they are applying against prior profitable years. Our revenues have
decreased dramatically, while at the same time our expenditures
have soared. You're aware of last year's one-hundred-fifty-billion-
dollar bailout. We may be faced with more of these situations.
Claims for unemployment compensation have exploded. For some
reason Medicare and Medicaid have outstripped their projected
budget. Naturally, the interest cost on our six trillion national debt
has increased. Based on current interest rates we could be looking at
several hundred billion of additional interest costs, and if we project
current rates into the future, the deficit becomes preposterous. We
expect to have better news on interest rates long before that.

"We have further concerns regarding government loan guarantees
on student loans, agency loans, small business loans, and sundry
other loans. And, of course, we have a growing concern about government guarantees of bank deposits, securities brokerage accounts,
pension plans, and others. Then we have agency obligations such as
Fannie Mae, Ginnie Mae, Freddie Mac, and many others. Most are
backed by the full faith and credit of the U.S. government. Others
have borrowing rights from the government.

"This still does not address the possible necessity of bailouts for banks, brokerage firms, insurance companies, and hedge funds. All in all, we have some heavy seas to negotiate and we certainly cannot allow any further deterioration in our financial affairs. I fully expect that interest rates will begin to drop soon. Current yields are too desirable not to attract attention, and if the dollar decline is finally out of the way, we should see more stability. Thank you for your attention."

"Thank you, Mr. Secretary. You have presented our problems in a clear and concise fashion," intoned the President. "Some of these issues are troubling. We have serious problems that we are going to have to resolve aggressively. Certainly we cannot have any citizen deprived of our help at this critical time. That's why I'd like to have the first item on our National Economic Rescue Package be an increase in the time limit on unemployment compensation from the current six months to one year. I know Congress will rubber stamp this proposal. I also would like to see us increase the amount of the unemployment benefits but I believe that's an issue that will prove to be more contentious in Congress, so I will not include that proposal at this time.

"Now I'd like to throw this meeting open to discussion. Senator, you've been fidgeting in your seat over there, why don't you lead off."

"Thank you, Mr. President," replied the senior senator from Delaware. "I'm happy to endorse your plan to increase benefits to our unemployed working people. I don't believe we can reduce the level of our financial commitments to these important programs. But that said, we have some serious realities to face up to and deal with. I've prepared a bill that I'd like to include as item two in our National Economic Rescue Package. My Federal Public Works Bill will provide forty billion dollars this year for construction projects that improve our national infrastructure. We need to build new highways, bridges, federal buildings, and airports. By pumping this money into the economy now, we can put many people back to work and hopefully get the economy moving again."

"Wonderful idea, Senator," said one of the economists. "The problem today is that people are saving rather than spending. Your program will help to replace their spending. That will maintain output and mend the economy. Eventually people will start spending some of their savings and turn things around."

"The problem with that," growled another economist, "is that we currently have the lowest savings of any major country. I don't think it will work the way you hope, savings are just too low."

"It's a good idea," inserted the president. "Let's make it item number two."

After a lengthy discussion there was general agreement on the inclusion of the senator's bill until the chairman of the Federal Reserve reminded them of their dilemma. "We currently face a runaway budget deficit. The government has shrinking income but growing expenses. Additional spending will be difficult. We need to restore our financial health and the best way to do that is through investment in new plants and equipment that produce goods for the market."

A congressman spoke up. "I agree with you, Mr. Chairman. However, we have agonizing losses in the markets and that translates into much less available capital for investment."

The same economist who had previously raised the issue of savings spoke up again. "We have the same old problem with low savings, sir. Capital investment comes out of savings and we don't have any."

"You're exaggerating," interjected the other economist. "We have savings."

"We have low savings then," came the reply. "And worried people are not going to turn this meager savings into risk capital for business. Not now, anyway."

"How are we going to get a handle on this deficit?" questioned another economist, "If it keeps growing like this, the government won't be able to borrow the money to fund it."

"That's correct," said another. "We need to cut the deficit."

"I propose we make item three a general resolution to cut spending," offered a congressman. "Nothing specific for now, but it will show we intend to come to grips with the problem."

"I'd support that," said the president. The debate on item three lasted for an hour before there was general agreement. A Wall Street economist spoke up. "The consumer price inflation index has been rising rather dramatically lately, as you all know. It's a consequence of the increase in the cost of imports and higher interest rates. The rise in oil has been most damaging. I believe we need an inflation-fighting program. If we can control inflation, stock prices are bound to improve."

Most of the attendees agreed that a program to fight inflation should be included as item four. The debate on the precise nature of an anti-inflation program continued throughout the balance of the first day.

On the second day, the discussion turned to interest rates. Several senators wanted to make lower interest rates one of the key elements of the National Economic Rescue Package. "We believe interest rates will soon come down, gentlemen," pointed out the chairman. "But no one should delude themselves that we are going to see the kind of low interest rates we once enjoyed any time soon. However, if you wish to make the goal of low interest rates a part of our rescue program, the Federal Reserve will certainly concur."

One of the senators made another proposal. "I believe we need to establish a moratorium on home foreclosure. At the very least, we should require a two-year waiting period before the lender can foreclose."

The idea was greeted warmly. The president liked the idea. "This will take the financial pressure off many of our people. I don't know about a general moratorium, I think we should set a specific time period and your idea of two years sounds like a good start."

One of the government economists asked to be heard. "The only problem with a moratorium on mortgage debt is the pressure it puts on the lenders and mortgage holders. It's going to create liquidity problems for them and if they ultimately foreclose after two years they're back in the same boat. It's also going to make it impossible to get any mortgage money."

They buzzed for a while about the negative impact of the debt moratorium and finally could come to no conclusion.

In the afternoon of the second day, a bailout package was proposed for failing banks, brokerage firms, insurance companies, and hedge funds. The amount was one hundred billion dollars.

"I can't see helping these damn hedge funds," said a senator.

Someone explained that the hedge funds in question were counterparties on swaps and futures contracts that would cause other financial entities to go broke and threaten a chain reaction of failures.

"They're insolvent, Senator. They owe money. We are giving them the money they owe to pay their debts so others won't become insolvent, too," explained an economist.

"This bailout sounds good," intoned the Treasury secretary. "Unfortunately, right now we can't borrow the money."

"I think we can come up with half of it from a special account we have," said a presidential aide. "And the other half we hope to get from the International Monetary Fund in the form of a loan. We'll be working through the Treasury, Mr. Secretary."

On the third day the National Economic Rescue Package was

complete but for one final item. The president introduced the last subject. "As you know, this country owns extensive gold reserves which are kept at Fort Knox. With gold now at $690, the total value of the one hundred forty-seven million ounces there is now almost ninety billion. We want to sell it. We can use the money to help pay for the National Economic Rescue Package. We know that once we announce this gold sale, the price will probably drop by half. There will be a national debate on this issue, as with many of the proposals in our economic rescue package. But once we have broached the subject to the public, we can get the O.K. from Congress to sell it. We would like to sell smaller amounts and get the best price, but we can't keep the matter a secret. In any case, at half of today's price, we will still get fifty billion."

Most of the attendees thought the president's idea to be sound.

"What good is it?" questioned a senior government employee. "It's buried underground."

"It's agreed," said the president's aide, "the final item on the National Economic Rescue Package is the sale of the U.S. gold supply."

Later, as the group was filing out, one of the senators turned to the other and giggled. "I wonder how that little prick in Minnesota, who made the billion bucks in gold futures is going to feel tomorrow after they announce this gold sale. He'll lose it all."

"Didn't you hear, Senator?" interjected an aide, "he sold out, I heard it on the noon news. He sold it all out over the past three days. He told all the commodities brokers he'd sue them if the word got out that it was him selling. He's supposed to have made a billion and a half."

Chapter 22

For three days Richie liquidated his contracts. He warned his brokers that there could be legal repercussions if they disclosed who was selling before he was done. He put the vast profits into T-bills and left them with the commodity firms. He planned to be back into action soon. He ordered out a check for five percent of the contracts he sold. By late morning of the third day he had completed his transaction. Then he told the brokers that it was fine with him if they let the cat out of the bag. His broker, Ken Ferguson, was so excited about his high commission that he immediately flashed the news to everyone in his firm.

The five percent of the contracts he sold garnered him seventy-five million dollars. Thirty million went to pay taxes on the prior year's gains. He put the balance in the bank and began to make plans for disbursing it. The terrible losses suffered by the dollar meant that the forty-five million he had in the bank was now the equivalent of twenty million in purchasing power. Nancy was thrilled to see bank balances for these astronomical amounts. She bought an expensive new wardrobe and some things for the house, but after that she was at a loss about what else to purchase. Richie had given her a diamond ring and a tennis bracelet that she'd always wanted, and she was now quite satisfied.

On the day after Richie had completed his futures transaction in gold, the government announced its National Economic Rescue Package. When the final item proposing the sale of the nation's gold reserve was announced gold prices on the futures exchange fell limit down. Meanwhile, the cash or spot market dropped much lower, creating interesting opportunities for arbitrage. The following day the market dropped limit down again and, in a week, the price of gold had fallen back to $450 an ounce. Richie watched it carefully, feeling for a bottom. He also paid close attention to the public reaction to the announcement of the proposed gold sale. The entire National Economic Rescue Package had been subjected to a withering criticism from various quarters. The most effective critique came from a group of congressional representatives who argued that the collapse in government tax revenues meant that none of the proposals in the plan could be funded. The deficit, they argued, was already projected to be four hundred and fifty billion dollars and because of government safety nets and guarantees more was piling up every day. This plan, they argued, would keep interest rates perpetually high and further devalue the dollar. It was a conclusion that, like bad tasting medicine, had to be swallowed. The president's plan quickly ran into trouble and the chance of Congress authorizing any of the proposed expenditures appeared slim.

The gold proposal was more of a hit. Many members of the House and Senate could see no reason why the gold should not be sold. Both senators from Nevada, the major gold-producing state, mounted a fierce counterattack. They bitterly admonished the administration for scheming to sell the national patrimony. Richie listened carefully to the arguments and began to believe that the nation's gold supply might never be sold. Further, he concluded, gold buying by foreign governments and individuals who were wary of paper assets would mitigate the damage to the gold price from a gradual sale.

With the huge profits from the sale of his gold contracts, he stepped back into the market and began to replace his five-million-ounce long position. At $450 an ounce he began to buy and, since selling was still heavy, he quickly filled his massive order, averaging down to $400 an ounce. The following week the chairman of the Federal Reserve, appeared before a congressional committee. He was asked about the proposed gold sale. "The nation's gold supply at Fort Knox," he told them, "acts as a de facto backing for the dollar. Although our currency is no longer convertible into gold as it once was in the early part of this century, it maintains a psychological link to the metal. Please understand that paper money by itself could never have been accepted as money had money not first been gold. You all know that gold evolved in ancient times as money because gold was in demand. It was the linkage of paper money to gold, the convertibility of paper into gold that created the confidence in paper money. Originally, paper money was backed by gold. Then, when we removed the official link to gold, paper was still accepted as money. That's what gold did for paper money, ladies and gentlemen. Should we now sell our gold, then the thing that originally caused us to accept paper money will no longer stand behind our money. If we encounter further difficulties with the dollar, our gold reserve will help support it. I do not believe we should sell the nation's gold supply."

What the chairman had wanted to say but couldn't was that in case a new currency was ever required, it would only be accepted if there was gold in the equation. The implication that the dollar might someday be worthless made any such remark on his part impossible. Why did he ever think about such gloomy outcomes, he wondered.

The chairman's remarks reversed the decline in gold and sent it soaring every day for two weeks. Richie had hit a home run. The news of Richie's coupe sent the media into apoplexy. Just one month before, the news of his sale had set off a mighty controversy. Many in the media had accused him of trading on insider information. How, they wanted to know, had he been tipped off to the president's plan to sell the gold reserve? Who was getting paid off? A few members of Congress, pandering to the media frenzy, suggested a congressional investigation of Richie and his trading activities. Night after night, TV reporters combed through the details of his transactions while talk show hosts argued with guests as to whether his profits should be allowed. One well-known guest, an attorney, recommended the government confiscate all his profits. Another proposed an excess profits tax of ninety percent on all commodity profits over one million dollars. The local newspaper lambasted Richie, editorializing about his obscene profits and the squalid method of speculation that enabled him to profit while the country was experiencing a severe economic contraction.

Now that he had reinstituted his position and his incalculable profits were soaring again, the media started a feeding frenzy that hadn't been seen since the Lewinsky affair. The "Golden Boy," as some were now calling him, was scrutinized down to the gold-toe socks he wore. Richie and Nancy were dumbfounded by the furor. Twenty to thirty reporters and cameramen gathered in the street outside their home and monitored the family's movements. Reporters followed Nancy to the grocery store. The school that the girls attended banned reporters from their grounds. Richie did a broken-field run every morning from his underground parking spot to his office. One morning, as he swerved through the popping flashbulbs, TV cameras, and shouting reporters, he decided he must make changes to protect what little privacy he had left.

Richie hired a guard at his office to assist Carol Olson in prohibiting the entry of any uninvited person. He hired a sedan and driver from a limo company temporarily to take him back and forth to work. He ordered a large fence built for the front yard of his house that would block the view of the unrelentingly nosy paparazzi. He began to carry his lunch to work so that he could stay in the office at noon and bypass the dozen photographers and reporters who followed him everywhere he went. This had made for a news service story about his frugality. Billionaire carries brown bag, read the article. Ultimately he knew this attention would pass but, for now, it was taxing.

The country was split down the middle about Richie. Half the people thought he was a rogue trader, a greedy speculator and a slick manipulator. They wanted him stopped, even punished. The other half thought him to be a nimble trader who deserved what he got. To some, he was a folk hero. He had a fan club. For many suffering the pain of financial reversals and insolvency, his exploits helped to lighten their load. The surveillance people, exchange governors, bureaucrats, and lawyers who monitored his activities on the commodities exchange were also torn in two directions. Some wanted to stop him and others wanted to let him continue. The overriding factor that thwarted any final action detrimental to Richie was their fear of a lawsuit should they shut him down. If he were to prove that he had violated no rules or policies, their liability could be enormous. The volume of gold contracts on the exchange had increased greatly and he still held only four percent of the outstanding contracts. A general consensus developed that they would not take action until he reached thirty percent of the open interest.

"The hell with staying in, I'm not taking my lunch. I'm going out to lunch with Bernie today," Richie had announced to Nancy. "Good for you," she had reassured. His friend had returned from Florida the month before and warm weather had followed him. They had talked on the phone almost daily and Richie looked forward to seeing him in person and having a relaxing lunch. Richie's profits had continued to soar to mind-boggling levels. Gold had returned to the $700-an-ounce level and his five million ounces were in the money to the tune of one billion three hundred thousand. This, on top of the nearly billion and a half he already had locked up, served to continue the media's relentless tracking of his daily activities. When he set out for lunch a bevy of photographers, cameramen, and reporters were in lockstep. They peppered him with questions along the way. Bernie was agog when he saw Richie enter the restaurant with his unwanted entourage. Every head in the place was on him as he worked his way toward Bernie's table. Richie could see the grin on Bernie's face across the room.

"Is this nuts or what?" he greeted his friend as he sat down.

"Unbelievable," sighed Bernie. A flashbulb went off in Richie's face, but fortunately there were no open tables anywhere around them, and the media people had to settle for a distant table or wait in the lobby.

"What a score you've made, Richie. It's made you into a big star."

"We all get our fifteen minutes of fame."

"Some don't," countered Bernie.

"My privacy is shot."

"I can see that."

"They're everywhere. It's the same way at home."

"This, too, will pass," sympathized Bernie.

"I'm thinking of leaving for a while."

"Where to?"

"Europe, Canada, I want to tie up some loose ends."

"How long?"

"Week, ten days."

Bernie didn't want to ask why, so he changed the subject.

"You still like gold?" he asked, then wondered if Richie's gold position was so large that anything he told him would constitute inside information.

"Yes, I don't think the economy is out of the woods yet."

"Me, either," Bernie agreed.

"They bailed out a bunch of brokerage houses and hedge funds again. That and the extension of the unemployment benefits are the only part of the president's rescue package that got enacted."

"Yes, his rescue plan turned out to be a bomb," Bernie commented.

"For a while it looked like they might sell off the gold at Fort Knox."

"I thought so, too," said Bernie. "How you played that gold swing I'll never know."

Richie grinned, "Dumb luck."

"Sure it was, I should be such a nebbish."

"What are you thinking about the markets now?" Richie queried.

"I do not like the looks of the bond market. I'm not talking about the junk, Richie. It's already riddled with so many bankruptcies that nobody wants it except at some hellacious rate. I'm talking about double A corporates. There's so much debt and business is so bad that some of the biggest companies are going to go under."

"I believe that. Listen, investors are already on to it. They've deserted corporate bond funds and switched into governments," added Richie.

"That's one reason interest rates came down," agreed Bernie.

"They were so high."

"They're still high in comparison to a few years ago and I don't see them going any lower," Bernie concluded.

"I concur," said Richie. "Here's another thing, a lot of these money market funds are in commercial paper. If these big corporations default to any extent, a lot of people who thought they were totally safe are going to be holding their heads."

"What about the money markets that hold mortgages?" asked Richie.

"Same thing," agreed Bernie. "Unless the government's behind them."

"The only thing anybody wants is government guaranteed paper. No new money is going into anything else."

"A few want gold," countered Bernie. "And some have switched into foreign bonds."

"Heck, the rest of the world is following us into a depression. I'm not sure about foreign bonds," opined Richie.

"There's not too many options," said Bernie.

"So much money has evaporated, it's lost, gone for good."

"Man, the capital markets are toast."

"How's the economy ever going to improve?" questioned Richie.

"A slow process. Savings, investing in new facilities, working hard, no frills, same way we did it a hundred years ago."

"Uff-da."

"Credit, I suppose."

"We tried that," said Richie.

"There's always going to be bank lending for commercial activity. Got to be."

"It's when it gets to be more than the available savings that things get overheated," Richie responded.

"Maybe they learned that," observed Bernie.

"No chance."

James R. Cook

"I'm not worrying about the next cycle. I'm wondering how the hell we're going to get out of this one," concluded Bernie.

With lunch over the same crew of photographers and reporters trooped after Richie as he strode back to his office. He noticed there were a few less than the prior week. The photographers never seemed to leave, but the number of reporters had waned.

As May rolled into June the media sentinels outside his home and office took their leave and soon were no more. "Things are finally back to normal," he told Nancy over the phone on a day when he came to the office and found no one waiting in the hallway. "Thank goodness." He began to drive his own car again and relieved the guard in the office of his duties. Despite the spotlight that his moves in the gold market had put him under, he now began to accumulate additional contracts at prices around $700 an ounce. He tried to trickle his orders in so they wouldn't be noticed, but a story soon appeared that he was buying again.

One evening after the kids had gone to bed, Richie told Nancy that he would like to go away with her for ten days.

"Where?" she asked.

"Europe, specifically London and Zurich."

"What for?"

"Vacation and some financial stuff."

"Oooh, that sounds great," she enthused.

"What about the kids, Nancy?"

"I'll call my mother tomorrow and see if we can leave them with her."

"I want to go to Canada, too, probably on the way to Europe."

"Where in Canada?"

"Vancouver."

"That's the wrong direction," she joked.

"We'll come back."

192

"Sounds good to me."

The following day Nancy's mother agreed to take the two girls and Richie called his travel agent to make reservations. In four days they would leave.

"That soon?" Nancy questioned.

"Why not. Nothing is happening here."

"Except a big depression," she replied.

"Everything's slowing down. All the markets are quiet."

"No more fireworks, hon?"

"Oh yes, there will be a grand finale."

"There will?" her eyes widened.

"What are you going to do?"

"Get rich."

"Oh, you," she exclaimed loudly. "You've made more money than Rockefeller and you're thinking about making more."

"It's a game. I love the action."

"I love you," she announced.

"It's mutual," he laughed.

"Tell me," she said, growing serious again. "What's going to happen?"

"Nobody knows for sure."

"Some of those people are writing terrible things about you."

"I know."

"It worries me, Richie."

"Don't let it."

"This one nasty little shit on television said the government should take it all away from you and put you in jail."

"Nobody's listening to him."

"But if things get worse, they might."

"Maybe."

"I don't want anything to ruin it for us."

"If things get really bad, we'll have a fallback plan."

"What's that?"

"I'll tell you about it when we go on this trip."

"Tell me now."

"I want us to get a couple of other places pinned down to live."

"You do?"

"Yes, that's why we're going."

"We might have to leave some day?"

"For a while."

"Why?"

"If things get desperate."

"Desperate? Like who's going to get desperate?"

"Like the government."

"Our government?"

"Yes."

"I've never heard you say that before."

"It never hurts to be a little bit paranoid."

"I can't imagine the government causing us problems. We pay our taxes."

"For the most part we follow the rules. I'm talking about a desperate economic situation. I mean really bad. Much worse than now."

"You think that's possible?"

"Yes. All I'm saying is a desperate government will do desperate things."

"You're scaring me!"

"Don't worry. I'll take care of us, no matter what happens."

"Are you sure?"

"Yes, I'm sure."

"I feel better."

"Kiss?"

"Kiss."

Chapter 23

———

"Interest rate risk, credit risk, liquidity risk," wailed Jeffrey Turnbull of Vintage America Fund Management. "How are we going to get through this?" As the overseer of sixteen bond fund managers, Jeffrey had been under enormous pressure the last few months. All of the managers had turned to him for direction and advice throughout the crisis. Lately a stabbing little pain below his left nipple nagged at him. He had dashed to his physician six blocks away from Vintage America's downtown Boston office. After a fingernail-chewing wait, the doctor had checked him over and ordered an electrocardiogram. Jeffrey had a meeting so he scheduled to come back the next day. The doctor told him his pain was probably stress related and he should wait for the test. He didn't have any problem accepting that it was stress, but he refused to wait.

Jeffrey had grown up with Vintage America. He was an analyst and then a fund manager. Eventually he became a boss. It was a good life. He saw himself as a connoisseur of the finer things in life. He made enough money to dine in the finest restaurants daily. He loved a martini or two straight up, before dinner. Then he drank a bottle of good Cabernet Sauvignon with his meal. He had a reputation in the company as a gourmet, and people often came to him for advice on where to eat and what to eat. As a result of his affinity for fine dining, the six-foot-three manager sported an extra forty pounds around his middle. Some of the younger managers would challenge him to a game of handball or tennis, to which he made a standard reply, "Exercise is against my religion." Lately he had been cutting back on the desserts. Worries about the fund business were curbing his appetite.

First it had been the junk bond fund. The initial rise in interest rates put pressure on the low-rated corporate bonds in their high yield fund. As rates rose, the bonds fell. The net asset value of the junk bond fund had plunged. Redemptions picked up immediately. Then the bad economic news hammered the fund further. Next had come a flurry of defaults on interest-rate payments by the corporate issuers of the bonds. Then came a series of bankruptcies by companies whose bonds were in their portfolio. Investors had been switching out of the fund in droves. Now, the huge slide in the dollar accompanied by a sell-off in U.S. government bonds had caused the junk bonds to collapse in value as the yield spread soared into the stratosphere. The bond fund was down eighty percent. As the growing numbers of fund share holders sold out or tried to switch to other funds, liquidity in the bond fund had dried up. The junk bond fund owners were trapped. As a consequence, the switchboard at Vintage America Fund Management had become unmanageable and stayed that way for several weeks.

"Did you ever see the *Exorcist*?" one of the switchboard operators had asked him. "Yes," he replied. "These people who are calling, they're like that girl in the movie."

Jeffrey Turnbull sat in his office with Walter Drysdale, the youthful manager of their high-grade bond fund. Walter, a Harvard MBA, sported a bright pair of suspenders over his button-down, snow-white shirt. He was glad he wasn't in charge of the junk bond fund but, nevertheless, Walter wasn't smiling. His fund had encountered rough weather and he felt like the tail gunner in a B-17 over Berlin. The fund he managed was huge, with several billion under management. He had run it as smoothly as a well-oiled ball bearing until the "great downturn" as he called it. His fund was ninety percent invested in high-grade corporate bonds, with much smaller percentages of U.S. Treasury bonds and U.S. agency obligations, usually Ginnie Mae mortgage pass-throughs.

Walter was having a tough time dealing with the savage reversal of his bond fund's fortunes. He wasn't sleeping at night and he'd developed a tic in his right cheek. The past twenty months had been a nightmare and he was sick of the whole thing. A few dis-gruntled clients had gotten through on the telephone and tore into him. That completely unnerved Walter.

"We're having trouble selling the corporates right now," he was telling his boss, Jeffrey Turnbull. "That Hill Corporation bank-ruptcy scared everybody to death. We're not getting the interest payments from TRT and we got a possibility of some other defaults on interest payments. I mean I'm talking about double-A rated companies."

"Ouch."

"Redemptions have flattened out, but they're still high."

"How about liquidity?"

"Still a problem. We're up another fifteen basis points. But ever since the dollar collapsed we've had problems. You know that."

"Yes, of course. Even before that."

"T-bonds dropped out of sight, but they've come back some.

That's helped us a little."

"High rates, huh? Everybody's a yield pig," said Jeffrey Turnbull.

"We got a tremendous amount of switching still going on. We'd have less if I could pitch out the corporates and add Treasury bonds. They all want governments. They want that government guarantee."

"Look at the yield spread," said Jeffrey. "The corporates are yielding at incredible levels."

"Sure, but everybody who owned them got their butt kicked the way the bond price collapsed. They lost a lot of money. They want out."

"I suppose with all the downgraded ratings, people are worried."

"Some of the biggest corporations may fail. They've got so much debt," said Walter. "Who can blame investors for getting out?"

"They bolted from everything, even our Liquid Asset Money Market Fund."

"Did they ever," confirmed the younger man.

"Nothing left in it."

"Commercial paper market dried up anyway," said Walter referring to the fact that their money market fund was primarily invested in the short-term commercial paper of large corporations. "If these big companies need money, there's nobody going to give it to them. It's one thing to have bond or stock offerings dry up, but short-term paper. Wow."

"Look at the economic indicators, Jeff."

"I hate to."

"Did you see how much the leading indicators were down?" asked Walter.

"Yes."

"That's the economy's early-warning system. When the index that predicts upcoming economic activity is in the tank, what's that tell you about the future?"

"It tells me things are going to get worse."

"Personal income is dropping like a rock," continued Walter, his voice rising.

"Yeah."

"Industrial production is down the tubes."

"Yeah."

"Retail sales are way down." Walter's voice kept rising.

"O.K., Walter. Enough already!"

"Durable goods orders are in the crapper."

"I know all that shit, Walter." There was an edge to Jeffrey's voice.

"Capacity utilization sucks," said Walter, louder than before.

"Damn it, Walter. Knock it off."

"Home sales are dead," Walter shouted.

"What did I just say to you?" Jeffrey yelled back.

"Housing starts are kaput," he proclaimed, louder still.

"I'm warning you, stop," replied Jeffrey angrily.

"Construction spending is dead," boomed Walter.

"Shut up you little piss ant."

"Car sales stink."

"Damn it, Walter. Have you lost your marbles?"

"Factory orders are down," said Walter, tears welling up in his eyes.

"You like your job here, Walter?" hollered Jeffrey.

"Business sales have collapsed," roared Walter.

"One more word, asshole, and I'm going to fire you," yelled Jeffrey.

"Consumer confidence is falling."

"You're fired," screamed Jeffrey, his face twisted in rage.

"Gross National Product is sinking," screamed Walter.

"Get the hell out of here." Jeffrey jumped to his feet, his face crimson and his adrenaline pumping.

"Consumer spending is dropping," chanted Walter, his voice

breaking.

"I'm calling security, you frigging lunatic. Better yet, I'm going to throw your over-educated ass out of the office myself." Walter rushed around his desk, his chest heaving.

"Inflation is up," shrieked Walter.

Jeffrey grabbed him by his suspenders and jerked them upward with a vicious pull. Walter was part way out of the seat when the suspenders snapped, sending Walter crashing into the bookcase along the wall. He lay there for a moment, his chest heaving. Then he closed his eyes.

"Unemployment is up," babbled Walter.

Outside the office Jeffrey Turnbull's secretary had heard the rising voices through the closed door. It sounded like an argument. Then she heard a loud thump. She walked to the door and put her ear to it. Someone was talking inside. It was the fund manager.

"Down, down, down, up, up, up."

"Down, down, down, up, up, up."

She opened the door a crack. Her boss was slumped against the wall and Walter Drysdale was talking to himself. She let out a little scream, ran to the phone and quickly dialed building security. "We've got a problem here, come quickly," she told them.

Chapter 24

———

In order to get from Minneapolis to Vancouver, Richie and Nancy flew first to Winnipeg and then direct to the British Columbia city. Vancouver had changed since Richie was there last. The population had swelled to almost two million people and a flood of affluent Chinese immigrants had driven up real estate values. The city was noticeably more cosmopolitan. Once they had checked into their room at the Bayshore Hotel they called for a sedan and driver. Richie wanted to ride through the city and find a neighborhood close to downtown where condominiums were being constructed. In the West End neighborhood they spotted a condo building under construction. It looked like a luxury development so they made plans to return the next day to look it over. They had their driver drop them off at a restaurant next to Stanley Park, Vancouver's answer to New York's Central Park. Then they walked the short distance back to their hotel. They admired the beautiful flowers along the way, especially the hydrangeas with their large blossoms of pink, red, white, or blue.

Richie liked Canada and he liked the Canadian people. They weren't cynical like some of their American cousins. They had a sort of wide-eyed innocence and they weren't afraid to let their true feelings show. Americans, on the other hand, were far too concerned about being sophisticated and cool to ever let it all hang out. He relished the unabashed enthusiasm the Canadians often evoked over something new. It wasn't like that in the U.S.

The following day the two of them went to the condominium sales office at the building site. An attractive brown-haired woman in a gray suit greeted them. She gave them brochures on the project and then took them on a tour of the eight-story facility. There were forty-eight units and Richie and Nancy selected one they liked on the sixth floor that overlooked English Bay and the ocean. The price was a million one hundred thousand in U.S. funds. Prices have gone up, thought Richie, this amount would have been five hundred thousand before the currency turmoil had debased the dollar. They agreed to make the purchase and decided to title the property in Nancy's name. The agent gave them the name of the attorney who would handle the closing and escrow the money. She also gave them the name of a local attorney who would represent them and look at the closing documents. A closing date was set four months hence when they would have to return for a day to sign the papers. The following day they stopped at the office of the attorney who represented the condominium project and left a check for the total amount of the purchase.

Nancy was excited. She had never thought of owning property other than her own home. Now she was going to have a luxury condominium in a beautiful city in a neighboring country. The fact that they had the money to make such a purchase bedazzled her. She felt elation, but also puzzlement for it was difficult to grasp the radical change in their fortunes. She could not fully comprehend it and wondered if she ever would. She knew she would enjoy selecting the flooring, drapes, fixtures, counters, and paint colors. She had two days to accomplish all this and to shop for beds, furniture, and other necessary items. She started immediately, and since Richie had people to see, she left him after lunch and started her shopping.

Richie had the car and driver go with Nancy, while he took a cab downtown. He planned to chat with geologists and executives at several mining companies with headquarters in Vancouver. The city had spawned numerous successful mining companies in the past. Risk capital always seemed to be available. Many local exploration companies traded on the Canadian Ventures Exchange. Although there had been a few companies that practiced stock manipulations and fraud, the exchange did a good job of policing the companies that traded on the CDNX. Richie knew that most of the mining companies in Vancouver were run by honest, hardworking people.

He stopped at Pacific Gold Exploration to visit with Doc Winslow, geologist and president of the small firm. The rising gold prices had brought firms like this to life and their enthusiasm rose with their stock price. Five years earlier Richie had talked on the phone with Doc Winslow about a promising mining claim the company had in Argentina. He owned a hundred thousand shares of Pacific Gold back then at .75 a share. He sold it at $2.50 three months later. Although the first drill holes had shown a quarter ounce of gold per ton, further drilling failed to prove the prospect up. It turned out to be a small deposit of five hundred thousand ounces and no major company was interested. Most Canadian junior exploration companies searched for discoveries that they would eventually sell off to a large mining company.

"Richie Stenquist, yes indeed, I remember we talked about

Argentina. Then I read your name in the *Financial Post* recently and I wondered if it was the same person," said Doc Winslow as he shook Richie's hand and greeted him with a big smile. "What an honor it is to have you here."

Richie squirmed. "Nice to meet you in person, Doc."

"George, George," Doc called to his assistant geologist. "This is Richie Stenquist the big Cahuna. You've heard of him, eh?"

"Doc told me you'd called and were coming in to see us. I called my wife and told her. She got so excited she knocked over the parakeet cage. Shook the little bugger up. Guess he's going to live, though." They had a good laugh.

The three of them adjourned into Doc's office where Richie got a rundown on their various mining properties.

"We're selling at over $3.00, Richie. We'll be drilling in B.C. this summer, up close to the Yukon. We've got spectacular surface samples and we think we might have something. It's winter in Argentina now, but we've got another great-looking gold prospect down there that we farmed out to Teck. They'll be drilling it this fall."

"Sounds good," replied Richie. Both mining prospects had sounded a little too grass roots for Richie's liking, but he hesitated in passing along his sentiments. To be polite he asked a few questions about the geology of their prospects. Soon they were passing generalities about Canada's economy which had suffered from the U.S. downturn.

"This bloody government here will probably raise taxes again," complained George.

"Too damn many rules and regulations," groused Doc.

Richie knew that most miners thought they were being picked on so he smiled in agreement. After a half hour he thanked them and left their office.

His next stop was at Horizon Mining, a small gold producer

with mines in Quebec. He met with Ian Walton, the controller. Richie contacted Ian on occasion to get his readings on the gold market. Ian explained that his company would soon be mining one hundred thousand ounces per year and expected their stock to rise over $10.00 a share soon. Richie got a rundown on the major producers in the gold business and how Ian thought they might fare now that gold prices were up. After an hour Richie was on his way.

His next stop was Victoria Securities, the largest brokerage firm in Vancouver. Years ago he had done some trades with Ed Misanchuk, a broker there. He would send Richie reports on gold once or twice a year and Richie appreciated the consideration.

"So, Richie, you're here in Vancouver, eh?"

"Yes. It's a lovely city."

"When it isn't raining, eh."

"We got nice weather today," Richie small-talked.

"What brings you to town?"

"I want to open an account."

"That's great, knowing what I know about you. The only thing is that our firm is leery of U.S. customers. Seems that your SEC has been putting pressure on to keep us from doing business in the U.S. I'll have to run it by management. Knowing who you are I think they'll make an exception. You're not the ordinary investor. Sit down here, I'll be right back."

Richie took a chair and waited. Trading on the CDNX had just ended and brokers were trooping by him. Before long Ed Misanchuk was back.

"They'll do it, Richie. Thank goodness, eh?"

"O.K., I'm going to have the account in my wife's name. Give me the papers. We'll fill them out tonight and I'll have her sign them."

"Good."

"I've got a certified check here for five million dollars. I'll leave it with you now."

Ed swallowed hard and croaked, "O.K."

"When I come in with the signed account forms in the morning, buy me a million dollars of Barrick, Placer Dome, Newmont, Anglogold and Goldcorp."

"Sure."

"Have you got that? Better write them down."

"O.K., I got it."

"Send the confirms to the attorney whose address I'll include on the application. She's in town."

"Sure."

"Keep the shares in street name."

"Got it."

"O.K., thank you, Ed. I'll see you tomorrow."

"Richie, thank you. It's a pleasure to take care of you."

Richie walked out in the busy downtown street and walked toward his hotel. He'd missed his morning run and wanted some exercise. In the morning he would run through Stanley Park and catch up.

The following day was a flurry of activity. They stopped at the Royal Bank and opened an account in Nancy's name. She could use it for paying bills on their condo, but Richie also wanted to have the bank account should he sell the gold stocks or in case he might want to transfer funds to Canada. Then they went to the brokerage firm and dropped off the application. Next it was the attorney the condo people had recommended. They visited with her for a half hour about the condo closing and Richie also explained she would be getting stock confirmations from Victoria Securities. He explained to her that if there were not confirms for five million, divided equally into five stocks, to call Victoria Securities and advise them of the discrepancy. He wanted everything about their affairs to stay in Canada. Next they were off to a series of vendors and contractors to select the finishing touches on their new condo. In the evening they talked over their busy day while enjoying dinner at Bishops. "This is so much fun," emphasized Nancy.

The following day they were at the airport early for a flight to Chicago. In the windy city they transferred to a United flight to Boston, where they caught a Swissair flight to Zurich. They kicked back in first class and got four hours sleep before their plane landed in the Swiss city. Richie had ordered a car and driver who met them as they got off the plane. He knows how to do this the right way, Nancy mused. They had reservations at the Doldergrande Hotel and the driver soon had them up the hill to the famous lodging.

After checking in, the driver took them to central Zurich. Richie told Nancy he would meet her in two hours outside the Rolex dealer where their car had dropped them off on the Bahnhofstrasse. Nancy was thrilled at the chance to shop along the elegant boulevard and kissed him good-bye. Richie left her, climbed back into the car, and asked the driver to take him to Mat Securitas, Switzerland's largest transporter of money and valuables. The company also stored assets, including gold, gems, and famous works of art in climate-controlled rooms and safes. He planned to buy gold while in Zurich and store it there, but first he wanted to inspect the facility. Thirty minutes after his arrival he was duly impressed with the storage facility and the polite treatment by the Swiss.

The driver took him back to the spot on the Bahnhofstrasse where he met Nancy. Then they rode a short block to the Zeughauskeller on the Paradeplatz for lunch, where Nancy bubbled about the shopping opportunities. "Richie, I've never seen such glorious shops anywhere." Richie considered their lunch at the cavernous restaurant to be one of the best he'd ever had. What a fabulous place, they both agreed. After lunch Nancy continued her breathless shopping while Richie walked into the Swiss Credit Bank and opened an account. Then he used their fax machine to send wiring instructions to his friend, Duke Peterson, at the Apple Valley State Bank. Richie had deposited the thirty-five million from the sale of his contracts in Duke's bank. He'd left most of it sitting there in a savings account. Richie had prepared Duke, who was expecting his fax. The next morning the Apple Valley State Bank would wire twenty million to the Swiss Credit Bank. Richie advised the woman who had helped him open the account that he would check with her to see if the wire arrived.

The next day Richie pulled Nancy away from her manic shopping to ride along with him to Lichtenstein. It was only a few hours from Zurich by car. Once there he opened an account at a bank and made a small deposit. He explained that a larger sum would be wired from Zurich and he requested the funds be kept in Euros. They left the little principality and were driven back to Zurich. That evening they dined at the Krononhalle, famous for its food and impressionist paintings that graced the walls.

On the following day Richie returned to the Swiss Credit Bank while Nancy continued shopping. It wasn't that she was buying so much, it was more the thrill of seeing the array of luxury goods in the couture shops, jewelers, candy stores, and floral shops. Richie went to the bank and confirmed that the wire from Duke's bank had arrived. He left five million on deposit in Euros. Then he requested five million be wired to the bank in Lichtenstein. With the balance of his ten million, he instructed the Swiss bank to purchase Austrian Philharmonic one-ounce gold coins to be stored at Mat Securitas. His business done, he strolled down the Bahnhofstrasse in search of his wife.

Early the following day they caught a flight to Frankfort. They would have lunch with Dr. Klaus Furstenburg and that same day fly on to London. Richie talked frequently with the doctor on the phone and he'd met him previously on a trip that Furstenburg had made to the U.S. They talked so much on the phone they had become friends. Furstenburg met them at the airport and drove to the Frankfurter Hof for lunch.

Klaus Furstenburg was in his late seventies. At age eighteen he and his twin brother had been inducted into the German Army. In 1943, two weeks before his unit was transported to the Russian front, he was struck with polio. It broke his heart to watch his young friends and brother march off without him. There were two hundred troops in the unit. For days they traveled by rail, toward the east. Finally, they could hear the distant thunder of artillery. It was mid-July. Sometime around midnight, as their train closed on the Kursk salient, the slow-moving train came upon torn up tracks and a partisan ambush. They fought off the partisans with heavy casualties, but early the next morning a Russian tank probe, accompanied by two thousand troops, stumbled upon them. Without anti-tank guns or armor they were no match for the T-34s. As the Russians closed in on them, one hundred survivors made a dash back down the tracks. They left the wounded behind. Within a quarter mile they ran into heavy machine gunfire and mortars. Twenty-eight survivors tried to surrender. The Russians shot them down where they stood. Then they killed the wounded. Three men who left the main body escaped. When they came across two dead Russians, they quickly discarded their uniforms, donned the Russian outfits, and exchanged rifles. Then they marched the third German away as if he were a prisoner. It worked. Several Russian officers put their binoculars on them and were satisfied. A day later they reached a German position. One of the three survivors lived through the war and related to Klaus Furstenburg what had happened to his brother.

Furstenburg had worked in the economics department of a big German bank until he was offered a job with the Bank of Internal Settlement in Basil, Switzerland. Upon retirement, he began to write a financial newsletter. Richie valued his opinion.

"This crisis will not pass soon," he told Richie and Nancy as they ate their lunch. "A depression liquidates the excesses of the previous boom. Past recessions in the U.S. were never allowed to run their course. Credit expansion and low interest rates were always invoked to cure the recession. Now it appears you must suffer through the liquidation of the credit excesses of more than one business cycle. I am sorry."

"We don't need more than one cycle, the credit extremes of the last cycle were bad enough," added Richie.

"The greatest ever," Klaus Furstenburg agreed.

"My theory," Richie continued, "is that credit will expand indefinitely if there's no brake on money creation and debt. Eventually it goes too far and that's when you have a crisis."

"Perhaps," said Klaus. "My concern for the U.S. was always the high levels of consumer borrowing and spending at the expense of savings. A prosperous country with negative savings, that's unique in economic history."

"We're paying for it now," said Richie.

"I only hope you will learn your lesson in the U.S. and avoid these bubbles in the future."

"I doubt it," said Richie. "With our money and credit system we're always going to have excesses. The only thing that stops it is high interest rates. It could be that it's an inherent problem with paper money. Maybe we need gold."

"I know you like gold, and perhaps a gold standard, but I have never seen the need for it. We Germans have never relied much on gold."

Their discussion continued until they'd covered most of the important economic events taking place in the world. Then after lunch Klaus Furstenburg drove them back to the airport.

By evening they were in London. They stayed in the Stafford Hotel located in a cul-de-sac behind St. James Palace, alongside Hyde Park. In the morning Richie ran down Birdcage Walk, past Buckingham Palace, looped around St. James Park and came back to the hotel. The two of them went to Barclay's Bank after breakfast and opened an account in Nancy's name with a small balance. He planned to wire money into the account later. Then they toured a residential area behind Harrods Department Store. This was the area where Richie wanted to buy an apartment or residence. He contacted several agents who promised to keep him posted on anything that came up for sale. At noon the next day their Northwest flight left Gatwick for Minneapolis.

Chapter 25

———

Jack Stallworth ran the Texas Teachers Pension Fund. He was having lunch with Gary Kinneli who ran the Texas State and County Retirement Fund. It was a drizzly day in Dallas and the gloom at their table was palpable.

"We're taking some big hits, Gary," said Stallworth, a former linebacker for the Houston Oilers when they were in the American Football League. Now silver gray, his muscular frame showed that he was still in trim condition.

"We've got these damn uninsured mortgages that have me terrified," replied Kinneli. "Foreclosures are rampant, that's for sure." answered Jack.

"The way it looks to us, home prices are down by half," offered Kinneli. "Anybody that's borrowed over eighty percent of the value of their house is better off going into foreclosure. They can buy the same house for half."

"That's half the mortgages in the country, Gary."

"I know."

"The mortgage insurance companies aren't going to be able to handle it all," Jack Stallworth continued. "Some of them are in trouble already. That's what worries me. If they default, we take the hit."

"We've already started to figure our losses on two of them," worried Gary.

"Thank goodness for FHA insurance. We've got a lot of Ginnie Mae certificates," Jack told him.

"Where they going to get the money? This is going to cost the government billions," responded Gary. "They've got to bail the mortgage agencies out because if they don't, everybody else is finished."

"So many foreclosures," agreed Jack. "There's one block in Houston they figure half the houses are foreclosed on."

"We've got losses on our jumbos, too," worried Gary, referring to larger mortgages popular with Wall Street. Although the fifty-eight-year-old manager had been in charge of the government employees' pension fund for almost twenty years, he was thinking about an early retirement. The investment committee had turned the heat up and he was sweating.

"I'm taking the blame for this," he told Jack.

"How can they blame you?"

"They think I should have limited our exposure to Ginnie Maes."

"There's a lot of mortgages out there besides that," assured Jack.

"I told them that. They don't listen. Our bond portfolio is in trouble, too. That doesn't help."

"I'm up against some of the same things," reassured Jack.

"At least we've got those Freddie Mac and Fannie Mae pass-throughs," Gary pointed out.

"The only thing," said Jack, "is that Fannie Mae and Freddie Mac have to go to the government to borrow money if there's a problem. There's no federal guarantee as with Ginnie Maes."

"Supposed to be almost the same."

"Yes and no. I read they're borrowing heavy from the government now."

"Man, the government is propping up a lot of basket cases," offered Gary.

"What worries me is that these mortgage defaults are rising. Hell, the unemployment rate has gone over twenty percent."

"The whole damn real estate market is going down the tubes," said Gary.

"Yes."

"Then there's all that foreclosed property, it's a glut on the market," he added.

"They can't sell it," agreed Jack.

"We're so damn heavy into mortgages," Gary fretted.

"Our mandate has always been to invest heavily in real estate," said Jack. "Now we've got a hell of a lot of bad commercial stuff. It's bleeding us dry. We're hemorrhaging money. A lot of retired schoolteachers are not going to get what they were counting on."

"That's why our committee wants my scalp. They can see their retirement checks shrinking before their eyes," said Gary.

"We should be okay on the pass-throughs," said Jack, referring to Ginnie Mae and Fannie Mae certificates.

"How much money do these agencies have?" asked Gary.

"All they need, I hope."

"They could be looking at $100 billion in defaults, maybe more," said Gary.

"Well, if the problems get too big, the state will step in for us."

"I don't know, the state is running a big deficit, too. They might not have the money."

"I wish we had government pension insurance like the private plans," offered Jack.

"Like the Pension Guaranty Corporation," said Gary enviously.

"If the pension plan goes haywire, they step in and make sure the benefits get paid."

"Where are they going to get the money with all these bankruptcies and underfunded plans?" asked Gary.

"I think they got almost twenty billion."

"What if a few million people lose their benefits? It would take that much or more every year," continued Gary.

"Times would really have to get bad," responded Jack.

"What the hell do you think they are now?"

"I suppose. Where's the government going to get all this money?" worried Jack.

"It isn't going to come from taxes, that's for sure. They're going to get less than half of what they got two years ago."

"Jeez, the deficit. It's damn near unmanageable."

"Could be a trillion," Gary remarked.

"Imagine that."

"You've heard about Sakura Financial?" queried Gary.

"Yes."

"They're buying up foreclosed homes and renting them out."

"The Asians have got money," said Jack. "Money's drying up in this country."

"It's lost," agreed Gary. "Just vanished in the markets."

""The wealth of America is disappearing, Gary."

"Looks that way."

"It worries me," continued Jack.

"Hey, I'm worried about my job and my retirement."

"They might fire you?" wondered Jack.

"Maybe. Hell, that's not the worst of it. I've built up a nice portfolio of tax-free municipal bonds. Some of the state and local governments have defaulted on the interest payments. I'm worried

about a lot more of them defaulting. There's no liquidity, either.
The dealers got them spread wider than Toby's arse."

"That's nasty," responded Jack. "I've read about more defaults
lately. It must be spreading."

"It is," said Gary. "That's my retirement."

After lunch Jack and Gary walked together a few blocks toward
their respective offices. They bid each other good-bye and Jack
continued alone. What a pickle, he thought to himself. No one
could have imagined this mess. Bad things were happening. The
day before he had talked with Billy Joe Tollefson, his pal from the
old days. Billy Joe had been a star running back for the Oilers.
Then he'd become one of the nation's first successful sports agents.
He and a few others had pioneered a revolution in the salaries of
pro athletes. Billy Joe had told him about several basketball stars
who had lost millions in bad investments. It seemed impossible
that so many sports stars could lose everything, but they had. Now
the owners were cutting salaries and releasing some of their biggest
stars. All professional sports were downsizing and a lot of players
were out of luck.

It was that way with everything, he thought. The Boyd brothers,
an aggressive family of Dallas takeover artists, recently hit the wall.
Some of their corporations were failing and the huge debt load
they ran up had begun to choke them. Banks were closing in and
since they had signed personally on some large notes, the banks
had grabbed valuable paintings off the walls of their homes. Not
that the paintings were worth that much anymore. In New York, a
Mark Rothko had just sold for four hundred thousand dollars,
down by ninety percent. Jasper Johns, Rauschenbergs, Warhols,
and de Koonings were selling in the same price range. The high-
octane market for art and antiques, which once rose to scintillating
levels, was dashed. The art world was surprised that foreign buyers

216

didn't pick up the slack on art prices, but they were too battered and frightened by events in the U.S.

The morning Dallas paper had carried an article about the huge mansions and multimillion dollar homes that were coming up for sale on the real estate market. The owners could no longer afford to maintain them with their high heating and cooling costs, taxes, repairs, and staffs of housekeepers and gardeners. The world of the wealthy had turned upside down. Over the years families that inherited fortunes had come to rely on money managers and bank trust departments to husband their wealth. Now, the imploding markets had devastated the rich. The managers had failed to preserve their capital and suddenly they were faced with unpleasant financial choices that would have seemed impossible only a few years ago. Over the past ten to fifteen years a hundred- million-dollar inheritance could have easily grown to a half a billion dollars. Now some fortunes were down to a fraction of what they were while others were locked into illiquid investments. Nobody knew the exact value of these commitments or the real net worth of once-rich investors. For some, it was the financial equivalent of the *Titanic* sinking. Some formerly wealthy individuals had to worry for the first time in their life about paying a bill. They were terrified.

It was brutal, thought Jack. Of course, he had his own worries. Commercial real estate had collapsed in value. He had invested the pension fund's money into three major office buildings, two in downtown Dallas and one in Fort Worth. The sorry state of business had meant that a lot of branch-office tenants had closed while others went out of business. His three buildings were now less than half occupied. One of them faced foreclosure by the primary lender because its occupancy rate had dropped to thirty percent. To make matters worse, two area shopping centers, in which the pension fund had a high equity stake, were going under.

He reached the thirty-eight story tower that held his office. It was one of the three buildings that threatened a big loss to the pension fund through foreclosure. His secretary greeted him with a worried look on her face.

"Mr. Stallworth, I'm quite concerned."

"Why, Janie?"

"The pension committee is here for an unscheduled meeting."

"They are?"

"They came in while you were at lunch. They're in the conference room."

"I wonder why," a grim look crossed his face. His stomach fluttered.

"They're waiting for you."

Jack crossed the carpeted office and tread down the hall to the conference room. The door was partially open and he pushed through.

"Hello, Jack," said one of the committee members while the others mumbled greetings and nodded. "Sit down."

"Why are we having this meeting?" asked Jack. "I wasn't notified."

"I won't beat around the bush, Jack. We're replacing you."

Chapter 26

——

It was fall again. Over two years had passed since the original crisis with the dollar and the stock market. Richie continued to hold his futures contracts. He had doubled his position to ten million ounces the past spring when gold had snapped back to $400 an ounce. The president's plan to sell the nation's gold appeared to be permanently mothballed. Gold rose back to $700. Since then the yellow metal had continued to rise. Any day the dollar fell, stocks dropped, or a bad piece of economics news surfaced, gold would rise two or three dollars. By fall it was over $840 an ounce and at a new high. The last time gold had been quoted at that level was 1980. Richie's incredibly large position of ten million ounces meant that every $10 rise in the gold price netted him one hundred million. He was now over four billion dollars to the good.

This had pushed him back on to the front page. More and more the media leveled brutal criticism toward him and his trading activities. The local newspaper now ran an editorial every week demeaning him and the market. One morning he found yellow paint sloshed across his office door in a crude message. "Screw the Rich," it read. Another person had tossed a bag full of dog feces over the fence of his front yard. A union leader gave a speech and suggested that all gold in the commodities warehouse and all the profits in gold commodities contracts be confiscated by the government. He censured Richie for profiting while so many others were suffering.

Suffering they were as unemployment and personal bankruptcies continued a steep climb. Richie had come home one evening to find Nancy in tears. Their friends, Charlie and Debbie Newcombe were going to lose their home. Charlie was working nights stocking shelves at Rainbow Foods and his income, along with Debbie's part-time paycheck from Target, wasn't close to the one hundred thousand he'd previously made. Their house payments were geared to his large salary and now they couldn't make them. Richie and Nancy had previously loaned them money and the Newcombes were too proud to ask for more. Nancy also explained that Geoff Larson and his wife Carrie were losing their house, and Brett and Cindy Peterson were also foreclosed on. She was also deeply distressed by the rude treatment she'd received from two women at the beauty salon. One of them had announced in a loud voice for all to hear that some people on earth were too greedy for their own good. The other woman had replied that no one should get rich at the expense of another person.

It was clear to Richie that people were growing envious of his profits. Sentiment in the country now seemed to be running against him. He would persist, he knew that, but he had to be more cognizant of the risks that his publicity presented to him and his family. You never knew when some screwball might decide to make a name for himself and physically harm him or his family. The possibility of a crime against him was growing. He thought about hiring a full-time guard at his house, but decided against it for the time being. He had never been a hunter, but years before he had done some trap shooting with a borrowed gun. He bought a new black Benelli twelve-gauge automatic shotgun and kept it on a rack in his bedroom closet with four shells in the magazine.

Nancy found herself worrying more about the condition of the country and her friends. She saw the pain her neighbors were experiencing. Some had lost jobs or were forced to take low-paying jobs. Others had filed bankruptcy or were close to it. She hated what she was seeing.

"Richie, the price of gas went up again."

"Yes, I know."

"How can people afford to pay double for gas?"

"They can't."

"Everything's so expensive now. What are they going to do?" she asked.

"This whole thing with the dollar and the economy means that people's living standards are going to be lower."

"That sounds terrible."

"It isn't pretty," he replied.

"I just hate what's going on. We have so much and they have so little."

"Right now, I don't see it improving any time soon," he told her.

"These prices for everything, they're so high."

"It's inflation."

"I know that, but how can you have inflation in the middle of a depression?"

"Imports are two to three times more costly," he replied.

"But people don't have any money, there's no demand."

"There's demand for the basics like food, energy, clothes, and a lot of that comes from overseas and it's higher now," he told her.

"Not food," she argued.

"Farmers have super-high energy costs now and there's overseas demand for our grains. That's why the prices are higher."

"There's no good news," she complained. "Everybody's hurting but us."

"We shouldn't have to feel bad because we're sitting pretty," he admonished.

"Well, I do."

"Maybe we should go back to where we were a couple of years ago?"

"Maybe," she harumphed.

"Nancy, you're not making sense. We're not responsible for anyone's misery."

"That's not the point. We're not doing anything about it."

"What the heck can we do?"

"You've got billions of dollars."

"You want me to start giving money away?"

"Maybe you should."

"Well, I'm not going to. As far as I'm concerned, giving money to people is the worst thing you can do."

"People are suffering and you're a big tightwad," her voice quavered.

"I can't solve the world's problems."

"You're too cheap to try," she lashed out.

"I'm not an airhead," he snarled back.

"I am an airhead to want to practice charity?"

"Only a fool would give all their money away."

"I'm a fool, too?" she yelled. "Well, you are a stubborn blockhead."

"Grow up."

"You go to hell, Richie Stenquist," she shouted, tears welling in her eyes as she dashed out of the room. Richie was upset by the encounter and sat reflecting on their disagreement. She would cool down and he would feel remorse over their dispute. Soon they would be forced to communicate about some daily household event and hurt feelings would mend. Most often at the culmination of this ritual they would wind up in each other's arms.

On the way to his office Richie turned on the radio and listened to the news. A plant closing in Philadelphia had led to a riot. When the workers were turned out, they tried to burn down the factory. The police had made arrests and three people had been injured. One of the senators from Pennsylvania was calling for the government to take over the large employer and keep it operating. Another senator was demanding that unemployment benefits be extended once again and that a moratorium on home foreclosure be adopted. After the news a talk radio program began. A guest bitterly criticized the Federal Reserve and the administration for allowing interest rates to climb. He claimed they had ruined the country. A series of callers denounced the monetary authorities, Wall Street greed, and the fools in charge of the country. Responsibility for the depression was placed at the doorstep of those who had profited the most in the boom. All across the land the economy had become a burning issue and strong opinions were voiced from all political quarters.

Richie was aghast at the animosity that people felt toward the rich. There was a growing sentiment to raise taxes to punishing levels and for the government to directly confiscate wealth so that all government safety nets and bailouts would be adequately funded. The multibillion dollar demands on government for unemployment benefits had doubled and redoubled. Many politicians and union leaders were insisting on an increase in benefits as well as across-the-board government funding of health care. The negative economic scenario contributed to deteriorating health, and medical clinics were overwhelmed by sick and depressed people. Health insurance companies and HMOs were bleeding red ink. This caused them to raise rates and the premiums were now so exorbitant that many people couldn't afford them.

Wealthy people were keenly attuned to the wave of envy and the proposals for redistributing their money. The nature and makeup of the rich had changed. Old wealth had dissipated, but nimble traders, arbitrageurs, and contrarians had become a class of newly rich citizens and they were determined to hold on to their gains. Money began to flow out of the country. Offshore bank accounts and assets held in foreign havens became exceedingly popular. Large amounts of money flowed into Swiss annuities and much more into Swiss banks. Capital outflows became a problem and when an administration official raised the issue of capital constraints, the amount of money leaving the country turned into a deluge.

Richie was alarmed enough to wire a large additional amount to his Swiss bank account. He also wired lesser amounts to Nancy's bank accounts in Vancouver and London. Some of it he converted into yen and some into Euros. He also bought more gold to be stored in Zurich. No matter what happened now, he thought they had enough tucked away to be secure.

He had a stack of phone calls on his desk. A Stephen Arlidge had called him from New York City and left messages at least six times. He didn't know the man but decided to return the call to see what the insistent Arlidge wanted. He hoped it wasn't money.

"Arlidge Fine Antiques," the receptionist answered.

"Stephen Arlidge, please."

"Could I tell him who's calling, please."

"Richie Stenquist."

"Can I tell him what it's about?"

"He called me."

"Hold on, please."

"Yes, Mr. Stenquist. Thank you for returning my call. I have a unique opportunity that you might be interested in. Have you got a moment for me to explain?"

"What's it about?" grunted the wary Richie.

"We have a wealthy client, or should I say a formerly wealthy client, who has a marvelous collection of art nouveau items made by Louis Comfort Tiffany in the early 1900's. They are splendid examples of Tiffany lamps, Tiffany glass, and Tiffany leaded glass windows. The prices of these items have collapsed. My client needs money. He wished to maintain his residence in the Hamptons and his town house here in Manhattan. The auction companies are reluctant to do much these days and the prices realized are terribly disappointing to the sellers. This is a first-class collection of the finest examples. Would you have an interest in perusing it?"

"I don't know much about it."

"Well, you know the Tiffany name."

"Of course."

"I would like to have a book delivered to you on the subject. Could you find time to look through it?"

"Probably."

"Good, I will call Barnes and Noble in your city and have it couriered to you today. I'll need your office address."

"Fine."

"I'd also like to E-mail you photos of the best items."

"O.K."

"I'll need your E-mail address."

Later that day a courier brought a large book containing an array of colorful Tiffany lamps and Tiffany vases. Richie looked them over and was amazed at the high values of some of them. Then he compared them to the E-mail pictures. The pieces in the collection for sale were truly splendid. He took the book and the pictures of the items home with him and studied them for a few days. He showed them to Nancy who agreed that they were beautiful and highly desirable.

He called Stephen Arlidge and requested the exact price.

"A large floor lamp like the Red Oriental Poppy sold at auction three years ago for over one million dollars. Of the two table lamps, the Wisteria sold in the past for three-quarter million, and the Spring Peony for about half that. My client will sell all three for one million. The twelve iridescent and flower-form favrile vases, which are all over ten inches in height are one hundred thousand dollars. The small lead glass window he will sacrifice for a hundred thousand, for a grand total of one million two hundred thousand. When you consider the demise of the dollar's purchasing power, this is an excellent buy."

"I'll send you a check today."

"Wonderful."

"How will you ship them?"

"We take exceptional care in packing. However, I will talk with my client. Perhaps we can have them delivered by a private courier."

"Excellent."

"Thank you, Mr. Stenquist."

"Thank you. I may be calling you with some questions."

"That would be fine."

Richie sat in his office pondering. The million plus price tag meant that he'd paid hundred and fifty thousand dollars for the lot in precrash money. It was a fabulous bargain. It didn't hurt to have some beautiful artifacts, he rationalized. He'd never collected anything, and these lovely things were a place to start. No sooner had he written out the check when Carol Olson told him that Stephen Arlidge was on the phone again.

"Mr. Stenquist, I talked to my client."

"Yes."

"He's delighted that you purchased his Tiffany collection."

"Yes."

"He has two other things that you might be interested in."

"What are they?"

"Do you know art at all?"

"You mean paintings?"

"Yes, in particular I mean American Impressionism."

"A little bit, you mean like Winslow Homer?"

"Somewhat, yes. Have you heard of Theodore Robinson?"

"Oh, yes, American Impressionist. He was Monet's son-in-law."

"That's correct."

"What about Childe Hassam?"

"Yes, I remember his flag painting in the National Gallery."

"Exactly, Mr. Stenquist. My client owns a large and important painting by both artists. I would like to E-mail you photos of these two paintings."

"You're throwing a lot at me."

"These opportunities are rare. Normally these paintings would be sold at auction, but my client must act quickly."

"Send them."

"I've already E-mailed them, sir. Please excuse me for this liberty."

"No problem."

"Perhaps they are there now."

Richie called to Carol Olson to bring him the E-mail photos of the paintings. He looked them over and was struck by their quality.

"How much are they?" he asked Arlidge.

"A million each."

"Ouch."

"You will never get this opportunity again, sir. The price is remarkably low."

"This is a little crazy. I don't usually do anything on the spur of the moment, but in this case I'm going to go ahead. I'll take them."

"Thank you, Mr. Stenquist. Given the size of your purchase, we will be delivering these items to you rather than shipping them."

"That's fine, and thanks. For now I'll store them in the bank vault."

Richie felt a pang of guilt on the way home. He was acquiring priceless art treasures at bargain-basement prices while the guy two doors down was losing his house. Nancy would probably be uncomfortable with his purchases. Guilt is a powerful force for good, he thought. Once home, he sought out Nancy.

"I've got an idea," he told her.

"What's that?"

"You know the Newcombes and your other two friends who are losing their houses?"

"Yes."

"Why don't we buy their houses for the remaining mortgage amount. We'll own them and they can pay us minimal rent. Then when times get better, we'll sell them back to them."

"Richie, that's wonderful."

"I know it will make you feel better."

"Yes, it will. This is so exciting. I'll walk over and propose it to Debbie after supper."

"Fine."

"When can we do it?"

"Right away."

"Terrific."

"One other thing, dear."

"What?"

"I bought a couple of paintings today."

Chapter 27

———

Miles Tenpenny was Commissioner of Financial Management Service for the Department of the Treasury. He had been requested to make a presentation to the secretary of the Treasury and two of his aides that afternoon. He knew what it would be about. The government's situation was deteriorating. Revenues had fallen from almost two trillion to eight hundred billion in two years. Projected revenues for the forthcoming year had fallen further to six hundred billion. The shortfall between tax revenues and government expenditures would soon be over a trillion dollars for one year. The current financing needs of the government were huge. They had to sell bonds in the amount of one trillion dollars to cover the current deficit and they had to roll over part of the six-trillion-dollar national debt. Trouble is, thought Miles Tenpenny, the Treasury had shortened up the maturities on its bonds to save on interest, and now they were going to pay through the nose. Interest rates on short-term government debt were stuck at fifteen percent and the interest on the debt was going to eat them alive. At the present rate they would soon be paying a trillion dollars a year for interest.

His secretary's voice came over the intercom, "Mr. Tenpenny, your meeting is in ten minutes." He rose from his chair and stuffed some papers from his desk into a beat-up leather briefcase. Then he walked out into the hall of the huge building and crossed the marble floor toward the secretary of the Treasury's office. In moments he was there. The receptionist sent him in and he was soon seated with two of the secretary's top aides across from the head of the Treasury Department. He knew both the aides. One of them, Tom Sciboli, was a friend whom he often sat with in the cafeteria at lunch.

"You all know why we're here," the secretary began.

"Yes," continued Tom Sciboli. "We're faced with a government financial crisis. Can you summarize it for us, Miles?"

"Sure. Basically we've had to finance a trillion dollars so far this year. We'll need another four hundred billion next quarter. For the coming year we're projecting over two trillion. We have a lot of refunding coming up."

"The thing is," added Tom, "we're having trouble selling our debt. The auctions have been going badly. We have to keep pushing up the rates to sell."

"That's why we have these high interest rates," interjected Miles. "I'm afraid they will have to go quite a bit higher to sell the debt for this quarter."

"Ouch," said the secretary. "If we push rates any higher the president's going to kill me."

"And it's going to kill the country," offered the other aide.

"That's right," said the secretary. "We have a full-blown depression and we desperately need lower interest rates."

"I don't see how, sir," said Miles.

"Tell him the bad news, Miles," said Tom Sciboli.

"Well, I've talked to our finance office quite a bit. They say a lot of primary dealers won't be bidding on our bonds. They don't have customers for them."

"What exactly does that portend?" questioned the secretary with a grimace.

"It's not pretty, sir. It's possible we won't be able to sell all of our bonds anymore. We may not be able to borrow the money we need."

"That's crazy," replied the secretary. "We'll have to raise the rates high enough to attract buyers."

"The interest expense raises the deficit and requires more borrowing," replied Miles.

"You mean we're in a box?"

"We will be if we can't sell our debt, sir," offered Tom Sciboli.

"What happens if we can't sell it?" inquired the aide.

"We can't pay our bills," said Miles.

"The U.S. government can't pay its bills, you must be joking," responded the secretary.

"It can't happen," said the aide.

"Well, it might. That's one of the reasons for this meeting," said Tom.

"I have to think this through," said the secretary. "Would we default on the bond interest or would we just not redeem them?"

"Both," said Miles.

"What would that do to the financial markets?" inquired the aide.

"It would be disastrous," offered Tom.

"They'd have to get used to it," said Miles.

"Well, we've had enough financial disasters, another one wouldn't be the end of the world," said the aide.

"It could be the end of our prestige in the world," suggested the secretary.

"Who knows what it will do to world financial markets," said Tom.

"I believe we could structure some sort of short-term borrowing from our largest trading partners," added the secretary.

"It's a bigger problem than they have the resources to help us fund," replied Miles.

"My God man, how large a problem do we have?"

"I'd say it's two trillion at a minimum," answered Miles.

"I'll tell you right now, a default is out of the question," the secretary blurted.

"Yes, sir."

"We have to get the Fed to play ball with us," continued the secretary.

"How's that?" asked Tom.

"We need them to start buying bonds. They can buy up to half a trillion or so and take us off the hook," explained the secretary.

"It's debt monetization," said Tom.

"Hell, we've monetized some debt before."

"Not like this, sir."

"All we're doing," interjected Miles, "is indirectly selling bonds to the Fed. They buy the bonds from the banks and flood the country with newly created money. It's inflationary as can be. We're just debasing the currency when we do that. Everybody is watching us now because they know we've got problems. When they see that we are creating billions of dollars more, nobody will touch the dollar."

"Plus, it's highly inflationary, sir," added Tom. "It's the kind of thing that leads to hyperinflation."

"I don't care, it gets us off the hook," replied the secretary. "That way the Treasury won't take the blame. Listen, if we can't sell Treasury bonds we take the blame. If we sell them and there's hyperinflation, the Fed gets the blame. I'm calling the president as soon as we're done here and I'm going to make this recommendation to him. He'll listen to me. He doesn't like those clannish economists at the Fed."

"Sir," responded Miles. "Do you understand that if one arm of the government sells something and another arm buys it then it didn't create anything? It doesn't mean squat, sir." Miles sounded peevish.

"It's more complicated than that," answered the secretary. "Hardly anybody in Washington knows how the ██it works. You know, the whole banking system and that fractional reserve stuff. Who knows how it works and who even cares? About one person in ten thousand has a clue. We've got to get the Fed to play along. I'll see to it that the president insists."

"I don't think the Fed will go along, Mr. Secretary," advised Tom.

"Maybe up to a point," said Miles, "but not to the extent we need."

"They are independent," said Tom.

"The central bank doesn't answer to the president," agreed Miles.

"Only if the chairman wants to get reappointed," said the aide.

"O.K., gentlemen," said the secretary, "this meeting's over. Don't tell a soul about this discussion, and whatever you do, don't let anyone know how damn precarious things are."

Miles and Tom walked out together and down the hall.

"Let's get a coffee," said Tom.

"Sure."

"Here's what I told him before you came. The government's going to have to cut way back. The budget needs to be reduced by three-quarters and it's got to happen fast."

"What'd he say?" queried Miles.

"Just stared at me and shook his head. Then he asks who is going to sell that crazy idea to the president?"

"I've heard some people in Congress mention cuts," said Miles.

"Not anywhere near what's needed."

"No," agreed Miles.

They walked into the cafeteria, got their coffee, and sat at a table together.

"I'd like to know what the Fed's thinking," said Tom.

"Yes. Everytime we can't sell our bonds and rates go up, we undercut them. They're trying to lower rates and we're forcing them up." ![scribble]

"They're not going to buy the secretary's plan, that's for sure."

"That's a fact."

They talked for twenty minutes and agreed to meet the next day.

Miles was looking forward to the evening as he walked to his office.

Once a week Miles got together with Angela Dvorak, an economist at the Federal Reserve. The portly Miles relished his weekly interludes with Angela. She wasn't beautiful he knew, but she was hot. Each date followed the same routine. After work he would drive to her Georgetown apartment. She would be waiting, clad only in panties. They would go directly to her bedroom and exhaust themselves. When finished they then went to a nearby restaurant to drink a beer and replenish their body fluids. Then they would sip wine, eat dinner, and talk. Angela was a gossip. She knew everything about everyone at the Fed. Furthermore, she was brilliant and knew monetary policy and the history and evolution of money like few others.

"The debt's getting unmanageable," he told her.

"You having trouble?"

"Yes."

"Can't sell it?" she asked.

"Not all of it."

"Push up the rates."

"I don't think that will work anymore."

"Ouch."

"The interest makes the deficit a lot worse and then there's more debt to finance. Catch-22," he told her.

"We've seen it coming," she said.

"Some of us have at Treasury, but not the brass."

"I know what they're thinking. You don't even have to tell me."

"You do?" he queried.

"Sure. We buy it."

"Yes."

"Won't happen."

"Why not."

"The chairman's returned to his roots. He's death on anything inflationary and he never wants to see a credit expansion again. Monetizing government debt will be out of the question."

"He's going to get pressure."

"From the White House?" she asked.

"Maybe."

"Won't matter. He won't budge. Plus that, he doesn't like the president."

"I'm not saying the president's right. I think he feels trapped. He's just trying to do the best thing for the country," countered Miles.

"Maybe so, but these politicians usually operate on short-run principles. It's the long run you've got to worry about."

"I guess this is the long run now, huh?"

"I'd say so," she confirmed.

Chapter 28

———

The financial world was electrified by the news that the Treasury had cancelled its October auction for a twenty-billion-dollar refunding and fourteen billion of new bonds. The truth was that most of the bonds were not going to sell anyway. If rates were forced higher to sell the bonds, the bond market would sink out of sight and the high rates would make business impossible. It had gone too far. The chairman of the Federal Reserve had won. The Fed would buy no great quantities of government bonds and take the Treasury off the hook. The chairman argued his case before the president who deserted his allegiance to the secretary of the Treasury and endorsed the chairman's ideas. The president also relied heavily on his economic adviser who supported the Fed chairman's position. The chairman had greatly aided his cause in testimony before Congress where he warned that driving up interest rates to sell bonds could bring on a financial dark ages. He had frightened them all with his pessimism.

Unfortunately, the government's announcement caused a panic

anyway. Despite assurances from government officials that the cancelled auction was a temporary phenomenon, the markets buckled. Government bond prices plummeted and interest rates rose again, much to the consternation of everyone who had just been told that a further rise in rates would ruin the nation. Stocks settled lower and the dollar made another low against all but a few third-world currencies. Capital for business was now either too expensive or unavailable. Business failures exceeded business start-ups. Gates and Jobs, two of the great capitalist heroes of the computer revolution, went on national TV to counter the gloom. They promised that the Internet and other components of the digital revolution would ultimately resurrect the economy.

On the news of the cancelled bond auction gold jumped $30 an ounce. Richie Stenquist watched the price cross $900 an ounce. That added another billion and a half dollars to the over four billion he had. At $900 an ounce he managed to add another two million ounces, or twenty thousand contracts. The fear of a government default on its debt threw people into a tizzy. It was only a rumor, but it elicited great discussion across the land and caused an eruption of interest in gold. Richie sensed that a gargantuan problem was brewing for the government and he stepped up his buying as gold rose above $900 an ounce. At $950 he had a total of fifteen million ounces and, when it hit $1,010, he was seven billion to the good. The number was so huge that it had lost its precise meaning to him. He had become the greatest speculator of all time and his legendary investment prowess would be the subject of books and articles for as long as markets existed.

Both *Time* and *Newsweek* called and were planning cover stories about him. These articles would, for the most part, be neutral and convey the facts. Others were bombastic in tone, highly critical of both him and the system that allowed him to profit. He was increasingly nervous about the negative commentary and tried to shy away from more publicity. It didn't work. By being aloof and uncooperative he only heightened the criticism.

Nancy had continued to fret about their great riches in the face of spreading impoverishment. Richie had read a story about a group of nuns who had started an orphanage for infant children who were removed from parents who were addicts, drunks, or criminals. He sent them a check for a million dollars. Nancy was pleased with him. Lately she had started riding into the office with him two days a week to help handle the load of correspondence and endless phone calls. She was a great help in running interference for him.

Richie sensed the profound and terrible impact that a government bond default would have on the country. Retirees would be hurt the worst. Many of them counted on income from bonds or bond funds. Even worse, Social Security funds were invested in government bonds. Pension plans, both private and government, were also heavily invested in these bonds. The default must be stopped at all costs. Yet, he was perplexed as to how it could be done.

Richie had avoided interviews with TV newscasters or guest appearances on talk shows, but since he had a reasonably strong opinion about the government's dilemma, he agreed to appear on *Larry King Live*. He and Nancy flew to New York in the morning and that evening he did the show. The ratings for his guest appearance were the highest since the Clinton affair. He told the famous host that the government had no choice but to cut its expenditures down to the level of its income. Interest on government bonds, he suggested, could be rescheduled and extended out beyond the maturity date of the bond. This said, he and Nancy caught an early morning flight back to Minneapolis. As he reflected on his appearance, he regretted pontificating about the government's dilemma. He had offered suggestions, but the more he thought about the government's predicament, the less confidence he had that they could extricate themselves. Business was terribly depressed and tax receipts from corporations remained minimal. With the exception of some short sellers, there were few, if any, stock profits. Individual taxpayers were out of work or doing something that paid less. Many of those that still had their jobs had endured salary cuts. Government costs had soared as a host of safety nets were called on to support a suffering populace. Worst of all, the debilitating interest costs on the government's mammoth borrowings were making budgeting impossible. The government teetered on the abyss of a massive default.

All markets continued to suffer with the exception of oil, precious metals, and some of the grains. Richie had read an article that short-term borrowing by the government was growing difficult. T-bills and notes were not being renewed for fear of a default. This was putting further pressure on the government, which on the surface appeared calm, but behind the scenes scrambled to hold off a default. Richie could see the handwriting on the wall and now began to pyramid his gold contracts. If the government hit the wall, gold was going to be dear.

Over the past few weeks he had opened accounts with commodity firms that traded futures contracts on foreign exchanges. He sold off some of his profitable contracts in the U.S. and used the proceeds to add contracts overseas. In this way he built his position to twenty million ounces. He was concerned that the Commodity Futures Trading Commission and the commodity exchange might move against him and thwart any future trading on his part. The foreign trades would keep him out of sight of the regulators. Not that what he did was illegal, but the move would keep him less visible. Once again, gold cooperated with Richie and on every rumor and story of the government default, gold jumped ahead until it finally stalled at $1,400 an ounce. Richie's twenty million ounces had gained eight billion more. He now had a profit of fourteen billion dollars and he still wasn't selling.

Richie was amazed at the scope of his success. He never intended to make such a vast fortune, only an amount that would give him financial freedom. He had started his speculation with a specific goal, but had far transcended that amount. Everything had clicked for him. It was the nature of the leverage in futures contracts that if the price of a commodity rises five hundred percent, tremendous gains were possible, and if a speculator pyramids all the way up, a vast fortune can be accumulated. The commodities price only need travel in one direction and never retreat from that path. That's what gold had done. It had gone straight up and never corrected. One large downturn in the early stages of his gold commitment would have finished Richie.

His success grated on the nerves of a wide range of officials. Politicians frequently mentioned him in their speeches as an example of what had gone wrong with America. James Cosgrove, the FCTC watchdog, called and left a message for him. When Richie returned the call Cosgrove warned him that sentiment among the commodities exchange compliance group had turned against him. Cosgrove warned him that the purchase of any further contracts or an attempt to take delivery would likely cause them to require that he unwind his position. "No more," Cosgrove had barked.

On another day Carol Olson came into his office to advise him that a Mr. Blakely from the Internal Revenue Service was there to see him. The unsmiling Blakely conveyed the fact that he was there to conduct an audit of his trading activities. Richie stalled on providing the records and they established a date one month hence when Blakely could come by and procure the records. Blakely suggested he work in the outer office, but Richie didn't want to have him close at hand while he conducted his trading activities. He could take copies of the trades.

Another day an auditor from the State Sales Tax Department showed up to conduct an interview. He wanted to see if any of Richie's activities might be subject to a sales tax. He determined that a few out-of-state purchases for the office and catalogue purchases were subject to tax. The state dunned Richie for a small amount.

In early December Richie was notified that he would be required to appear before a Senate subcommittee investigating the role of speculation in the decline of the U.S. economy. He must appear in ten days. His testimony would be given in the Senate Office Building. Richie and Nancy flew to Washington and stayed at the Willard. He was scheduled to appear first thing in the morning. They rose early and Richie nibbled at an order of toast. He was nervous. Nancy reassured him that he would be fine.

The media coverage of his appearance was overwhelming. Cameras clicked and whirred. "You'd think I was Al Capone," Richie whispered to Nancy as they walked into the hearing room. Several senators sat at a large circular wooden bench or desk that dominated the room. Behind them sat their aides and below them a banister stretched across the room, separating the witnesses and the audience from the senators. Richie was directed to a seat behind the banister and Nancy sat beside him. Richie had considered hiring counsel to represent him at the hearing, but he thought that would give the appearance of guilt and decided against it. What he had done was legal.

The senators were slow in assembling and, after a half-hour delay, all seven were finally present and they began. The senior senator from Rhode Island presided over the hearing. He turned the initial questioning over to the senator from Maryland.

"Mr. Stenquist, I'd first like to verify that the stories about you are correct. Is it true that you have profited in the amount of fourteen billion dollars?"

"Yes, Senator, that is correct," Richie responded, his mouth feeling dry.

"I'm curious as to how someone feels after accumulating that vast amount."

"I really don't feel much different than I ever did. There's a sense of financial well-being, I suppose."

"I would think so. It certainly would give me a sense of well-being and then some," grandstanded the senator as the audience chortled.

The senator continued her line of questioning and it soon became clear that she held no animosity for Richie. As he answered her questions he felt his confidence grow. The questioning moved to a senator from Michigan who had previously voiced criticism of speculators like Richie.

"Do you ever feel guilt, Mr. Stenquist?"

"No."

"You've managed to pile up enough money to take care of the needs of an entire state and you don't feel any guilt?"

"I don't feel guilt. I've certainly felt bad about the problems some people have experienced, but no guilt."

"These futures markets that you've profited in have caused others to suffer losses, is that right?"

"Yes, there's profit and loss."

"So, while you prosper, others are wiped out."

"Not necessarily, most commodities transactions are done by large companies who hedge their business activities."

"Mr. Stenquist, it's my view that any system that allows one person to generate these obscene profits is fundamentally flawed. Would you concur?"

"No, Senator. I wouldn't."

"Why not?"

"First of all, I'm the exception to the rule. Most small speculators like I once was wind up with losses. The futures market takes the risk out of certain kinds of transactions by allowing companies to hedge. It's good for business."

"Apparently not good enough for business to keep us out of a depression."

"Other factors were responsible for that," replied Richie.

"I'm not so sure that excessive speculation isn't responsible for this whole mess. By buying gold you've turned your back on the dollar. How patriotic is that?"

"You can't expect people to hold something that's losing value, sir."

"It's speculators like you who started the decline in the dollar, too."

"The fall of the dollar was inevitable. There were too many dollars."

"That's what you say. People advise me that that's not necessarily the case."

"There's always going to be disagreements on economic issues," responded Richie.

"Well, when you help to ruin the currency, your actions are extremely damaging."

"I didn't do the damage, Senator. It was going to happen with or without me."

"How did you know exactly what was going to happen?"

"I sensed that we had excesses in the country."

"What kind of excesses?"

"Too much credit, too much leverage, too much speculating on margin, not enough savings, things like that."

"Are you an economist?"

"No, Senator."

"Then your opinion is no better than any other. Making some money doesn't validate your views."

"I don't claim to have all the answers. You asked me."

"Yes, and I'll ask you this. How is it that you are the only person to ever experience such a run of luck?"

"I don't know."

"Whatever it was I don't want to see anything like it again, and I'm urging the Federal Commodities Trading Commission to more closely supervise trading activity and place some kind of profit limitations on futures transactions. Your case may just be a fluke but it's the government's role to keep the playing field level and not let any one person or group get too far ahead of the other participants."

The senator from Nevada cut in. "I disagree with that. What Mr. Stenquist did was perfectly legal and the trading system in which he operates transacts billions of dollars worth of problem-free trades that eliminate risk for all sorts of enterprises. It is definitely in the national interest to keep this trading system intact and free of unnecessary rules and regulations that cramp and constrain market activity."

They interviewed Richie for an hour and a half. Some were hostile and some were friendly. Then blessedly, it was over. Richie came out of the hearings satisfied with his performance. Two senators had tried to rough him up but they hadn't rattled him. The suggestion that he was a mindless, self-serving speculator didn't get off the ground.

Chapter 29

——

The bond pits were quieter than Lisa Farley ever remembered them. She had walked over to the Treasury Bond pit at the Chicago Board of Trade. Up to a month ago she stood on the top step of the bond pit yelling and signaling her trades. She was the best trader that Yamaha Securities had on the trading floor. She was aggressive, took big positions, and made money. She started there in the early nineties when bond futures trading was still embryonic. She had developed the experience and the instincts that gave her an edge. Not only did she do the company's trading, she worked with their derivatives trader to hedge the firm's bond positions.

Now she was back in Yamaha's Chicago office trying to clean up mismatched hedges on Yamaha's large remaining U.S. bond portfolio. The firm was trying to sell off their bond position but it wasn't happening. The bond market had frozen up like a burnt-out pump. Rumors had begun to circulate early in the fall that there would be problems refunding the U.S. debt and financing any new government borrowing needs. At first she found it hard to believe. The

245

rumors persisted and trading activity reflected these concerns. On balance selling of governments continued day after day. Attempts to hedge large bond portfolios proved difficult. When everyone wanted to hedge the same way, derivatives became impossible.

Then came the October announcement that government bond auctions were discontinued. At first they said it was for October, then they said it was until further notice. The bond market crashed and burned. Liquidity vanished and the growing fear of a government default eliminated any domestic or foreign buyers. Lisa Farley's bond trading activity in the pit ground to a halt.

The government cancellation put tremendous financial pressure on the primary dealers who held large bond inventories. First the price dropped; then they couldn't hedge; finally, they couldn't sell. Everyone in the bond business now waited for a sign from the Treasury, but none came. November and December passed into January. The Christmas holidays had been grim. The government had still managed to pay its bills. No one was sure how. There was talk about slush funds and secret borrowings from other nations, but no one knew for sure. The stock market could not take the uncertainty and had collapsed again, down another fifty percent from its summer trading levels.

The outcry from the financial world had been enormous. The public had gone wild. The drop in bond prices was a massacre like no other. The worst part was the total absence of liquidity. The bondholders were stuck and they suspected the worst. Their greatest fear was a default. They could stand a few missed interest payments, but the government must redeem them on the maturity date. So far they had made both the interest and redemption payments. But the checks had been a month or more late. They must keep up, screamed the financial world.

To make matters worse, a number of stock and bond firms were failing. Already there were heavy claims on SIPIC, the Securities Insurance Protection Corporation, which guaranteed brokerage customers that they would not lose money due to the failure of their brokerage firm. They were protected up to five hundred thousand on securities and a hundred thousand dollars in cash. A number of banks had also failed, which called into play the FDIC. They were the purveyor of federal depository insurance for over two trillion of bank deposits. That so many banks were heavily invested in government bonds gave birth to a whole different set of worries. If the banks failed because of a government default, depositors would make claims on the government for their losses. The deposit insurance was close to being worthless.

"Hello, Francis," she called to an exchange clerk who was her friend.

"Nothing doing here, Lisa," he responded.

"Who'd believe it," she replied. A half dozen traders were seated in the area chatting or reading the paper.

"Hi, Robby," she said softly to a sitting trader. Robby Silverman was a "local" or independent trader who worked the bond pit.

"How you doing, Lisa?"

"I'm doing."

"You're missing nothing," he assured her.

"They've got me sorting out the position mess and the portfolio mess."

"What's to sort, you're locked in."

"I know, but just in case."

"I'm moving out of here," he confided.

"Where to?"

"Oil or grains. Trouble is, I don't know anything about them so I'm slow to move."

"Put your toe in. Make a small start."

"I'm reading," he said, holding up a government crop report.

"Maybe we'll know something after tomorrow night when the president speaks."

"Yeah, it's a major address, not just a press conference."

"They been lying to us?" she asked him.

"I think so. The market says it's a lot worse than what they're telling us."

"This is no time to bullshit us," she stated.

"You got that right. It's time to come clean."

"People are in a permanent panic," she continued.

"They're nuts," Robby agreed.

"They've lost everything if the government defaults."

"Tell me about it. My whole family is terrified. My parents, my grandparents, they talk like it's the end of the world."

"We still got our health, Robby."

"I got more than that. I stuck some money into oil contracts. I'll be O.K."

"Good," she responded, wishing that she had taken more precautionary measures. Most of her money was in bonds. She wandered away from the bond pits and noticed the arm-waving activity at the oil pit. Robby was a shrewd trader. A tanker full of oil would look pretty good right now, she thought.

Her cell phone rang. It was Mack Forester, her boss.

"How close are you?"

"Board of Trade."

"Good. Can you come back?"

"Sure."

"We got the bigwigs in from New York. They called from their airplane. They want an assessment of our bond derivatives. They think they have a big foreign buyer. A pigeon, if you will."

"O.K., I'm on my way."

She strode out of the exchange onto Jackson Boulevard and turned down LaSalle toward the office of Yamaha Securities. In minutes she was walking into Mack Forester's office. The two executives from New York were waiting. She had met them both briefly before. Lance Hodgins was the head of the bond department and Conrad Cashman was the financial officer. She shook their hands.

"We've got an angel," began Cashman.

"That's right," agreed Lance.

"Let's face it, the company's in big trouble. I mean insurmountable trouble if the government keeps up this crap," continued Conrad Cashman.

"We've got someone with a lot of oil money," added Lance. "They want twenty-five percent of the firm and a half-billion dollars out of our bond position for a quarter-billion- dollar cash infusion."

"Haven't they heard about the president's speech tomorrow?" she asked.

"Yes, but they're not sure his speech won't restore confidence," replied Conrad.

"Fat chance," offered Mack, her boss.

"You never know, Mack," responded Lance. "We don't care about that right now. All we care about is shoveling out a shitload of illiquid bonds. The buyer will do the deal first thing tomorrow morning."

"We know most of what we have. We want to biff off all the thirty years and anything else long-term. What we're not sure of is the amount of the leveraging and hedging of the shorter term stuff, and how it plays out if liquidity returns."

"You have that information," she reminded them.

"It'll take us awhile. We got no time, Lisa. You have to help outline it for us," directed Conrad.

"Let's go to work," she said.

Within two hours they had the information they needed to put together a half-billion- dollar portfolio of their most illiquid holdings.

When they were gone she sat with Mack Forester in his office.

"I didn't know we were that bad off, Mack."

"I knew there was red ink. Hell, everybody in the business is losing their shirt."

"What happens if they don't get the infusion?" she asked.

"I don't know," said Mack.

"Let me get this straight. The U.S. operation has a big enough liability to sink the ship. This is an international securities firm. We can't be dragging Tokyo down, too."

"I guess they had a lot of their money in our bonds."

"There's not going to be anybody left," she moaned.

"We'll see what the president says tomorrow night."

"It better be good," she emphasized.

Lisa went back to her office. The monitor showed another dismal day in the markets. It never seems to end, she thought. She looked through her messages. There was one from Ken Ferguson, a commodities broker whom she'd dated years ago. They had kept in touch. She knew he was one of the brokers who handled transactions for Richie Stenquist, the billionaire speculator. Stenquist was always in the news and she liked to talk to Ferguson about him. Fergy, as she called him, always had an interesting story to tell. She dialed, hoping she might still catch him. In moments he was on the line.

"Hello, Lisa."

"How's your big client, Fergy?"

"Pretty quiet."

"He quit buying?"

"Looks that way, Lisa."

"Why?"

"I think they might have clamped down on him."

"Who?"

"The government."

"Really. Did he do something cute?"

"No, I don't think so."

"There's so much talk about him," she said.

"Every day."

"You heard what Senator Jacobs wants to do?" asked Lisa.

"You mean confiscate his contracts?"

"It's more than that. He wants to confiscate all the gold in the country. I mean he's talking about all the gold in the commodity warehouse, the coins people have, and gold jewelry, too."

"I think he's goofy," responded Ferguson.

"A lot of people are listening to him, Fergy. They like what he's saying."

"He doesn't want to use it to prop up the dollar like they did in the dirty thirties. He wants to use it for Social Security."

"That's what I mean, Fergy. Who's going to argue?"

"Then he wants a ten percent value-added tax on everything anybody owns over a hundred grand," Ferguson groused.

"I think that retirees will be so desperate they'll stand for anything."

"That kind of thing will just make matters worse. It eats up the capital that's left in the country. How the hell can we get the economy going again if the government keeps spending the little capital we have left?" questioned Ferguson.

"It's going to free-for-all if they stop sending out checks," she said.

"Everybody's going to have to pull their own oar."

"What about the people that can't, like the elderly?" she asked.

"There ought to be enough left for them. There's going to be some revenues."

"You mean it's going to be a dog fight to see who gets the scraps," she stated.

"This is a big mess, Lisa. It isn't going to be easy for anybody," he replied.

"I guess all of us are going to have to live with less, except for Richie Stenquist and a couple of brokers like you who are lucky enough to make big commissions off him."

"You sound a little testy," Fergy needled.

"Not at all. But when you think about it, this guy owns a lot of gold. He turned himself into King Midas while the rest of us went down the tubes."

"You can't hold that against him," said Ferguson.

"I guess I don't."

"It's the American dream. He started pretty much from scratch."

"He's got so much. Why doesn't he sell?"

"I wish he would. I'm looking at a new Jaguar," joshed Ferguson.

"You just bought a Mercedes."

"I want two cars."

"Haven't you heard? We got hard times now!"

"Not if you got Richie Stenquist for a client. My commissions are huge. It's like an annuity. He rolls them over and I get commission on the new contracts. I love that man."

"Maybe gold will drop after the government's speech."

"He doesn't think so, Lisa."

"He doesn't?"

"No, he doesn't think we're going to beat the rap."

"He didn't say that on Larry King," replied Lisa.

"Wasn't he good?"

"He's so handsome."

"Happily married."

"Lucky girl."

"He calls me every day for advice."

"Sure."

"Wants me to give him my opinion on the gold market."

"I thought you shorted gold at $500."

"Did I tell you that?"

"Yes."

"I didn't remember."

"What you call me for?" asked Lisa.

"I'm having a big party tomorrow night for the president's speech. You want to come?"

"I promised my mother I'd watch it with her."

"Well, I tried."

"Thanks anyway, Fergy."

"See you, kid."

The following day Lisa Farley heard from Mack Forester that the potential buyer of their bonds refused, at the last moment, to pull the trigger on the deal. There was no help coming.

Chapter 30

———

The president had been meeting with the two of them off and on for a week. He was crafting his speech and he wanted all the input he could get from the Treasury and the Federal Reserve. Today was the last time the three of them would ever meet. One week ago, on the second day of January, the secretary of the Treasury had resigned his position effective the first day of February. He had already rented a house at Bal Harbour for February and March.

This was the morning of his speech and he was preparing a final draft. From the beginning the chairman and the secretary had differed.

"You have to make a complete disclosure of our predicament," argued the chairman of the Fed.

"I wouldn't do that," countered the secretary. "The fact of the matter is that the government can't pay its bills. Are you going to tell the people that we've gone broke?"

"We have to," responded the chairman.

"That's crazy. We should tell them we'll have the problem corrected soon."

"That would be a lie," emphasized the chairman.

"Do you think that's the first lie a president ever told?"

"In this case lying won't help."

"If you tell the truth you're going to create too much fear. There could be a panic, chaos, riots, who knows what."

"I don't think so. If it's done right we'll be O.K. We tell them the truth about our predicament, we flush the markets out once and for all, and we start from scratch to rebuild."

"You're going to tell them that the United States of America is bankrupt?" questioned the secretary.

"We have to tell the truth," reiterated the chairman.

The president had gradually swung around to the chairman's idea of full disclosure to the people. In the past they swept the bad news under the carpet and were secretive about their problems. The president knew that further fudging would be useless. All their secrets were eventually uncovered anyway. The financial markets reacted negatively to endless rumors and leaks surrounding their financial affairs. The bond market had already ceased functioning. He was sick of half-truths. It was time to bite the bullet.

The solution to the financial predicament facing the country appeared elusive. There were no good answers and consequently there would be pain. Already the country had been ravaged by a rising tide of bankruptcies, massive unemployment, and plunging incomes. Charities were operating overtime to help the worst cases, but many people were still going without basic necessities. The demand for government services had skyrocketed and although his social sympathy and compassion had helped get him elected, the government now had no choice but to turn their back on the burgeoning population of needy.

Either they had to make massive cuts or they had to somehow capture an enormous amount of additional income. He expected a visit from Senator Werner Jacobs at any moment. The senator and his staff were the chief proponents of a plan to raise government revenues. They were coming, one final time, to try and convince him to embrace their revenue-raising plan and announce it in his speech. Most of his proposals would have to be okayed by Congress, but as desperate as things were, anything he suggested had a high probability of getting through Congress and becoming law.

His meeting with the chairman and the secretary was winding down when his aide notified him that the senator was waiting. He let them cool their heels while he finished up. He thanked the secretary and chairman for their advice and watched them exit from the Oval Office. No sooner had they gone when Senator Jacobs and two of his aides entered. The president also had two of his aides in the meeting. Everyone shook hands and sat down.

"Here's what we suggest," started the senator. "There should be heavy cuts in defense spending, some trimming of agency budgets, and a large increase in government revenues. One of the first things we'd like to do is confiscate gold. There's a lot of coins, bars, and jewelry that we can use to prop up the dollar. Gold was confiscated in 1934 so there is a precedent for this kind of action. Secondly, we strongly suggest that we add revenues through a value-added tax of ten to twenty percent. This would be a one-time charge on all assets in the country. We would have a one-hundred-thousand-dollar exemption per person or company."

"I think we could get a bridge loan if we get this passed now," said the senator's aide.

"It means we can keep sending out checks," said the other aide.

"We'd have to send out the army to collect it," said one of the president's aides. "The value of everything is in the tank," he continued. "It won't work."

"Talk about tax cheating," said the other aide.

"It will cause an enormous amount of screaming from everybody in the country who has any kind of net worth," added the president.

"It won't get through Congress," interjected the second aide.

"Mr. President, if you insist that it be included, and if you threaten to veto any legislation without a value-added tax, we think it will pass," argued the senator.

"What will it do to the economy?" inquired the president.

"It's going to hurt, maybe slow things down, but it will adequately fund a lot of important programs," replied the senator.

The president's aide stood up as if to give a speech. "People will have to sell off their assets to raise the money. So it will further depress the price of real estate, stocks, art, land, you name it. None of that capital will be available for investment in plants, equipment, or computers. It will do more harm than good."

"Defaulting on our promise to the people will do a lot of harm, too," replied the senator.

"We have to raise revenues," said his aide.

"We have to bite the bullet," said the president's aide who was still standing up. "We can't possibly continue to spend the way we have in the past. Look at the economic damage it's done."

The discussion continued twenty minutes more before the president called it to an end. He had their input and now he must decide the exact nature of the cuts that had to be made and whether there would be an increase in taxes. For days he'd wrestled with the problem in his mind and only now had satisfied himself how to proceed. He was finally sure that the course he would take was the right one for the country. He sat alone at his desk, making a few small changes in the draft of his speech and rehearsing his delivery.

Later he sat at the same desk while TV cameras from the networks were brought in. Then they applied makeup, checked the lighting, and made ready to go. He tapped at the perspiration on his lip with a handkerchief and then they began to count down.

"Good evening," he began.

"I am not going to waste your time this evening putting a good face on a bad situation. We have a national emergency. This crisis must be met head on. First I am going to spell out the exact dimensions of this financial emergency and then I am going to give you our plan for a resolution. We will need the full cooperation of Congress and the American people to enact our program. Together we can extricate ourselves from this predicament, but it will take time and patience. Our program may cause suffering and hardship for some. We will do everything in our power to ease these difficulties, but it would be a mistake to promise you relief and then find it impossible to deliver.

"For all intents in purpose our government is bankrupt. This is not the kind of bankruptcy where you go out of business. This is the kind of bankruptcy that calls for a reorganization. We must bring our expenditures into line with our revenues. First of all, we must address the issue of debt. At this time we have no choice but to suspend all payments on government bonds and declare a moratorium on all bond redemptions. We don't have the money to do anything else. At a later date we will attempt to restructure this debt so all hope is not lost for bondholders. Naturally, we will no longer be borrowers in the capital markets. We have discontinued our activities in these markets. Since we can no longer borrow, we can no longer run a deficit. We must balance the budget because we have no choice.

"Next we must cut our overhead. This will begin with our defense budget. We need to reduce defense spending by half. This cut must be immediate. I have asked the secretary of Defense to have a plan for this reduction on my desk within fifteen days. The plan will begin to be implemented within thirty days. We will be closing bases and discontinuing weapons research and armament production that's in process. There will be significant discharges of military personnel. This cannot be helped. I apologize to the military personnel who have so faithfully served their country, however, every citizen faces these hardships.

"The following agencies of the government will be required to provide us with a plan on how they will cut their size and costs by half. This will include the Department of Education, Health and Human Services, the State Department, Justice, and the Treasury Departments including the Internal Revenue Service." The president stopped as if to take a breath. "The following agencies must be reduced by seventy-five percent; the Departments of Commerce, Agriculture, Energy, Transportation, Interior, Labor, and Veterans Affairs. Certain agencies may be eliminated altogether. The U.S. Postal Service must be cut by half.

"Please do not conclude that all is lost. We still have tax receipts and fees. The first dollar of revenue from our new reduced budget will go to maintain Social Security benefits. We may have some Social Security payment reductions forced on us by our current financial constraints, but we will be sending out checks. Our goal will be to not reduce these checks by any more than fifty percent. We will also maintain food stamps and other welfare benefits but they will be reduced by half. Our expenditures for Medicare and Medicaid must be slashed by an equivalent amount. Many subsidies must be eliminated altogether. All business subsidies will cease immediately. All grants will end. All agriculture subsidies must be eliminated, including gasohol. Until further notice there will be no further spending on highways and infrastructure. We need to stop aid of any kind to state governments for funding of any state programs.

"We must also discontinue any further federal guarantees of bank accounts, brokerage accounts, and retirement programs. Our guarantees on mortgages are hereby abolished and borrowing rights for any government agency are suspended. Student loans and small business loans are both suspended indefinitely, as well as all other loan programs. Our goal is to reduce our budget to twenty-five percent of its former level. We anticipate tax revenues and receipts of approximately four hundred billion. That's down from almost two trillion dollars. You can see just how much cutting we must do to reach this level. Nevertheless, it can be done and it must be done. The fiscal integrity of the country has been badly bruised, but we cannot stand to have it ruined.

"I have asked the secretary of the Interior to ascertain what government lands and property we have that could be sold or auctioned. We are considering privatizing the post office and selling it to the highest bidder. We promise you we'll be unstinting in bringing our costs under control.

"Now I want to briefly change the subject. As of today I am declaring a moratorium on foreclosures on one- and two-family dwellings. This includes all homes currently in foreclosure. We will keep this moratorium in place until further notice. I am also prohibiting any repossession of automobiles for the next twelve months. This will give our citizens a chance to get on their feet and resume their home and car payments at a later date. No interest charges or penalties will be added to these contracts because of this moratorium." The president calmly took a sip of water from a glass on his desk.

"We have had many discussions with various government officials and members of Congress on how we might increase our revenues. We have concluded there is no way to take more from the American public at this time without causing further economic dislocation.

We have given careful consideration to various tax proposals and we have concluded they will do more harm than good. Some suggested means of raising revenues, if enacted, would abridge our basic freedoms and put the government in a position of violating the people's rights and our constitutional safeguards. I will not be a party to this. Although these are desperate times, we cannot resort to measures that our founding fathers specifically prohibited.

"I know that many of you will be hurt by these stringent budgetary requirements. Others will be faced with additional financial struggles. Without question this is a painful period. Our great nation is being tested. Together we must face this adversity and ultimately we must prevail. If you, the public, accept these radical cuts and if the congress enacts my programs into law, then our valiant people will have put into place the remedies that will secure our future. Light will begin to shine at the end of the dark tunnel we currently traverse. Thank you and good evening."

The TV commentators immediately began to analyze the president's speech. For days they sorted out the nuances of his strict budgetary and financial requirements. At first criticism was mild and even the opposite party's remarks were muted. However, this quickly changed and resistance rose. There were many difficult days ahead and the criticism of his administration proved to be loud and long. Yet, it would eventually come to be told by historians and biographers that this was his finest hour.

Chapter 31

———

Rumors of a government default had been one thing. The president's announcement of a national bankruptcy was quite another. It represented the final blow to financial markets. Stocks crashed once again down to prices last seen in the early nineteen eighties. The bond market gasped and wheezed, asphyxiated by zero liquidity. The default sounded the death knell of mutual funds. Stock funds turned into quicksand and bond funds were comatose. Money market funds froze up and could no longer be liquidated. The gargantuan size of financial losses reached beyond anyone's ability to comprehend. This financial disaster would be written about for centuries to come.

A large segment of the population accepted the painful prescription the president laid out. Others were incensed. A minority in Congress mounted a furious counterattack. They would not accept the cuts or the reductions in subsidies and benefits. The president's advisers made it clear he would veto any bill that tried to restore his proposed cuts. Spokespersons for special interest groups plied

the airwaves with pleas for minimal reductions in government programs. They refused to face the bitter truth that there was little or
no choice. The argument raged on TV talk shows and a great
debate reverberated across the land.

In Washington demonstrations began in earnest a few days after
the president's speech. People get angriest when something they
consider to be theirs is taken from them. Two hundred farm trac-
tors, big green John Deeres, blue Fords, red and white Massey
Fergusons stormed up Pennsylvania Avenue, chewing up the
boulevard. Behind them came two hundred thousand farmers led
by congressmen and senators from farm states, walking together
with their arms linked. The demonstration lasted two days, only to
be followed by the next and larger protest. This became known as
the "Day of Destruction" student riot. Park police estimated that
the crowd of college-age participants was almost four hundred
thousand strong. The size of the crowd made the demonstration
impossible to police properly. After a parade down Pennsylvania
Avenue they turned into an unruly mob. Then the demonstrators
went berserk and fought for a day with police and with special
units of the army brought in to disburse the crowd. Thousands
were arrested and hundreds injured. Two students died.

The following week the "Parade of Poverty" took place. Poor
people from across the nation came to Washington to stream down
Pennsylvania Avenue. Some estimates of their numbers went as
high as half a million. They were led by congressmen and clergy
who walked together with their arms linked at the head of the vast
assemblage. They passed through cordons of police and military
units and they behaved in a peaceful way that brought relief to the
denizens of the capital who feared more violence.

That was followed by another huge demonstration of government employees. These were people who faced layoffs. They were

led by congressional delegations from Maryland and Virginia whose inflammatory speeches worked the crowd into a frenzy. They began to throw their handheld signs at the surrounding police who quickly terminated the demonstration and broke up the crowd. By now the authorities had little patience with misbehavior.

Then came a massive turnout of union members and unemployed workers. They marched behind the leaders of the largest labor unions. Several hundred of them became unruly and accosted a group of reporters and TV cameramen. Five members of the media were beaten to a pulp before the cameramen, photographers, and reporters fought back, grudgingly giving yardage to the attacking union members. Television footage on the national news showed one encircled TV cameraman holding his opponents at bay while swinging his camera. He knocked two unionists senseless before he went down before his attackers. The police, swinging billy clubs and zapping people with stun guns, rescued the bleeding cameraman before his injuries were serious. He quickly became a national hero as the TV news built him into a celebrity.

Smaller demonstrations followed with mortgage bankers, environmentalists, lighthouse operators, and teachers making noisy marches down the avenue. It was all to no avail. The money no longer flowed to the many constituents who had come to rely on these disbursements. It wasn't there anymore. Congress had little choice but to endorse the president's proposal. They needed a plan in a hurry and he had one. Anything else would be chaos. The government could send out a few checks here or there, but then they would likely start to bounce by the tenth of the month. If there was to be order, the president's plan must prevail.

As it was, the president's policy proposals had already been partially adopted. The lack of money made it necessary to cut costs and layoff government personnel. Otherwise they would be working for nothing. Many supervisors, hoping to preserve their own jobs, went overboard on terminations and fired everybody in sight. Some let more people go than the president's plan called for. Soon bitter recriminations swirled around the agency supervisors and Congress promised to investigate.

Demonstrations erupted across America. Often these protests would turn into miniriots. Although these demonstrations got out of hand, nothing evolved like the great city riots of earlier decades when whole neighborhoods were burned. For one thing, state governors quickly called out reinforcements to thwart outbreaks of violence and police were better prepared to cope. Only a few scattered examples of violence caused injury and death. These protests tended to be spontaneous outbursts rather than planned demonstrations.

In time, people became resigned to their worsening condition and acceptance set in. The poor reacted in a most unexpected way. Rather than curl up and die, they showed surprising resourcefulness and in many cases found that through applications of their own ingenuity, their situation improved over their former sorry state. At the very least they found that their mental outlook had improved. Most unexpectedly, the use of alcohol and drugs among all stratas of society began to decline.

Within sixty days the president's program passed Congress and he signed it into law. There was really no choice and even some of those who initially opposed the bill reluctantly endorsed its passage. It was either a helter skelter default or an orderly retreat. The reorganization went on and despite the cries of anguish, it soon began to bite into the government's overhead. Much remained to be cut, but at least the country could see some early results.

Esamae Walters had attended the "Poverty March" in Washington, then she had stayed with relatives and marched a second time in the "Government Employees March." She rode to

Washington from New Orleans among a bus load of demonstrators. The chartered bus returned without her and now she planned to ride a Greyhound back to New Orleans. Esamae worked at a government welfare office in the southern city. They disbursed payments to those unfortunates who found themselves in need. The checks were usually mailed, but they processed original entitlement claims at her office. Sometimes there would be visits from welfare recipients who felt the amount of their check was incorrect. She also handled complaints.

She was worried when her relatives dropped her off at the Washington bus depot. Crime had soared in the nation's capital and most major cities were plagued by robberies and thefts. Masked gangs were robbing banks, their antics reminiscent of Bonnie and Clyde and the Barker-Karpis gang. The Federal Bureau of Investigation had been subjected to budget cuts and forced reduction in staff had left their ability to respond impaired. She worried that someone on the bus might have ideas about robbing the passengers. After looking at the other passengers, she knew she was too paranoid.

The ride back to New Orleans was long and uneventful. She exited the bus depot and caught a streetcar to her apartment. Esamae was a portly woman and she loved to eat. She stopped for takeout and took the food back to her apartment. Her mail and newspapers were piled inside where her neighbor and friend had stacked them for her. She was tired from her trip and, after reading her mail, she nodded off with the light still on. She woke seven and a half hours later and began to get organized for the coming day.

The television news indicated that the people of New Orleans were suffering from the Federal cutoff. It was no different anywhere she concluded; they would all have to get by as best they could. At eight-thirty she arrived at the welfare office. Her work was piled up on her desk. She dug into it. By afternoon she was surprised to see a crowd of people gathering in the large lobby. It soon became apparent that these people were angered by the cut off of their payments. A few had been drinking wine and she noticed a faint smell of the alcoholic beverage. One scruffy character was questioning a young clerk when Esamae interrupted.

"There aren't going to be any checks," she told him. "Don't you read the paper?"

"I don't read nothing that makes me mad," he responded.

"I'm sorry, but programs like this are on hold."

"I heard the state was going to come up with our money."

"They haven't and I don't expect them to," she told him. By now another man had pushed up alongside the first.

"Somebody better do something," he blurted at her. She caught a rancid smell of wine on his breath.

"I'm sorry, right now we can't help you."

"Somebody better get us some money, now," he yelled.

"I'm sorry!"

"Don't give me no frigging apologies. I want my money."

"Yes, me, too," yelled the first one. Now several others had joined the ranks of the frustrated pair.

"Give us our checks, lady," called out one.

"Now," screamed another. They began to curse the two women.

"Watch your language," insisted Esamae. They cursed her all the more.

"Watch your dirty mouth," she screamed at the worst offender. Now the entire lobby was on its feet and new claimants full of seething frustration had entered the ground-floor office. Others could see through the plate-glass window that something was happening and they, too, pushed into the mob of people crowding toward Esamae and her staff.

Esamae was suddenly alarmed. Some of these people probably had police records and were under the influence of alcohol. The crowd had become increasingly loud and were now demanding their payments.

"Money, money, money," they began to chant. A woman grabbed the hair of the clerk and began to pull her into the crowd. A man swung his fist at the young girl and she went down. Someone gave Esamae a mighty push. The screaming crowd collapsed a rail that separated the office from the lobby. Seven employees of the office jumped from their chairs and stood helpless before the surging crowd. The howling mob stormed through the office and began to kick and beat at the terrified employees. Soon they were overwhelmed by the raining blows and fell to the floor or scrambled under a desk. Esamae held up her arms as the crowd enveloped her. A snarling man directed a punch at her forehead and she began to fall. She hit the floor and someone stomped her ear. Darkness enveloped her. All nine members of the office were injured and beaten unconscious. The crowd dumped out the contents of file cabinets and desk drawers, tipped over desks and threw chairs through the plate-glass window. Suddenly someone on the street threw a homemade firebomb through the broken window. The bottle didn't break, but the burning rag, stuffed in the snout of the bottle, came out. The gasoline inside the bottle poured out on the floor, ran toward the rag, and burst into flames with a loud poof. This frightened the mob who quickly dissipated. The fire was roaring in one corner of the office when the unconscious Esamae came to. She was blinded by heavy smoke. She crawled to a wall and began to feel her way out. As she breathed in the heavy billowing smoke, she struggled to stay conscious. A few feet from the door she passed out and crumpled to the floor. Ten minutes later a fireman found her and dragged her into the street.

The resuscitation equipment failed to revive her. Only one of the other employees escaped from the inferno. The tragedy made headlines. Unfortunately, no arrests were ever made.

Chapter 32

———

The president's announcement shocked world markets and started a panic into gold. There was a widespread loss of confidence in the currencies of all nations. Only those foreign countries with gold reserves were spared a severe devaluation. Richie Stenquist watched the gold price march upward until it reached two thousand dollars an ounce. He began to formulate a strategy to sell his contracts. The selling in itself was the easy part. It was more difficult to know what to do with the money and what currency to keep it in. If he kept it in dollars he could suffer big losses if the greenback continued its downtrend. Other world currencies seesawed back and forth in the volatile currency markets. Most of these currencies offered little or no stability and no assurance that he could ever retrieve the full value of his money.

Although he had become rich, a series of other circumstances were clouding his life. The problem with where to keep his money was currently the least of his worries. The IRS had informed him by letter that they were conducting an investigation into his finances. Two special agents had been assigned to his case and they were busily combing through his financial affairs for the past five years, right down to the amount of money he spent on his tailor-made suits. It had caused him embarrassment when they interrogated his tailor. They were looking for anything they could find in order to indict him. Duke Peterson at the bank notified him two agents had been there to interview him. They were asking questions about the silver coin-bag transaction where he had deposited the coins at face value and reduced his income. He knew that the agent who had originally been assigned to audit him had found this transaction. That agent then turned it over to the Criminal Investigation Division who had assigned the two agents. Richie had employed tax counsel and the lawyer had met with the agents. He wanted to keep Richie away from them. The lawyer wasn't sure if they would go ahead with a prosecution but he advised Richie that since he had paid the taxes he had a good chance of beating it. The only thing that concerned the lawyer and worsened Richie's case was the fact that he was a high-profile personality. He told Richie that the IRS liked to go after people who, when they were indicted, made the news. They wanted these prosecutions to get into the papers and frighten other taxpayers.

Another cause for worry was a letter from James Cosgrove at the FCTC. He advised that the FCTC was conducting an investigation of his trading in overseas markets. Richie read between the lines. They were trying to lay the groundwork for a case against him because he had increased his position without reporting this fact. It was a weak case he was sure. He had never come close to getting a corner on the gold market and he had not taken delivery which would have dramatically reduced the available supply of gold in the commodities warehouses and driven up the price. Nevertheless, it was something else to worry about.

Then there were the lawsuits. He had been sued by the Commercial Gold Users Association, a group of jewelers who wanted damages for driving the price of gold up and slowing sales of gold jewelry. The Environment and Pollution Guardians of America had sued him for causing gold mining to become more profitable, thus encouraging new mines to start-up. Some mines were in wilderness areas and they accused him of ruining the environment. Then he had been sued by the American Poverty Association, who claimed to represent the poor. They charged him with willfully running up excess profits and also with gross income disparity between his income and the national mean. While their case had made the headlines and the editorial page of his local newspaper had virtually swooned in favor of the lawsuit, his lawyer assured him that they had no chance of winning the case. He was sure that a judge would dismiss it before it ever came to trial.

All of these things had piled up quite suddenly and put Richie in an uneasy mood. Then he was thunderstruck by news from Nancy that she had found a lump in her breast and was going to the doctor. He fretted and worried about her discovery and went with her to the physician's office. The doctor was methodical but not the least bit comforting. He ordered a biopsy and told her to come back for it the next day. Then they waited two more days for the results. Richie feared the results and spent each day around the house close to Nancy. He found himself praying steadily for good news. He knew that the health of his wife was more important to him than anything else in his life. The thought of her possible affliction upset him terribly and the thought of losing her was too distressing to contemplate. When they returned to the physician's office for the results of the test he was terrified.

They waited in the lobby while Richie paced impatiently back and forth. The nurse brought them into an office where they continued their wait. Richie was exasperated beyond measure by the delay. Finally the doctor came into the office, looked at them over the top of his glasses and told them the lump was benign. Nancy smiled broadly and Richie let out a whoop, jumped from his seat, and smothered her with a long hug and kiss. This was the best news he could ever receive. Nothing else mattered but that his Nancy would be all right. On the way home he told her how much he loved her and gave thanks for the good news.

Over the next few days Richie continued to think intently about where to keep his money and what to do with it. He felt that gold had topped out and would probably not rise much higher. On the other hand, the gold contracts were a good place to keep his money for the time being, so he had no need to rush.

One day Richie took his two daughters, Chrissy and Kimberly, to the great Mall of America. The huge shopping center was almost empty of people on this Monday. They rode the moving walkway through the Underwater World Aquarium and looked at the spectacular mix of freshwater fish that swam overhead from one side of the aquarium to the other. Then came the river fish and finally the ocean fish. Next they went to Camp Snoopy, the amusement park in the center of the vast shopping mall. The girls went on the roller coaster and the Mighty Axe while Richie stood waving at them from the safety of the floor. Richie liked this quality time with his two girls. He thought his kids were well-adjusted and gave all the credit to Nancy. He'd always felt that a mother was most important in raising solid kids. A mother's love could overcome all other factors.

The country had begun to adjust to a new, slower, pace of life. The culture toned down, became quieter, less flamboyant, and more conservative. Extremes of dress and behavior were disappearing and there was less tolerance for bad behavior. Richie could see the impact of hard times everywhere. Jobs were more highly valued and people seemed to dig in and work harder. Excess and waste were replaced by caution and savings. Home gardening, especially backyard vegetable gardens were suddenly popular. Even sewing and canning made a comeback. The new lifestyle caused people to get by on less, stay home more, look for bargains, and eat at home. It was as if time was rolled back sixty years.

Richie talked to Bernie on the phone about the changes in the country and sought his advice.

"It's really changed things down here in Florida," he told Richie. "It's not crowded anymore."

"Everything's dead up here, too."

"Must have been like this in nineteen forty," Bernie guessed.

"People are working for less money and nobody thinks they're too good for a low-paying job anymore," said Richie.

"It's a depression, alright."

"It you go back and read about the thirties, you find a lot of similarities with today," said Richie.

"One big difference," replied Bernie.

"What's that?"

"This time the government can't help anybody. They don't have the money."

"What's going to happen now, Bernie?"

"It's hard to say. There's still a lot of agitation for draconian measures. You know, confiscation, a special tax on assets. We may see some of that."

"It will do more harm than good," said Richie.

"Yes, it will. I hope it won't get that far."

"What would you be doing if you had accumulated some money here?" Richie asked.

"You talking about yourself?"

"Maybe."

"I'd buy an island and retire."

"Seriously, Bernie."

"There's a lot of bargains around. I guess I'd think about picking some of them up."

"What if there's another leg down?"

"That's a risk. But people are saving again instead of spending. We may be able to work our way out of this depression."

"This is more than a depression," continued Richie.

"You're right. It's a nightmare. Who would ever guess the government was going to go broke?" said Bernie.

"Only a very few," came the reply.

"I have to give you credit. You seemed to know and you made a fortune."

"The question is, what do I do now?" said Richie.

"Why do anything? Keep your gold, buy some Swiss annuities, and relax."

"Maybe I should," came the reply.

Richie was disturbed by the sorry state of the country. The economy was intolerably weak and any financial progress looked a long way off. He debated on whether to stay in the country full-time, or live abroad part of the time. He knew that once the depression had run its course, it set the stage for recovery. But this time it could be different. With the low level of savings and the weak currency he wondered if too much damage had been done to restart the economy. He was also concerned that there would be a repeat of past mistakes. If money and credit exploded again, or if the government took a greater part in running the economy, a recovery could fail to get off the ground.

Another concern was personal safety and the well-being of his family. Lately there had been frequent examples of lawlessness. The "supermarket riots" were in the news. Whole neighborhoods would converge on a large grocery store and suddenly rush inside grabbing everything in sight. The raiders would then run out of the store carrying a basket full of goods. Their success spurned others to run in and get their share. By the time enough police got there, the mob had made good on their pillaging, and, while a few people were arrested, the others had spirited away a good portion of the store's inventory. Similar examples of lawlessness were commonplace.

Richie and Nancy returned to their home from a movie with the girls on Saturday evening to find the front door open and several rough-looking characters streaming out of their house with armfuls of their belongings. They were terrified. Richie locked the car and dialed 911 but by the time the police arrived the crew of burglars had fled out the broken gate. It was a smash-and-grab burglary. The alarm was howling, but the criminals only needed a few minutes to gather up their valuables. The police no longer responded to alarms with any alacrity. Almost everybody had home security systems and there were frequent false alarms. The police waited awhile to see if someone called in to report a false alarm. If not, they responded. The Stenquists surveyed the mess in their house and tallied their losses. Among other things the burglars had stolen their small TV, the computer, the fax machine, and Nancy's jewelry. It was a traumatic experience for them and it had made Richie's decision easy.

The next day he told them they would be going to Vancouver to stay in their condominium. The Canadian city had been more stable than large cities in the U.S. Natural resources such as mining, timber, fisheries, and agriculture in British Columbia made the economy sounder. The girls had two months of school left. Richie and Nancy planned to get them a private tutor to cover this time. They loaded their vehicles, locked up their house, said good-bye to the neighbors, and drove away. Nancy was behind the wheel of the car and Richie followed in the Suburban which was packed to its limit with their clothes and prized possessions.

As he drove, Richie turned the decision to leave over in his mind. The government was searching for a way to nail him. Every attorney with nothing better to do was trying to find a reason to sue him. He had become a sore spot for the media and a lightning rod for criticism. He had an embarrassment of riches that made him envied and widely disliked. His family's security was at risk. His personal safety could no longer be taken for granted. The country was down on itself and prospects for a better life looked grim. All in all, it was a good time to leave.

They drove northwest on the freeway to Fargo and then up to Winnipeg. They crossed Canada on Highway One and wound through British Columbia, down along the Fraser River and into Vancouver. Richie and his family would be unknown here and he liked that. No one would recognize him and the local newspaper would not be attacking him or publishing his picture, and the daily news on television would not be reviewing his financial exploits. It was a relief.

Nancy didn't like pulling up her roots and cried when she said good-bye to her neighbors. She knew, however, that their situation was deteriorating. As the politicians and media tried to shift the blame for the economic crisis on speculators and opportunists, Richie was shunted to the forefront of this list of villains. This had incensed many people. It even encouraged some rascals to justify things like the burglary of her home. She knew it was no good to live in a place where envy and resentment were the dominant feelings. They had made the right decision. On the other hand, their two daughters were outraged at the sudden move. They were young ladies now, fifteen and thirteen, and leaving their friends was more than they could bear. They cried on the way out of town and lapsed into tears, time and again, throughout the long drive.

After a few days of orientation in their new surroundings, the family began to adjust. They spent most of their time together and their tight-knit unit was a source of great strength to all four. They would not be lacking any of the finer things in life. This made things far more palatable than had they been struggling with economic hardships. Refugees in a new land they were, but the richest refugees in history. They stayed to themselves and made no effort to become acquainted with the people who lived in their building. Richie didn't call his Canadian broker or look up any of the mining people he knew. He wanted to stay as anonymous as possible.

He ordered financial newsletters and publications and used a local post office box for an address. He used his middle name on the order and they came addressed to Michael Stenquist. He bought a new computer and hooked it up to the net where he watched the markets on NYMEX and Bloomberg. He gradually began to liquidate his gold contracts in foreign markets and had the proceeds wired to his account in Switzerland where he let it sit in Swiss francs. Gradually the billions began to build up.

One week after they had left home a story written by Sarah Gordon broke in the Minneapolis newspaper that Richie Stenquist and his family had fled the country. Immediately it was a national story. Suspicions were voiced in the media that he left, knowing he was soon to be indicted for some unknown wrongdoing. The question was raised as to where he had gone and several of their old neighbors disclosed they had gone to Canada. "Stenquist Flees to Canada," read additional headlines.

The Canadian authorities were soon aware of the Stenquist family's whereabouts. They were not violating any Canadian laws and since the U.S. had not taken any legal action against Stenquist, they were satisfied to leave him alone. An immigration administrator paid the family a visit to determine the exact nature and duration of their stay in Canada. Richie could not be definite, but felt the interview went well. In the U.S. a number of commentators had stood up for Stenquist on TV, claiming that unless he broke a law his critics were out of line.

Richie contacted one of the realtors he had met in London and arranged to buy a flat sight unseen. They had E-mailed pictures of the place to him and when Nancy thought it looked okay he went ahead. He wired the money from Zurich to pay for it. He felt they needed a backup residence in case someone in his new country decided to put the squeeze on them. It was a touchy period in his life and he was sensitive to his family's vulnerability. He knew that if a government decides to move against you, it's hard to survive. The likelihood of the U.S. coming after him was remote. He felt he had broken no laws. But there was still outstanding issues with the IRS and the FTC. He also had a huge tax bill to reckon with. His contracts with their outsized profits had been marked to the market at the end of the year. That meant he owed the IRS billions of dollars. He had requested his accountant file an extension and he had an additional sixty days to pay. He could probably go a few months beyond that, but that would be all. Interest and penalties would be steep for any delay. He had no choice but to start unloading his U.S. contracts.

He wanted to do it slowly and he began to peck away at them daily. Fortunately, mistrust of paper currencies was rife and his gradual selling, although quite large by market standards, did not force a decline in the gold price. Gradually he was getting out. He knew the FTC would turn the records of his foreign transactions over to the IRS. He fully intended to pay his taxes on these transactions. If they moved against him on his silver coin-bag strategy, he didn't want additional problems. Then it would be he and his family fleeing from the U.S. government. It was a scenario he did not relish, and since he was a U.S. citizen they would eventually ferret him out. He was nervous about his predicament and frequently called his tax attorney in Minneapolis to see how the investigation of his financial affairs was progressing. His attorney had met once more with the two pursuing agents and felt that they had isolated their investigation on the silver strategy. He warned them he would defend Richie aggressively and that his tax move was not against any known law or regulation in the tax code. They would have a tough case. Richie pioneered the strategy and they couldn't arbitrarily pass a regulation and make it retroactive.

Each day Carol Olson, Richie's secretary, would pile up all the mail from his office and FedEx it to him. The Stenquists had routed their home mail to his office so that was included, too. One day as Richie sorted through the mail, he came across an envelope from the IRS. Inside was a one-page letter containing two paragraphs. The first told him that the IRS had discontinued its criminal investigation of his activities. The second paragraph advised that another investigation could begin if they found any additional evidence of wrongdoing. That was it. He was home free.

Chapter 33

———

The age of affluence had ended. Conspicuous consumption and splashy extravagance were dead. Luxury was replaced by necessity. The dollar had lost over eighty percent of its value. The price of everything rose fourfold while incomes remained the same. If you were lucky, you still had a job and a paycheck. It was now twenty bucks to rent a movie. The great entertainment binge was over. The production of new movies was negligible. Television became one endless rerun. Advertising income plunged for the networks and new productions dried up with revenues.

The average household stopped most of their consuming as the residents tried to pay off their bills. Everyone became more self-sufficient. There was little work for handymen, lawn services, pet groomers, housecleaners, tree trimmers, and snow plowers. If it wasn't absolutely necessary, people didn't want it. Stores and shops that sold art, souvenirs, knickknacks, gifts, and collectibles vanished. High-priced autos, furs, luxury goods, expensive jewelry, fancy furnishings, and pricey vacations were no more. Specialty stores of every description closed their doors. The revolution in consumption and spending habits wreaked havoc on merchandisers. Chains of super stores selling electronics, sporting goods, office supplies, clothing, and toys disappeared. The survivors were those who had not encumbered themselves with too much debt and those who quickly closed money-losing stores and discontinued slow-moving merchandise. It was a test of the management skills of business executives like no other. Most were found wanting.

There was bad news upon bad news until a kind of national resignation set in and the public became inured to the siege of negative news. As financial woes and adversity piled up, the anger that had once greeted the budding crisis was placed by a grudging acceptance which slowly turned to indifference and apathy. The best of times had become the worst of times.

Tewedros Tsehai woke up to the sound of shouting. It was early morning he could tell from the gray light in his window. The neighbors in his rent-subsidized high-rise apartment were squabbling. They never went to bed in his building until full morning light, he thought. Damn Americans, most all of them who got subsidized housing and welfare stayed up all night. Tewedros was an Eritrean who had been raised by his uncle in Addis Ababa, Ethiopia. The Ethiopians claimed that Eritrea was a part of their country but the Eritreans disagreed. A low-level war had been going on between them for years.

When Mengistu, the Ethiopian communist dictator, had taken power Tewedros' uncle came under the scrutiny of the police. He had been a business agent for Haile Selassie and in the eyes of the new regime he was tainted. When Tewedros was twelve years old, his uncle had taken him out of their house in the middle of the night and had brought him with him across the border to Sudan. The boy had no choice but to go. Both his parents were dead and he could not stay alone in Addis Ababa.

They had walked for miles until they were picked up by the authorities who interred them in a refugee camp. The uncle had been stripped of his money by the Mengistu regime but he had managed to keep a fat roll of U.S. twenty-dollar bills. This bought him passage out of the camp. Once he had presented himself at the U.S. embassy and advised he was a political refugee, the remaining money bought tickets for the both of them to America and then on to Los Angeles. His uncle had relatives in the city who took them in. Within weeks his uncle was driving a taxi and making enough money to support them.

Tewedros had difficulties in the U.S. school system. He had intelligence, but the language differences proved difficult to over-come. He always tested poorly. While in high school he began to work in a fast-food restaurant. He did not graduate from high school and continued to hold a series of low-level jobs. Now he was almost forty years of age and up until the prior week he had been working at LA International Airport at a coffee franchise. Now they had closed the coffee operation at the airport because of low traffic and all of them had lost their precious jobs.

He had originally tried to get unemployment insurance but they told him they were unable to take any more applicants. He had applied for benefits from a special California fund that paid the newly unemployed one hundred and twenty-six dollars a month. For days he had walked from place to place in search of work. There was none to be had. When his small dole was gone for the month, he joined a vast throng of people lined up at one of the missions to get a hot meal. After waiting over an hour each day he was fed his evening meal.

Things got worse. The California unemployment fund was reported to be close to financial exhaustion. He was afraid to walk in the streets of some neighborhoods to look for a job because muggings were rampant. The line at the mission was longer than ever. One day he ran into Juan Gomez, an illegal immigrant who had worked with him at the airport. Juan told him that the next time he was sent back to Mexico he would not try to return.

Tewedros had inherited twelve thousand dollars from his uncle. He had managed to save another three thousand. He never owned a car and always rode the bus. His slice of the American dream had been thin, but it was better than where he'd come from.

Tewedros kept his savings in the bank. When he saw the dollar start to drop in value, he went to the bank and asked them what other currency he could own? They gave him a list. He selected the Swiss franc because he'd heard from other Ethiopians that it was sound. Rather than keep his money in a Swiss franc account, he took the money in actual bills. He brought the roll of Swiss francs home and hid them inside his mattress.

He finally found work at a restaurant. They needed someone from 5 PM until 9 PM every day to run the dishwashing machine. He took the job and stayed with it a month until they let him go. A friend of the owners had a cousin who desperately needed a job. Tewedros cried in dismay. He kept searching for other work but jobs were harder than ever to get.

He was eating well despite his travails. Charities had sprung up everywhere to help the unemployed. Food shelves provided groceries and churches, missions and other charitable outlets served hot food. Neighbors helped neighbors. The fortunate helped the less fortunate. Families closed ranks. When someone had lost their home, they moved in with relatives. When someone lost their car, friends would give them rides. Car pooling and public transportation became huge. Volunteering also became a way of life. In the close-knit Ethiopian community of Los Angeles there was help and friendship at every turn. Tewedros took aid when he needed it and gave help when asked. He was reduced to odd jobs and infrequent placements by a temporary service.

Despite his newfound ability to survive without much work, he was chronically dissatisfied. He wanted to work and prosper. It had always been possible to do that in his adopted country, but for now that had changed. He had heard that his Mexican friend Juan Gomez had been grabbed by the immigration police and shipped back to Mexico. As he reflected on his friend's decision not to return, a thought flashed into his brain. He would leave the U.S. He would go back to Ethiopia with his savings and start a new life. Perhaps it would be difficult there, but it was difficult here.

He caused quite a stir when he announced his decision. The Ethiopians he knew were surprised, but some confided that they, too, had thought of such a move. He became a minor celebrity among the Ethiopians. One night at a party he was introduced as the man who was fleeing America to look for opportunity in his homeland. Somehow the Los Angeles Times got wind of his pending departure and decided to do a story on him. The article pointed out that things had become so tough in America that the Ethiopians were going back to Ethiopia.

A few friends accompanied him to the airport. He would fly to New York, then to London and on to Addis Ababa. They warned him that it would be different. He knew at first it would be strange, but he was tired of the struggle in America. Perhaps with his little hoard of Swiss francs and a new idea, he could find a way to prosper. The plane lifted off and he watched the lights of Los Angeles fade away as they climbed out over the ocean and swung back toward the mountains. He wondered if he would miss it.

Chapter 34

———

Richie's friend Bernie flew out to visit the Stenquists in Vancouver. Once he arrived the five of them decided to take an overnight trip to Vancouver Island, a land mass six times the size of Long Island. They drove their car onto the ferry that was the primary way to reach the island. As they crossed an open stretch of sea called the Strait of Georgia, they stood by the rail and talked.

"What are you going to do?" asked Bernie.

"I'm not sure."

"You going to come back?"

"I don't know. I was thinking of spending a year or two in London."

"It's nice here," observed Bernie.

"Yes, we like it a lot. Maybe we'll stay."

"You sound like 'the man without a country.'"

"There's one big difference. I can come back."

"Why don't you?"

"It got pretty hairy. Every day I was reading about what a son-of-a-bitch I was."

"Yeah. They were starting to blame you for the mess we're in."

"Then I come home and there's a bunch of freaks in my house stealing my property. It wasn't pretty."

"Scare the hell out of you."

"I shouldn't have to worry about my family," said Richie.

"No. I understand why you cut out."

"It's not good there anyway," observed Richie.

"I hear you. The wealth of the country is shot. Half the businesses are gone. People are pulling together but it's no picnic."

"I don't think I can take a chance on coming back," observed Richie.

"I don't think you'd still be at risk. Things have calmed down. There's not as much bitterness and unrest. The media has cooled off. A lot of them lost their jobs because people cut back on reading newspapers. Can you believe that?"

"Amazing."

"We hit bottom. It's been tough on everybody. People got no patience with excess or weird stuff. The other night a couple of guys wouldn't stand for the national anthem at wrestling. They kicked the crap out of them."

"Really," Richie chortled.

"And this victim stuff. Forget about it. Almost everybody's a victim now. People sucked it up. They quit whining."

"That's good."

"Listen, this may sound pretty far out, but I think the U.S. is gonna be better off for this in the long run," said Bernie.

"You do?"

"Sure, everything goes too far in one direction and then corrects back. Let's face it, the country was getting a little weird," said Bernie.

"Maybe," Richie nodded.

"I hope you come back."

"I'll think about it."

The ferry let them off on the island and they drove down to Victoria at the tip of the island and looked out upon the Strait of Juan de Fuca. The Olympic mountains rose in the distance far across the channel. It was a pretty place, they all agreed. They toured the famous Butchart Gardens and admired the gorgeous flowers. It was good to have his family and friend together with him in these pleasant surroundings, thought Richie. This was a time to remember.

Richie got frequent messages and calls at his office from the media and Carol Olson forwarded them to him. He ignored most. One request for an interview came from a national publication and for some reason he decided to go with it.

An editor from *Business Week* flew to Vancouver to interview Richie. They talked for two days. The magazine wanted Richie's take on what must be done to restore America's economic vigor. It's a simple prescription, Richie told him. The article appeared two weeks later under the title "Billionaire Speculator Advises How to Restore the American Dream." Richie advised them that first and foremost they needed sound money. "I would prefer gold, but anything that limits the unbridled expansion of money and credit will do. Although I don't know what would do that other than gold." Then he advised, "Savings are all important. Credit must not expand beyond the available savings." Finally he insisted that governments should never be allowed to borrow money. "It's their incessant borrowing in the capital markets that brings about all our economic afflictions. It gives the people who buy their debt a false security but it's a confidence betrayed. It's the mechanism for inflation and currency debasement. Until it is stopped there will always be problems."

The article attracted widespread attention and soon Richie was the center of a raging national debate. Now, however, he did not shun the media but took every call or request for an interview. *The Economist* did a feature on him. Articles appeared everywhere reciting his opinions and chronicling his successes. Before long he was referred to as "the guru of Vancouver." The local papers and television stations picked up on him and he became a Canadian celebrity.

Nancy was puzzled at this sudden turnabout. He had always shied away from the media and up to a few weeks ago, she felt that they were hiding out.

"What's got into you?" she asked him.

"What do you mean?"

"All of a sudden you can't seem to get enough publicity."

"It's not that," he replied.

"What is it then?"

"I agreed to the *Business Week* article because they wanted my opinion on economic matters. I thought I might be able to say something that did some good."

"Well, did it?"

"I think so. Now it seems a lot of people want to hear what I have to say."

"Amazing."

"Here's the thing. If our country makes the same mistakes again, we'll suffer again. I believe there's a few elementary economic principles that a country has to follow."

"The country did great up to a few years ago."

"Yes, but look at us now. We would be much better off not going through these boom and bust cycles. In the long run we'd be much further ahead not to expand money and credit so recklessly."

"It's hard to argue with you when you were so right," she replied.

By midsummer Richie had paid the IRS the billions of dollars he owed them. Also due was a few million in interest and penalties for his delayed payment. It was worth it, he thought, because it had allowed him to take more time to exit the futures market. A sudden sale of all his contracts would have depressed the price. Now he would send a check for the balance. It was amazing, the tax payment from a single taxpayer was important to the Treasury. They needed the money for defense and to maintain the law enforcement agencies that protected the people. He gladly paid for what he thought to be the proper function of the government.

This still left him billions to invest. He kept it in foreign currencies and in gold. Now he began to seriously reflect on what to do with the money. Retirement was out of the question. He needed the stimulation of work and the excitement of risk. It would come to him he knew, but for now he was stymied.

The FedEx delivery had brought a packet of letters addressed to his office. One of them came from Bob Rice, a commercial real estate agent in Minneapolis. He claimed to have a proposal for Richie. The following day, on a whim, Richie called him.

"This is Richie Stenquist."

"Who?"

"Richie Stenquist, you wrote me."

"You mean Richie Stenquist?"

"That's me."

"The Richie Stenquist in Vancouver?"

"Yes."

"Well, er, uh. I, uh, had, uh, an idea," he stammered.

"Go ahead."

"We have a lot of commercial property, you can get it for a dime on the dollar. It's a tremendous bargain now. You should buy it."

"Why?"

"For the day this depression ends."

"What happens then?"

"People will want factory buildings, plants, commercial stuff like that. We've got office buildings, too. They're empty now but someday they'll fill up."

"I wish I was that optimistic," replied Richie.

"This is America," explained the realtor. "We're going to bounce back."

"I hope you're right."

"We can package up a ton of stuff for you."

"To pay taxes on," commented Richie.

"Taxes are way down, they had to lower them."

"Really."

"If you've got any business ideas, you can use these properties for them."

"Right now I don't."

"You come back here ever?"

"Not lately."

"Listen, you come back and I'll show everything to you. It's the opportunity of a lifetime."

"I'll think about it a little."

"Do that."

"O.K. Thanks for the call."

Richie had other correspondence from people with similar ideas. Venture capital sources had dried up and he had several requests to fund companies that wanted to start-up again. One letter in particular intrigued him. A small manufacturing company had gone broke in the aftermath of the stock market crash. They had worldwide demand for their products, but had lost money on their inventory and goods in process everytime the dollar dropped. Nor had they hedged their receivables and in a few months they'd gone bankrupt. There were many similar stories. Richie had no interest in financing brand-new companies. He felt the risk was too high and that many new business ideas were half-baked. It was the once-successful companies that failed through no fault of their own that fascinated him.

"Richie Stenquist, you haven't heard a word I've said to you in the past two days," complained Nancy.

"Sorry, I'm thinking."

"I know what you're doing, but it's still rude."

"Hey, don't bug me."

"Just answer when I say something."

"I'll try to do better."

"Good. What are you cooking up?"

"I'm just thinking."

"I know when you're scheming. It must be good because you've been a space cadet since the weekend."

"I'm working on a plan."

"What kind of a plan?"

"I'll tell you soon. I just need to think about it a little more to make sure it's the right thing to do."

"Tell me a little."

"Please dear," he replied in exasperation.

"Come on, Richie."

"I'll tell you one thing."

"O.K."

"If I did it we'd be going home."

"Oh, Richie," she let out a jubilant cry. "I'd love that."

"I'll tell you what I decide tomorrow."

She jumped onto his lap and gave him a kiss. Then she left him alone. It was exciting news. She wanted to see her house and the old neighborhood. She dared not say anything to the kids until Richie assured her it was true. They would be too disappointed if it didn't work out. It just has to, she thought. Otherwise, she, too, would be badly disappointed.

The following day Richie dialed Sarah Gordon, the business correspondent at the Minneapolis paper. She had done previous stories on him and had visited his office. He remembered her well and hoped she was still at the paper.

"This is Sarah."

"Hello. This is Richie Stenquist."

The line was silent for a moment.

"How are you?" she asked.

"Good."

"Where are you?"

"Vancouver," he told her.

"So I've heard."

"Yes."

"What can I do for you?"

"Would you like a story?" he asked.

"Of course. What about?"

"I'm coming back."

"You are?"

"Yes."

"When?" she inquired.

"Soon."

"I'll write it."

"That's not all."

"It isn't?"

"Me coming back is no big deal. I'm coming back for a purpose."

"Which is?"

"I'm coming back to invest in America."

"You are?"

"I'm selling my gold and converting my Swiss francs and other currencies into dollars. Then I'm going to buy commercial property and provide venture capital for businesses that went under in the crash and want to start-up again."

"That's wonderful. This will be a great story. We need something like this now. Will I have an exclusive?"

"Yes."

"I know all the wire services will pick it up."

"Good."

"This story will help me a lot. Thanks."

"O.K.," he said. "What else do you need to know?"

The headline on the front page story read, "Billionaire Stenquist to Return," and the subheadline stated "Plans to Invest Fortune in America." The story was echoed in every paper and on every television channel in the country. They gave it a positive spin. Some even claimed it would be the turning point.

(Author's note:)

For reasons conducive to good storytelling, the time span of this novel has been compressed into three years. The real crash could unfold over a period three or four times longer.